15 SCIENCE FICTION SHORT STORIES - BRYCE WALTON

BRYCE WALTON

ELI JAYNE

BY EARTHLIGHT

By Earthlight by Bryce Walton

First published in 1953

This Edition Copyright @2020 by Eli Jayne

All rights reserved.

Cover art by Eli Jayne

We all have to die sometime, but it's more the manner of our going, and the reason why we must die when we do that's the rub.

CHAPTER ONE

The rocket skin was like a dun-colored wall in the dim light under the hill. Three anonymous men who were beyond suspicion, who had worked on the rocket, were taking Barlow up in the elevator, up along the rocket's curving walls.

Earlier, scores of men had climbed up many ladders to various platforms where doors opened into the rocket's compartments for the insertion and repair of the many highly-specialized instruments.

It was still—so damn still here!

Some guards were way down somewhere in the shadows, but they didn't notice anything. The three men were regular workers and there were last minute things to be done. It all looked quite logical.

Over in the blockhouse, some of America's most important political and military figures were sitting over instruments and charts, waiting, discussing.

One of the three men was talking, explaining things to Barlow about the rocket, about the pressure-suit he was to wear. Barlow listened and got it all straight. Barlow was helped into the suit. It weighed 700 pounds, and after they had encased him in it—all but the huge helmet-plate—he lay there absolutely helpless, on a dolly, waiting to be rolled into the rocket's compartment.

The anonymous faces he'd never seen before, and would never see again, looked down at him. He blinked several times and moistened his lips. The suit was like a lead coffin. He didn't feel dead, but supposedly dead and unable to tell any one. A ridiculous way to feel!

What was the matter with him? He'd expected to die, all the time, from the start. Everybody died! Few could experience what he was experiencing. Death was worth this. One last kick, the biggest kick of all for Hal Barlow. You lived for kicks, so what was the matter?

He couldn't move his limbs; he could barely lift his head. Encased in 700 pounds of suit. Helpless. A pencil-flash flickered on and off. A couple of eyes shone. A whisper. "The kit is fastened to your belt. The instructions are in an air-tight capsule inside the kit. If you're caught, and the paper's removed, it will disintegrate; now we'll slide you inside."

The helmet slid over his face. It was absolutely dark. The suit, all-enclosing mobile shelter, atmosphere-pressure, temperature-control, mobility and electric power to manipulate tools. Its own power plant. It reprocessed continuously the precious air breathed by the occupant, putting it back into circulating supply after enriching it. The rocket was cold and alien and it would support no life; the suit alone protected him. The rocket was just metal and gadgets; only the suit stood between him and an agonizing death from acceleration, deceleration, extremes of heat and cold.

The dolly was rolling him in through the small opening. His encased body being slid, stuffed, jammed into something like a wad of ammo into a barrel. His body was entirely constricted. He couldn't hear anything. It was black. He could shift his massive helmet slightly. It clanged against metal, and the sound inside the helmet was like rusty thunder.

His blood boiled softly. He felt like a child shut up in the dark. He thought of the radio in the suit, and desperately manipulated the controls by the small control-panel in the metal hand of the suit.

The voices seemed to quiet whatever had been boiling up in him. He had started to scream; he remembered that now. Somehow, with an intense effort, he had suppressed the scream, clamped his teeth on it. Now the voices helped. He realized how much time had passed in the quick pressured dark. Voices preparing to send the first rocket to the moon. Quiet voices with all the suspense and tension held down by long military habit.

He had started being afraid. More than that. He had been going to scream. He—Hal Barlow! Where was the excitement, the great thrill, the big kick he had anticipated, to compensate for a voluntary dying?

He felt only anxiety. Afraid the terror would return. He had never admitted fear before. He thought back a little, trying to recall something that would explain the fear.

"*X minus one!*"

He felt as if an immense cyst of suppuration had burst inside of him. Sweat teared his eyes.

If they had psyched me, I'd know. I wouldn't be afraid. What would they have found? Why am I afraid now when I've never been afraid in my life?

Or had he? He couldn't remember. He tried to think of something immediate....

CHAPTER TWO

Two hours before, Barlow had paused on the second floor of the men's barracks on the White Sands, New Mexico, Proving Grounds and looked put. He shivered a little. It was a lonely spot, maybe the loneliest in the world. Especially at night. Even here, Barlow managed to be with someone most of the time—but the same dullards got boring. Even women (like Lorraine), who said they loved him, were futile companions; a guy whose future was death couldn't get emotionally involved.

He went into his three-room dump and switched on the radio at once. He needed the sound of voices and the music. He started to undress in the dark. But the cold and frigid moonlight came in and shone on the bed; it revealed the body lying there. The face looking up at Barlow was his own! His breath thinned. His hands were wet.

It did him a lot more justice than any mirror, or the reflection in a woman's eyes. The half-boyish, half-man face with the thin wiry lips, the blond curling hair and the sun-burned, cynical face. The blue eyes that seemed never quite able to smile. The face on the bed never would; it was dead.

Barlow turned. Part of the shadow in the corner moved. A voice. "D-716."

The 16 meant that this was that number among the hundred possible goals of duty and sacrifice. The D of course meant Death, and Barlow had known since having been given the number years ago what his end would be.

There were many other ways, some worse than dying. Loss of identity by plastic surgery. Barlow's appearance had been thoroughly altered three times. Some had volunteered for the torture and concentration camps of the East. Barlow had done that, too; anything for kicks.

He'd never bothered to indoctrinate himself with the philosophy of the Brotherhood with its seven rituals of self-denial and discipline, its long program of learning the love of humanity, the unity of each with all people and with the Universe.

He had his own philosophy. You were born, and then you died; the rest was just a living job.

You lived as an individual, and not as a cog—if you had the guts for it. You lived for the excitement and the thrill of danger and the maintenance of individuality—if you could. Otherwise you might as well die when you were born—because then the stretch between wasn't worth the price.

That was Barlow's way. Only the *manner* of dying was important. Everybody had to die. All that the Brotherhood really worked for was the goal of enabling everybody to live as long as possible, and finally to die with dignity and moral integrity. Barlow didn't need their philosophy; basically, that was all he, too, really wanted—maybe.

The man was indistinct in the shadows. An anonymous figure without a name. "The man on the bed has made the supreme sacrifice for the cause."

"So he's dead," Barlow said casually. "So what?"

"It took a lot of work to make such an exact resemblance. One of our members brought him in through the guards in a supply truck. It's easy to bring in a dead man who'll never go back out—except as someone who was already in. You of course."

"No one will know what is to happen to the real me then?"

"No one. It will be assumed that you committed suicide."

Barlow grinned thinly.

"There's been no change in your attitude? Your willingness to—"

"Die? None. Willing Barlow, always ready to drop dead at a moment's notice."

"You're the only one of the Brotherhood who's never submitted to the rituals and the psyching; we hope that isn't bad. Your service has been excellent. But I wish you had submitted to a psyching before this assignment, because there's one basic weakness, an Achilles Heel, in everyone, and on an assignment so vital as this, it would be worth knowing, in advance...."

"Get someone else if you're worried."

"You're the only member we have, who's inside the grounds here, who can stand the acceleration and deceleration."

"Ah," Barlow exclaimed. "This sounds big."

"It couldn't be bigger," the anonymous man said. "Than a one-way trip to the moon!"

CHAPTER THREE

The man explained some things to Barlow. Barlow didn't say anything. Maybe there was a slight tremor in his lips, but he didn't think so.

The first man into space. The first man to the Moon!

"... a world atomic war may break within six months. In spite of propaganda being fed to the people, trying to paint this atomic war as just another war, we know it will probably be the last war, the end of civilization. So our philosophical revolution, the revolution of men's minds, will begin in approximately six months from tonight. But if this last war breaks, our centuries-old plan will fail; it will never even materialize.

"The revolution is quite delicate. Simultaneously, all over the world, at a specific time, and under rigidly-controlled and favorable circumstances, the movement we have been building so long will spring up. Nothing can stop it then, once the spiritual fires begin to burn! But it can't begin until the exact scheduled moment. Your job will be to attempt to prolong this present 'peace' until our plan can go into effect. That's why you're making this trip to the moon."

Barlow laughed. "That doesn't mean a damn thing to me. To me, the only important thing is that I'm the first man into space. That's enough for anyone to know."

"Is it?"

"I'm just Hal Barlow, a guy who's had several other names, and who's really only a number! I joined the Brotherhood for kicks, not lectures! I'll do this job, in my own way, because I want to do it. For Hal Barlow!"

The man in the shadows nodded slowly. "Can't you feel what it means? Our spiritual revolution? You've read some of the works we've printed on it. This feeling of oneness with humanity. That's the real value. Can't you—"

Barlow said. "Isn't the offer of my life enough?"

The shadow said. "Maybe—for us, for people. But what about you? Maybe there are some things even you can't face alone. And think of those people out there; they need and cling to each other, even to each others' madness. Living in futile hope while going on down the crazy toboggan-ride to their own destruction. The living loudly and in public, because to be silent allows reality to enter in on feet of terror; and because 'to be alone' means madness. The simulated gaiety of the bars every night, with the shadows outside that never seem to go away, even under the glare of neon. They've never had a chance to plan, to live with any hope for the future. Burdened down by anxiety, they've built up a defense of falseness, and underneath, the terrible fear of the atomic bomb is a constant inner sickness!"

Barlow grinned. "A nice speech, but I already know those things. What I'm really interested in is what I'm supposed to do."

So the man explained to Barlow some things about why he was going on a one-way trip to the moon in a rocket intended for no man to be in, in a rocket intended for no living thing.

After the man had gone, Barlow quickly snapped on the radio again, and he felt better with the music and human voices. For a moment there, he had seemed to feel a tinge of fear. What the devil? Psyche-screening? So he was capable of fear; who wasn't? He didn't need psyching. What indignity to the individual—to have the fingerprints of psychiatrists all over your brain!

I'm Hal Barlow! The first man into space. The first man to the Moon!

He had gotten to the rocket-launching site early and had sat in the moonlight smoking a cigarette. He felt odd inside and he didn't know why. The moon had a cold effect on him. He was worried, about himself.

The whole area had been painted and disguised with all the arts of camouflage; everything appearing from the air looked like sand and sage and rock and hill. The rocket itself was built inside the hill, which served as a giant launching-barrel to guide the rocket with the exact accuracy demanded in its take-off.

The moon had loomed large and still and cold.

"... *ten, nine, eight*...."

So he was back inside the suit, inside the rocket, jammed into a barrel like a wad of ammo. Now he was beginning to see what might cause his terror. His Achilles Heel. But it was too late. What would they have found if they'd psyched him?

A wild kid—old, but still driven by the urges of a kid who hadn't grown up. A lot of surface things, the inside of him covered over. Obsessed with exterior things, he had never given himself a chance to see inside himself. Afraid. Always been with people, beer, women, bars, juke-boxes, noises, excitement. Never alone—

No parents that he could remember. He'd run away from the middle-west orphanage and heard about the Brotherhood from a friendly priest, and the priest had taken him into the organization. Strictly for kicks though, Barlow had warned. The priest had smiled with wisdom —"You don't know your own true motives, my boy."

"... *seven, six, five, four*...."

Just Hal Barlow. That was all right, but the real Hal Barlow was unknown. He'd never realized, with all his screaming about individualism, how much he'd depended on people. He had loved no one. He had seemed to love them when he was with them, but could never form any solid associations. Now all the people he had never really known became as shadows thrown upon the wall of his brain. He felt the sweat soaking his skin. Alone. Destined for it like a twin, whose double has died at birth. Always—in league with those on the other side of the looking-glass.

"... three... two...."

He screamed; *no, I can't do it, I can't face it—*

Someone—listen—

The dull muted explosion miles away, and the terrific compression and the wash of numbing, deafening sound beating back around him. Everything inside him seeming to whirl up and come down in a crash. The seeming to slide around in the dihedrals of time and space, slipping in and out of being like a ball-bearing in a maze....

First man to the moon. In a rocket meant for no man. Not a rocket. A coffin—on a one-way trip—

And I—maybe the one, the very one they should never have sent.

CHAPTER FOUR

With each degree of returning consciousness, more and more capacity for fighting the fear. He cursed the fear and wrestled with it like a man with an invisible opponent down an endless flight of stairs.

He felt too alone, isolated; then he thought of the readings. They could be flashed into a small screen in the face-plate by manipulating the fingers of his right hand. He tried to concentrate on the readings as an aid in fighting the fear.

... in the stratosphere, eighty kilometers, rocket's temperature minus a hundred and fifty degrees. Hundred and twenty-five kilometers, lower part of ionosphere, up plus one hundred and fifty—and then on up where it was somewhere around a thousand degrees, and who cared? He was beyond that—away way out—somewhere—

It went on a long time and then ... nothing but darkness ... the lonely song of the gyroscopes. His own voice ... distant, alien ... raving ... a kind of delirium ... then sometime, an awareness of the cutting down of power, the brief warning of intuition, the concussion. And as consciousness came back again, the knowing that he had hit too hard in spite of the lighter moon gravity.

His head throbbing crazily and around him the absolute darkness and silence and the warm ache in his head, the dizziness and the warm stickiness flowing down his face.

He lay there, afraid of retching. He moved his finger to release more oxygen. He could smell himself, the sharp bite of fear and the odor of blood.

He felt panic. He experimented. He could move easily here where the seven-hundred pound suit weighed only 140 pounds. He switched on the suit's light beam. The anonymous man had said. "*Get out of the rocket at once, silently!*"

He squeezed out of the barrel, into the larger compartment. He got the compartment door open. Half blind by shock, he was out in the Lunar night. "*When you get outside, stop right there. Read the instructions!*"

He had a panicky desire to fall to his knees, cling to the rocket. He stood there stiffly. "It isn't fair," he whispered over and over. "I can't do it!"

Read the instructions.

Alone, a man—one man—on the moon. No movement, no sound, no air, no life. Only sharp black and white contrast of lifeless shadow to accentuate the awful and final loneliness. Occasional meteors striking into the pumice dust—silently, voicing the stillness of his own terror.

He read the instructions. He hooked the capsule out of the kit, opened it. The suit's single light beaming like a Cyclopean eye.

The giant walls of Albategnius the center of the moon's visible disk towered bleakly up around ... everywhere ... lifelessness, just broken rock ... no water to erode. No voices, no faces, no life anywhere. Just Barlow. Barlow and a rocket.

And the stars and somewhere, the earth in the sky, sharp as molten steel in the eyes. The rocket watched him and listened. This was a target rocket. 240,000 miles away in the New Mexico blockhouse, they were watching through the rocket's eyes, feeling through the rocket's mechanical nervous system. The rocket carried instruments to test out flight calculations, controls, conditions on the moon. It carried self-operating information about the range of temperatures, radiation, gravitational influences and other conditions to be encountered on the journey and here on the moon's surface. It wouldn't return; only the results of its sensory apparatus were returning now and would keep on returning until the rocket's power ran out.

The rocket was equipped with every kind of instrument—trackers, telemeters, and it was sending back sound and sight like a human eye and ear. Radar stations, television stations, G.E. wagons down there receiving information from the rocket....

The instructions told Barlow exactly where to stand so the television-eyes could pick up his image. He found himself leaning in using the kit, getting the radio apparatus out of his suit connected properly.

He was starting, making gestures, while the terrible fear of loneliness and isolation, his Achilles Heel, made the alien surroundings reel and slip and tremble as though at any moment he was going to crumble, fail, surrender.

The bleeding from his nose and ears had stopped. No pain; that wasn't the trouble. It was being alone, the idea of dying alone....

The bulbous suit carried him over the terrain. Clouds of pumice-dust drifted. He felt like an infant walking, his feet threatening to fold under him. The rocket seemed to be drawing him back toward it. It seemed warm and friendly as he walked the required distance away from it. On Earth they were seeing him now—a man on the moon where there should be no men. He would explain it to them; that was his job. To give them an explanation that would frighten them, freeze the inevitable war-drift for six months more. So the Brotherhood could act—the Brotherhood only needed time.

But what about Barlow? Sure, everybody had to die, but no one should have to die the way Barlow is being asked to. He couldn't do it!

But he stood there, and the rocket transmitted his image and his words back to the blockhouse at White Sands, New Mexico. He said what the instructions told him to.

"We've been observing you; we saw the rocket coming in. You think you're the first to send a rocket here, but you're not. We've been here quite a while. Long enough to have set up a small colony. We've built a city near a uranium mine. There are large processing works, rocket installations and living quarters. There are atomic warhead rockets too...."

He stopped. His legs were weak, so much pressure for such light gravity....

... rockets on the moon's dark side, out of your reach. But we can reach you. The world is just a target rotating beneath us. We have unlimited deposits of uranium and other radioactive metals; you are completely helpless. Any further attempts to come to the moon will meet with destruction. We will enforce peace if we can. Any indication down there of any power planning to start a war, and we'll send our own atomic warhead rockets down.

"We are primarily scientists and technicians. The annihilation of civilization would have been inevitable anyway, so we've nothing to lose by this last attempt to maintain peace by the only means left—by force. We'll bomb any power that attempts to launch atom bombs, or begins any form of military aggression. And remember—no more rockets to the moon!

"And who are we? WE are not America, Russia, France, Britain, Yugoslavia, China, Japan, Italy, Germany, Norway, Sweden, Denmark, Spain, Portugal, Canada, Texas, or any South American country. We are no country at all. We are of ALL countries. We are here to protect all countries from every other country, and we will try to do this by force if necessary. Remember—no more rockets to the moon. We will atom-bomb any nation attempting any form of military aggression."

CHAPTER FIVE

The Brotherhood was very old, the outgrowth of an ancient Eastern philosophical cult of non-resistance and peace. With six months more, the Brotherhood could win the peace, maybe forever. If the speech just made frightened the Americans enough, they wouldn't try anything. The only other powers that might start a war within six months were Russia, China, Yugoslavia. And they were too uncertain as to whether or not America had already reached the moon. Who controlled the Moon controlled Earth. They had been afraid for some time that perhaps America had already gotten to the moon. Mutual fear of retaliation had postponed the last war this long.

The Brotherhood knew social-psychology. They figured this would work.

Barlow felt himself backing away from the rocket. They were watching him, the rocket's eyes and ears. Taking his voice and image back to earth, back to voices and laughter and music and sound and warmth and women ... with a sob, he twisted away from the rocket, turned, fell to his thighs in thick pumice-dust, kept on struggling through lazy streaming dust ribbons and he didn't look back. He was watched; he mustn't look back at the rocket again.

Meteors exploded soundlessly on the beds of lava and seas of dust, shooting up thick motionless sprays that seemed almost solid. Above him, like splintered steel, stretched the thousands of feet of crater wall. He reached the sharp wall of rock, managed to get around it and out of sight of the rocket. He fell. He lay there, his suit blending with the cold and airless landscape.

He screamed. He clawed his way up, started back again, back toward the rocket. Hell with the Brotherhood. He was for Hal Barlow. Just for Hal Barlow. He'd tell the truth. It wouldn't be long then. They'd send other rockets up then. This was for Hal Barlow. The isolation pressed in, pressed him faster, throwing him crazily over the dust toward the rocket. Then they'd know the truth, send up other rockets, ... not this way, with no more sounds, voices, any moving thing. No way for a man to die....

It wasn't death; it was the way of dying. No one should die this way— so alone. Especially Barlow, who feared loneliness more than anything else.

He fell. One foot slid into a crack filled with pumice dust fine as powder. He hooked the big steel hooks on the ends of his arms at the rock, and clung there, his helmet barely pushing up through the dust. He struggled for a while, desperately with his mind filling with visions of the rocket. He wanted to live now, make up for all the living he'd missed for so long.

He looked around, still struggling. Light gravity, little weight, but he was so weak now, and still the rocket wasn't in sight. He crawled on his stomach, dragging the bulbous suit over the rock. He could get around the rock. He had to. Out of sight, but so near, was the warm human rocket.

He ran into the rock and collapsed with a long wet sigh. He gasped. Pain throbbed damply over his chest. He moved ... just enough to turn over on his back. He slid up a little so that he was sitting there staring at the frigid, barren, naked emptiness of utter silence and desolation.

What had the man said? *"No man is alone who has learned the secret of oneness with the world...?"*

He thought about the Brotherhood, seriously now, for the first time. Many men before him had died for it. An entirely new approach to society and the individual. Working from the inside out, there would be more than a mere deflection of evil. There would be suppression at the source, in the individual will.

An end of national idolatry that threatened the existence of civilization. Man was superhuman in power and glory, subhuman in morality. After the spiritual revolution, never again the monstrous evils arising when remote abstractions like "nation" and "state" are regarded as realities more concrete and significant than human beings.

And no man is an island unto himself....

Unity....

He looked up. He saw the Earth then.

It shone down upon him through the Lunar night, twenty times brighter than moonlight. He felt warmth. There were faces in the shadows, hopeful women's faces and the eager innocent faces of children who had not yet learned hopelessness and hate. They might never learn it now.

He grinned. It was funny, you had to get so far away to look back and see all the people on earth as one, one face, one heart—one world—it looked like one world from here.

It wasn't cold as Barlow lay there and looked up at the bright shining disk. He closed his eyes. The Earthlight seemed to warm him, as the sunlight had once warmed him, long ago in childhood, on a lazy summer afternoon.

DARK WINDOWS

Dark Windows by Bryce Walton

First published in 1957

This Edition Copyright @2020 by Eli Jayne

All rights reserved.

Cover art by Eli Jayne

Sooner or later it would happen, and after that he wouldn't ever have to worry again. He'd be dead, or worse, one of the silent living dead.

CHAPTER ONE

I was suddenly wide awake and listening. A gray light the color of wet charcoal lay over the chilled room. There it was again. Plain and sharp through the thin wall separating my room from that of old man Donnicker, the shoe-maker.

Maybe he was sick. No, that wasn't it. Another muted cry of pain, then a choking sound, and the unmistakable thud of a falling body. An odd whirring sound clicked off. Then a voice said, "Grab the verminous legs of this subversive, Marty. Let's get him in the wagon."

"You gave him too much bip. He looks deader than Einstein."

"I said grab his legs."

A door shut. I went to the window. I was shivering in the morning chill. A black car moved away down the broken pavement. It swerved to miss a large mudhole in the middle of the street and an old woman with burlap wrapped around her feet didn't move fast enough. She flew across the sidewalk like a ragged dummy and lay in a heap.

Goodbye, Donnicker. I had seen the black car before. Donnicker was dead. But it didn't bother me. I never had anything to do with neighbors, anybody I didn't know had a top clearance. I was clear and intended to stay that way.

You just never knew. Donnicker had seemed like a true patriot. My carefully distant and casual observations of him had led me to believe he was as happily stupid as I was. But he had been hiding something.

I turned from the window and started the day's routine that had been the same for as long as I could remember. I warmed up some mush on the gas burner. At seven, as always, the Tevee warmed up, and Miss Info with the lacquered lips smiled at me. "... and so don't worry, citizens. The past is dead. The future is assured, and tomorrow will only be another today. And today we are safe and care-free."

Amen. She said it every morning, but it was nice hearing it again. Then the news came on. There was a pile of junked tractors, trucks and harvesting machines, smashed and rusting. Then a line of farmers working with hoes and hand-guided ploughs drawn by horses.

"Machines took away sacred routine work from citizens. Eggheads built the machines to disrupt and spread the disease of reason. We are now replacing machines at the rate of a million a week. Soon, all of us will again be united in the happy harmonious brotherhood of labor. And when you see a rusting machine, what you are seeing is another captured Egghead, frothing and fuming in its cage...."

At a quarter to eight I walked ten blocks to work. There were the usual hectic early morning traffic jams. Wagon-loads of produce and half-starved horses blocking the streets. The same man was beating a nag with a board. A wagon piled with fruit and vegetables was stuck in a pot hole in the pavement. Two men were carrying a spinning wheel into the front of an apartment building. A peddler was selling oil lanterns, wicks and kerosene out of a barrel. The same women and boys in dirty sheepskin jackets were hauling rickshaws.

I really didn't see anyone or speak to anyone. I didn't know anyone. I knew I was safe and had nothing to worry about. Once a week I used up my GI liquor chit at a bar with a Security seal on the window. Twice a week, I slept over at a GI brothel, where every girl had a Security clearance number tattoed on her thigh.

I had nothing to worry about.

I was passed through three gates by guards and went to my little cage inside Pentagon Circle, local headquarters of the Department of Internal Security.

Until that Tuesday morning I couldn't remember ever having done anything but sort colored cards. My chief qualification for my job: I wasn't color blind. When a green card with figures on it meaning nothing to me came out of a slot in the wall, I pushed it into a green slot that led somewhere into a filing department. When a red card came out, I pushed it into a red slot, and so forth. There were cards of fifteen colors.

Another qualification: my unconscious efficiency. I never had even a hint of an abstract thought. I never remembered yesterday, let alone the day before. And until that Tuesday morning I never made even a tiny mistake.

I had no idea what I was doing. Nor was I at all curious. Curiosity was highly suspect. Curiosity was dangerous in the best of all possible worlds. It was ridiculous in a state where people had never had it so good.

Cards sped from my hands always into correct slots. Care-free hours slipped painlessly by into the dead past. I was sure I was safe and not thinking at all. I was a blessed blank. And then all at once—

"The eyes are the windows of the soul."

The thought meant nothing to me, except it was wrong, it didn't belong in the routine. The routine flew to pieces. My efficiency blew up. I felt like a shiny bottle in a row of bottles with a sudden crack running down the middle. Red cards hit blue slots. Green cards hit yellow slots. Cards piled up, spilled over the floor. The more I tried to return to my efficiency, the worse everything was.

My suit was wet with sweat. I thought of Mr. Donnicker. If a man's routine broke, it could only be because some inner guilt was disrupting his harmony. A happy person is an efficient person. Inefficiency is the symptom of a guilty conscience.

"Mr. Fredricks," a voice whispered. "You're replaced here."

A cold paralysis gripped me.

"Get up, Fred."

I jumped out of my chair. A thin, stooped little man in a cheap gray suit and dull eyes took my place. In no time at all he had straightened out my mess. Cards were blurs moving into the right slots.

A wide, fattish man in a wrinkled dark suit was watching me out of curiously shining eyes. He carried a black briefcase. I had seen the black briefcases before. Special Police Agent.

He opened the door of my cage and motioned for me to go out ahead of him. "Say goodbye to all this, Fred."

I felt the smile on my wet face as I nodded and tried to feel grateful while at the same time trying to suppress the flood of fear coming up through me and turning to sickness in my throat.

I simply couldn't be afraid. I had nothing to hide. And if I was hiding something inside me I didn't know about, I should feel glad to have it detected and get it all cleaned out.

"My name is John Mesner," he said as we walked down the corridor. I couldn't say anything. I felt like a string someone was beginning to saw on with a rusty knife.

Mesner's office somewhere upstairs was a dingy room with a dusty desk and a couple of chairs. The walls were made of cracked concrete lined with dusty filing cabinets. The window was so soiled I could barely see the shadows of bars through the panes.

Mesner sat down, put his feet on the desk. He took an apple out of his desk drawer and started peeling it slowly with a small penknife.

"You scared, Fred?"

"Of course not."

He smiled, held out a long ribbon of apple peel and dropped it on the floor. "You're scared, Fred."

I put my Personology Card on his desk right in front of him. "I just had a quarterly brain-check a week ago. There it is."

I stopped myself somehow from yelling out wildly as he stabbed the card with his penknife, then tore it in little pieces and dropped them on the floor.

"You've got nothing to be afraid of, Fred. But it'll probably take you a while to realize it." He went on peeling the apple. He had thick hands, stubby fingers, and the nails were dirty. He had a round pale face, a receding chin, thinning hair, and an absurd little red cupid bow mouth.

I tried not to hear the moaning sound that seemed to come from the other side of a door to Mesner's right. He got up, went to the door, opened it. "Shut that guy up," he said. He shut the door and sat down again. He sliced off a bite of apple and pushed it into his mouth.

"To make it short, Fred. I've investigated you thoroughly. And I can use you here in SPA. You're being transferred."

My throat was constricted. I leaned against the desk. "I don't understand, sir. I don't know anything about Police Work. I'm only a clerk, a card-sorter. I don't have any qualifications. And you can see— my card."

"A couple of field-trips with me, Fred, and you'll be a veteran."

"But why me?"

"You're already in the Security Department for one thing. That makes it convenient. Also, your Intelligence Quotient."

"It's a low eighty," I said. "That's the average. I'm well below normal, and this brain-check showed I was lower this time than the last. So how could my IQ make any difference?"

"Curiosity killed the cat, Fred."

I managed to sit down before I fell down. It was impossible that I should really become an agent in the SP, the most powerful and feared organization in the state. What then was Mesner really up to? One work error shouldn't have snagged me. I'd never been guilty of thinking above a rudimentary and socially acceptable level. My IQ was unquestionably low. I was little more than a moron. So why was I frightened. Why did I feel guilty? Why was Mesner interested?

Mesner stood up and dropped the apple core on the floor.

"We're going on a field-trip now, Fred. Your indoctrination as an SPA man is beginning."

CHAPTER TWO

Mesner piloted the heliocar. Mesner said the only heliocars left in operation belonged to SPA. He dropped it on a plot of dried grass on the side of a forested hill in the Tennessee Mountains. Until we got out of the heliocar, I didn't know Mesner had a gun. I couldn't remember having heard of a gun or seen one before, but Mesner told me all about guns. He slid the rifle out of a canvas case, checked it, called it his favorite little field piece. Then he handed me his black briefcase.

He led the way down a narrow path. It was a quiet sunny day. Squirrels ran between the trees. Birds hopped and sang up in the leaves.

In front of a gray, dilapidated shack was a rickety wagon. Two men were lifting a sack out of the rear of the wagon. They wore ragged overalls and no shirts and they were both barefoot.

Mesner yelled. "You. Dirksons! This is a security check."

The shorter one started to run. Mesner shot him in the back of the head. The tall man grabbed up a piece of iron with a hooked end and started yelling as he ran toward us.

"Open the briefcase," Mesner said calmly.

I opened it. Mesner leaned the rifle against a tree. He knelt down, brought a metal disc out of the briefcase attached to a wire. He turned a dial on a bank of controls inside the case. I heard a whirring hum. The tall hillbilly screamed. He stretched up on his toes, strained his arms and neck at the sky, then fell twitching on his face.

Mesner walked toward the hillbilly and I stumbled after him. I was going to be sick, very sick. The sun worked like pins in my eyeballs.

Mesner drew a round metal cap which he called a stroboscope from the case, fitted it on the hillbilly's head. The metal strip had a disc hanging down in front of the hillbilly's eyes and about two inches away.

Mesner worked the dials and the flicker began blinking off and on, faster and faster, then slower, then faster again as the hillbilly's eyes stared into it unblinkingly. His muscles began to twitch. He beat the ground with his flat hands. Grasshoppers jumped across his face.

Mesner pointed out to me that I was watching an on-the-spot brain-probe. The brain-prober, or bipper, as Mesner called it, was so effective he hardly ever had to use the other items in the case such as the psychopharmaceuticals, drugs, brain shock gadgets, extractors, nerve stretchers and the like.

Mesner sat on his haunches, worked the flicker and lit a cigarette. "These brain-wave flickers correspond to any desired brain-wave rhythm. You play around and you'll get the one you want. They talk. What they don't say comes out later from the recorder. With this bipper you can get anything out of anyone, almost. If you don't get the info you want it's only because they don't have it. It burns them out considerably in the process, but that's all to the good. They're erased, and won't do any meddlesome thinking again."

The hillbilly wasn't moving now as the flicker worked on his eyes and activated desired mental responses.

"Dirkson," Mesner said. "What happened to your sister, Elsa?"

"Don't know. She runned away."

"She was blind wasn't she? Wasn't she born blind?"

I felt an icy twist in my stomach.

"That's right. Borned blind as a bat."

"What happened to her?"

"Runned away with some river rat."

"You've hidden her somewhere, Dirkson. Where?"

"I ain't hid her nowhere."

Mesner turned a dial. The hillbilly screamed. His body bent upward. Blood ran out of his mouth. He was chewing his tongue. Mesner stood up and frowned. "Guess he didn't know. If he knew he'd have told us. He's no disguised Egghead. Just a damn collaborating, bottle-headed jerk."

I went over behind some brush and was sick. The hillbilly would never answer any more questions, I knew that much. Now he was laughing and babbling and crawling around on his hands and knees.

"It's rough at first, Fred. No matter how patriotic you are, and how much you hate Eggheads, it's always rough at first. But you should get used to it."

"What—I mean why—?"

"The Dirksons didn't show for their quarterly brain-check. You assume they're hiding something. It turns out they're not, then you haven't lost anything. Of course you have to burn them out a little to question them. But better to burn one innocent bottlehead than let one double-dome slip away." Mesner turned and looked at me. "Isn't that right, Fred?"

"Of course it's right," I said quickly. Mesner smiled at me.

CHAPTER THREE

On the way back to Washington, Mesner piloted the heliocar casually. He leaned back, smoking cigarettes, the ashes streaming down the front of his soiled lapels.

"I think you'll work out fine in SPA, Fred."

I was still sick. I had a throbbing ache in my head and sweat kept stinging in my eyes. I nodded numbed agreement with Mesner.

"I appreciate your trying to make an SPA man out of me," I finally managed to say. "But could you have made some mistake? Gotten the wrong file or something?"

"No. Your IQ is a nice low eighty, Fred. But you're just not aware that you have what is technically known as a quiescent IQ."

"What's that?"

"You're a true patriot, Fred. We both know that. So don't be scared. You know the sick and evil danger of a high IQ and so you've put an unconscious damper on your own intelligence. You're not really so dumb, Fred."

"But I am," I said quickly.

"No, Fred. You think you are, and you look and act normally stupid and believe me, Fred, I admire your patriotic suppression of your intelligence, even from yourself. But a fact is a fact, and you're not so dumb."

"I'm not pretending. I'm not a a subversive—"

"Easy now," Mesner said. "You're not a subversive, that's right. A real subversive knows he's smart, is proud of it and consciously tries to hide it from others. But you loathe your own inherent mental ability, and you've been able to freeze its operation, conceal it even from yourself. Now realize this, Fred. The only place we can allow intelligence to operate is inside the Government. The Government must have a slightly superior thinking capacity in order to run things —for the present anyway."

"But any IQ above eighty is subversive. It says in the—"

"That's an ideal, a goal for the future, Fred. When the transition's been made, when the last Egghead is captured and put away, then all of us will be normal. We'll get ourselves bipped, and burn our excessive intelligence down to the eighty mark. But until that time, Fred, some of us—especially the SPA—have to keep our wits about us. An unfortunate necessity that we pray will soon be ended."

I gazed numbly out through the plastic canopy at the white clouds streaming past. He was trying to get some admission out of me, I thought. That was the only explanation. Working some subtle game with me. But that was absurd on its face, because I was way below normal.

"My IQ's no good for you then," I said. "I just don't see—"

Mesner interrupted with an impatient laugh. "You're a hell of a lot brighter than you let yourself admit that you are, Fred. That's all I'm saying. You know it's a terrible thing to be smart, so you keep it under wraps. But now you know there's nothing to be afraid of. You know it's legal for a while longer to be smart as long as you're in SPA. Now you can start opening up, releasing your mental capacity. Believe me,

Fred, it's for the good of the state. I know it sounds like a paradox, but that's how it is."

"How can it be good when it's such an evil thing?"

"Because right now it's a necessary evil. SPA has problems, Fred. There are still a lot of Eggheads running loose, causing trouble. And the doubledomes still loose are the toughest ones to catch, and that's our job. We've got to track down the old maniac physicists, chemists, engineers, professors, psyche-boys and the like who are still working underground. Until they're all caught Fred, we've got to live with our own filthy brains. Because you see it takes brains to catch brains."

"But I have hardly any brains at all," I insisted.

"You'll see, Fred. You'll see."

CHAPTER FOUR

Before I left his office that evening he gave me an SPA identity card. My name and face were on it. Suddenly it seemed impossibly official. All at once, I was one of the most feared and powerful men in the State. Only I knew that the only one I really feared was me.

That card supposedly gave me a free hand. It could take me anywhere, even into top-secret departments in Security. With it, I was immune to curfew laws, to all social restrictions and regulations. But when I went for a walk that evening, I knew I was being followed. Wherever I went, eyes watched me constantly. Shadows moved in and out of gray doorways and dissolved around corners.

After nine, after the curfew sirens howled down the emptied streets, I walked fast toward the ancient rooming house in which I thought I had always lived. Hundreds of silent gray women and children came out onto the streets and began cleaning them with brooms. One by one, the gas lights along the rubbled streets went out. I started to run through shadows, and footsteps moved behind me.

A drunken man came out of an alley and staggered down the broken pavement where weeds grew. A black car whisked him away. But no black car stopped for me. I saw no one with a black briefcase either. I saw only shadows, and felt unseen eyes watching me.

The old woman who had been run down by a black car still lay there on the sidewalk. No one dared approach that corpse to get it off the streets. No one knew who it was, or why it was dead. No one would take any chances. One was just as suspect from associating with a guilty corpse as a living neighbor named Donnicker.

Upstairs, I saw a splotch of blood on the hall floor. This time I knew it was Donnicker's. It reminded me of the Dirksons now. And of who could say how many others?

I lay down and took all three of tomorrow's tranquitabs. We were allotted a month's supply of tranquitabs at a time, and we were all compelled by law to take three a day. They knocked out worry and anxiety usually. But now they didn't seem to do me much good. I couldn't seem to go to sleep. This had never happened to me before.

Maybe Mesner was right. Maybe I did have a high IQ but wasn't consciously aware of it. This being true, then I *had* to be in SPA. SPA was the only place a high IQ could be tolerated.

What really bothered me the most, of course, was why I should be worried about anything. If my IQ was useful, I ought to be glad of it. A true patriot should be glad also to have unconscious subversive elements detected. A true patriot would be grateful for whatever treatment could cleanse him. What was the matter with me? Didn't I want to be purified, cleansed? Didn't I want to be bipped a little?

I didn't trust Mesner. I didn't believe he really wanted me to help him track down Eggheads. But so what? If he was trying to find out something about me, I ought to be glad to cooperate.

Only I wasn't.

I had bad dreams. I dreamed of Dirkson babbling and crawling and smiling at me with his bloody mouth. He kept smiling and whispering to me: "I never did know nothing, and now I'm just all burned out."

I dreamed of old man Donnicker being dragged down the stairs.

Then I dreamed that Mesner came in and looked down at me sleeping. A light bulb came down from the ceiling. It turned bright, then dull, then bright, then dull.

Mesner smiled as he lit a cigarette. "That really bothered you didn't it, Fred. Bipping the Dirkson boy."

"It made me sick."

I wanted to wake up. I tried my best to wake up because I felt that if I didn't wake up now, I never would. I would die in my sleep.

"Let's talk about it, Fred. I'm uneasy about it myself sometimes. I've bipped so many of them, maybe my conscience bothers me. You think it might bother a man's conscience, Fred?"

"What do you mean, conscience?"

"Maybe you think there's something immoral about bipping a man."

"If the State does it, it's right," I said. "If it helps bring about the Era of Normalcy and absolute and permanent stability, then any method is right."

Was that the correct answer? I was beginning to feel confused. Thoughts, words all jumbling up. There was an orthodox thought and an orthodox answer for everything. I'd learned them all. But had I answered this one correctly?

"That's right, Fred. But the old crackpot Egghead moralists used to say that the end doesn't necessarily justify the means. They would claim that bipping a man was wrong, and that no good results could ever come from it. They would say that a destructive means would always create a destructive end. Violence, they said, could only create more violence. What do you think of that, Fred?"

"That's wrong," I said. "That's confusing, double-dome stuff."

"I know. But we've got to identify with Egghead thinking if we can. No matter how repulsive it is, we've got to understand how they think if we're going to track them down and put them away. Now think hard, Fred. Have you ever heard a man say, 'Better that the whole world should die than that one man's brain should be invaded against his will.'"

"No, no, that's subversive," I screamed.

There was more dream, more questions, more and more confused answers. I woke up in a cold sweat. I found several electronic spy-eyes concealed about the room. Just outside my door I saw one of Mesner's cigarette butts. It was yellowed with spittle, twisted and pinched in the way his always were.

I didn't know if all of that night, or only part of it had been a dream. I didn't know if Mesner had actually been questioning me in my sleep or not. The spy-eyes could do that. But I knew Mesner had been outside my door. Probably he had been questioning my dreams.

CHAPTER FIVE

That day was worse than the night. Mesner had said to wait until I heard from him, but there was no word from him that day. I tried more tranquitabs. The hell with tomorrow's supply. They didn't help me. A blinding headache hit me at regular intervals.

What was Mesner using me for? What did he want from me? What was I supposed to know?

The Educational Tevee came on also at regular intervals.

"... so if you might think, Citizens, that a machine could do your simple work better, just remember what a terrible thing the machines did to us during the cataclysmic age of reason. As you know, the machines were invented to replace human labor by Eggheads who have always tried to destroy normal, comfortable and simple ways of life. The disease of free-thought was only possible after the machines replaced human beings, gave us the time to develop excessive and self-destructive thinking...."

I watched the light outside my window turn a duller gray then black, and after that an edge of white moon slid partly across the pane.

Why should I care what Mesner was trying to get out of me? If it was subversive then I should be glad to get rid of it. If I was clear and clean, then I had nothing to worry about. Why wasn't I simply bipped like Donnicker and Dirkson had been? Why should a true patriot care?

I shivered and stared into the darkness. Something horrible had happened to me. For the first time I realized I was entertaining unpatriotic thoughts. I didn't want to be bipped. And I knew that when Mesner finished with me, I would be bipped. When he found out whatever I was supposed to know, I'd join Dirkson and the rest of them. It had been all right, going along with the routines, as long as I actually hadn't seen what happened to a man if he didn't.

I didn't want to be erased. Whatever I was, I suddenly wanted to stay me, guilty or not. Maybe this attitude was all that Mesner wanted to be sure of. But I doubted it. Because a simple bipping would have determined that.

I didn't think I could stomach any more of Mesner's field-trips. On the other hand I had to go along. It all seemed to boil down to whether I wanted to get bipped now or later.

"Bipping isn't bad at all," Mesner had said yesterday. "After you're bipped, you can do routine work like everyone else, never worry again about worrying. That guy who replaced you, for example. He was bipped. He's never made a mistake for 20 years. He never will."

I closed my eyes. I thought of all the happy bottleheads walking the streets, out on the farms, doing their routine work, happy and carefree as long as they didn't worry. Human vegetables, the erased ones, and the terrified ones who didn't know they were even scared. Cities full of dull-eyed ciphers, and now that I was outside it a little, I could see them with an awful clarity.

And I thought—how many are as dumb as they appear to be? How many were just too frightened and numbed to think? How many would stay frightened and numb so long that they would never be able to think even if they sometime decided to try?

It was easy enough to assume that too much intelligence was an evil, a virus to be burned out. Was it better to have too little and become like the hillbilly?

Oh, Mesner had set my so-called quiescent IQ going all right. But how far would it go before it had gone far enough for his purpose?

CHAPTER SIX

That night I had another bad dream. Only it didn't really seem so bad as it should have been. A blind man was talking to me. Then I dreamed that a blind girl with a seeing-eye dog was looking at me. She was about fifteen, maybe younger, dressed in a plain flowered dress tied in back with a ribbon. She had a soft round face and her eyes were wide and opaque. The girl and dog seemed to come out of a mist and they whispered to me. It was frightening, but important, and I didn't remember what it was.

I woke up shivering. I seemed to smell wet hair, and the window was open. I couldn't remember whether I had shut the window before I went to sleep or not.

Mesner called me early the next morning.

He looked the same in his wrinkled suit with the food stains on the lapels, and peeling an apple.

"Fred, have you ever heard a phrase sounding like '... and the blind shall lead them?'"

I appeared to be trying to think about it, then said I had never heard anything like that.

"You're positive about that?"

"I don't remember it."

"You mean you might have, but you just can't remember it."

"I didn't say that. I doubt if I ever heard such a phrase."

"What about this one, '... and the blind shall see again.'"

"No, I said.

"You're sure?"

I looked directly at him and he stopped peeling the apple. "If I'm supposed to have such a damn high quiescent IQ, why not let me in on a few things?"

"What few things?"

"These references to the blind. The Dirksons. Some blind girl named Elsa. What are you trying to find out?"

"I thought maybe you remembered something, that's all. I'm pretty much in the dark myself. All I have are a few clues and theories."

"Clues, theories, about what?"

"Eggheads. Sabotage. What the crackpots could build, they can best destroy. They're blowing up factories, manufacturing and power plants, machines, production."

"That's sabotage? I thought the whole idea in bringing about the Era of Normalcy was to do away with all mechanization. Do everything with the hands, like in the good old days."

"That's an ultimate goal, Fred. Drudges don't think. They're happier. But the transition has to be more gradual. The Eggheads want to take away all mechanization at once, create chaos and anarchy. They figure that will cause the bottleheads to revolt against the Government. We can't catch the saboteurs. The saboteurs inside a blown-up factory, for example, we never know who they are. We bip every worker, not a sign of a saboteur. So whoever does the dirty work is a mindless tool of the Egghead underground, having no memory of having committed sabotage. Who are the couriers, the ones who make vital contact between the Egghead underground and the saboteurs? The dumb saboteur has to get his highly complex directives from the Eggheads. Who are the couriers?"

"Why ask me?"

"I know this much, Fred. Blind people are used as couriers."

My knees felt weak. I couldn't say anything. All I could think about was my dreams.

"I want to show you something, Fred." Mesner led me through the other door. A bleak concrete cubicle, no windows, a damp walled gray cell. Two naked men lay on slabs. Stroboscopes on their heads. Behind them, styluses recorded brain-wave patterns on moving white strips. One of the men, the one on the left, was blind. His eyes staring up into the flicker were opaque.

"Look at those brain-wave recordings, Fred. They're getting the same stimulus. We can give a thousand bottleheads this stimulus with the flicker, and get identical responses. But not the blind boys. We can't successfully bip a blind boy. The brain-waves are radically different and we've never figured out a way of codifying them. A blind bastard's never *seen* anything. The seeing eyes are trackers, like radar. But a blind boy takes in reality and records it and keeps it in a different way. We can't get at the code easily. But I'm getting it. I've bipped plenty of blind boys and I'm getting it, Fred. The blind are used for couriers. I know that much. For the simple reason that we can't bip meaningful info out of their scrambled think-tanks."

The naked men on the slabs moaned. One of them opened his mouth and a bloody foam spread over his chin.

"What I'm looking for now is a known courier who is also blind. Then I can bip him, and check the info with the code I've worked out."

He unbuttoned his coat and took a black hand-gun out of a holster strapped beneath his arm. "Meanwhile, Fred, these bottleheads have had it. They're burned out."

I heard the two sharp echoing reports as Mesner shot them in the head. One of them beat his heels on the slab. Mesner pointed the smoking revolver. "Even dead, the blind brain records differently. See there?"

I leaned against the wall. Through a crumbled hole down in the corner of damp concrete, I saw two red eyes and heard the rat squealing.

"Let's go, Fred. We've got some important field-trips on today's schedule. And you still have a lot to learn."

We went to Chicago. We set up some hidden electronic spy-eyes in a big apartment building. They were to be checked later for evidence of someone there who was hiding an IQ of over a hundred.

And that afternoon we ran down a renegade bio-chemist hiding in a tenement. He had disguised himself for a number of years as a plumber. Mesner bipped him, and an official Security heliocar came down from Washington to take him away.

When Mesner finished with the old man he was hopping around like a monkey, making grotesque faces, giggling and yelling. Tevee cameramen were on hand. A reporter was commenting on the capture of another, "... insane crackpot who has been living here under an assumed name while plotting and planning and building some diabolical machine with which to blow up the city. Our department of Internal Security excercising its eternal vigilance, captured him in time...."

Mesner and I took the heliocar back up into a clear blue sky and headed for Sauk City.

"Do you wonder, Fred, why we just don't kill them after they're bipped?"

"What could it matter?"

"It doesn't to them, but to us it matters. Public likes their scapegoats alive. More satisfying to hate live people. Public likes to see their dragons behind bars, humiliated, treated like crackpots. Makes a bottlehead feel good to see an Egghead dancing like a monkey. Also prevents martyrs. Living men are never martyrs."

"So why are we going to Sauk City?" I asked. I wanted to change the subject.

Mesner had information that an ex-professor from some long-extinct University had been concealing a high IQ after having supposedly purged himself of it years before. He was supposed to have been caught by a brain-probing spy-eye and was reported to have an IQ of over 160.

Mesner talked of such an IQ as though it was a living time-bomb that might go off any minute and blow Sauk City and the entire State to hell. He shot the heliocar along at 500 miles an hour. He held the T-Bar in one hand and lit cigarettes with the other.

"What upset you so much, Fred? I mean that morning when I interrupted you sorting cards?"

I felt a warning click in my head. I remembered it. *The eyes are the windows of the soul.*

Mesner, I thought, couldn't look into the windows of a blind man. Could I?

It hadn't been my own thought that had disrupted my idyllic, care-free life sorting cards. Mesner had said it to me.

"Just the unexpected break in the routine," I said. You've already explained it. My quiescent IQ is just too high to be a successful card-sorter."

"It wasn't *what* I said?"

"What did you say? I've forgotten."

"The eyes are the windows of the soul. But I was only quoting, Fred. Some crackpot said that long ago."

"Why probe me about blind people? I never knew any."

"Ninety percent of a human being's mental activity is underground, like most of an iceberg is under water. How much of your past can you remember, Fred?"

"Very little. The past is dead. Why should I remember it?"

"Because a good intelligence depends on the past. Memory is a part of it. Without a past, you don't have a brain. And we've got to release our brains, Fred, for awhile. Until we can catch saboteurs and Eggheads."

"I guess I've just been a patriot too long," I said.

"Remember attending Drake University ten years ago, Fred?"

"Sure," I said, fast, as though it was unimportant. I was really beginning to sweat. "I can remember if you keep prodding me. Sure, I can. So what? I purged myself. I forgot it. Schools weren't illegal then."

"But we've got to reawaken all those past memories, Fred. Make our brains work better, even if a lot of double-dome stuff comes up. You remember a psyche prof named O'Hara?"

I felt suddenly dizzy, sick. A wavering wheel started turning in my head. I managed to stop it from turning so fast. "I don't remember that at all," I said.

"Then of course you wouldn't remember that he was blind?"

In the darkness behind closed lids I could see patterns of light begin to flicker and threatening whispers dug at a fogging curtain.

"Don't push it, Fred. It'll come. I'm patient. If I weren't, then by this time I would be bipped myself and safely put away."

He would get it all right, I knew. Sooner or later he would tap it. First I would tap it, then Mesner would tap it. And after that I never would worry again. I'd never worry about remembering or forgetting anything. I wouldn't even be me. A body with a bipped brain would walk around doing routine work, and looking like me. But I'd be dead.

I didn't want to die that way. Genuine physical death would be all right. But not that, not that bipping treatment.

Mesner turned quickly and caught me staring at the outline of the hand-gun under his coat. He smiled. "You want one of these, Fred?"

"Not yet," I said. "I don't remember enough yet. I'm not smart enough yet."

"Tell me when you're ready."

CHAPTER SEVEN

By the time we closed in on the professor in an old deserted house on the outskirts of Sauk City, he had managed to hang himself to a waterpipe in the basement. He wore a pair of ragged pants. He was terribly thin and his hair was white, and his toothless mouth gaped open and his jaws sucked in. I had never seen anyone appear so pitiful and so harmless as that old man hanging there.

We untied the rope and the body fell to the floor. Mesner took a small disc from his case and put it over the dead man's heart, then stood up. "He's too dead. We should have gotten here a few minutes earlier."

He seemed tired as he sat down on a soggy box. His hands were dirty with coal dust and a smudge of it was on his face.

This is it, I thought. Now was as good a time for it as any, because there wasn't any good time for it. He had all the advantage. And the longer it went on, the greater advantage he would have. It was only a question of time anyway, and I couldn't stand waiting.

I lunged at him. I heard the faint whining sound, saw the flash and the glint of the disc coming out of his pocket. A sudden, painless paralysis hit me and I was helpless on my knees looking at Mesner. He just stared at me morosely, tired, irritated a little.

"You should know better, Fred. You're smart."

"Go to hell," I said.

He shook his head. "Not now, Fred. Nor you either. It isn't me you want to get, Fred. You just don't want to get bipped. You ought to trust me. I don't want to bip you, now or ever. I mean it. We need brains to catch Eggheads and that's my job. You're valuable. Everybody getting bipped, it isn't easy to get smart people these days."

"Bip me now then, you bastard. Get it over with."

"You'd better trust me. I'm being honest. Some of these other orthodox jerks in Security, they wouldn't fool with you. They would bip you sooner than look at you."

"Why don't you?"

"I've told you, for God's sake. You're a bright guy, and I'm eager to learn. And I don't want to burn up any important info."

Then I got it. Then I knew why he was keeping the bipper off me.

I thought about it all the way back to Washington while Mesner fed himself apples. I was supposed to have valuable unconscious info. Mesner wanted it. But the old crackpots were right. The means not only created the ends, but could destroy the ends if the means were bad enough. You probe and pry into a man's brain deep and hard enough and you come up with nothing. Your methods have destroyed the end. You've burned out the truth you're trying to get.

Mesner was trying to get info from me without burning it up.

The bastard was trying to have his bloody cake and eat it. But the insight didn't make my position any easier. He was going to get it some way. His talking and hinting and probing was designed to awaken vital memory in me, get it up into total consciousness where he could get at it with his instruments without the danger of burning it up.

Soon as he got what he wanted he would bip me. I couldn't keep him from getting it because I didn't know what it was. I couldn't keep on suppressing something if I didn't know what it was, and I knew that no one can consciously suppress knowledge in himself in any case.

CHAPTER EIGHT

For two more days I didn't hear from Mesner. I indulged in feverish and ridiculous escape fantasies. There could be no escape for me. The educational voices from the Tevee drifted in and out.

"... the greatest threat to man's happy survival is reason. Man was never intended to go above a certain mental level and become thereby a victim of his own imagination and complex fears. This disease of reason has been carried to its final suicidal limit by Eggheads...."

No mention of sabotage. The care-free public must not hear of such disquieting things. All the public heard 24 hours a day was a voice telling them about the evils of reason. The destructiveness of overly-developed brains, and the vicious criminality of Eggheads.

After listening to that long enough, and having all subversive level IQs purged, who could believe otherwise? How many believed otherwise now? Did I? What in hell did Mesner want to dig out of me? Who, what, why was I?

I was still a bottle. But now there were countless cracks appearing in it.

Then Mesner called, said we were going on another field-trip that next afternoon. All right, I said. Someway or other, I knew, I would make this my last trip with Mesner.

He had located a blind man, he said, who he knew had been a courier, a blind man definitely linked up with a recent sabotaging of a motor parts plant somewhere in Illinois.

Mesner looked down on the shanty town from a high bluff above the river. The river rats' shanties were built half in, half out of the water, some of them on stilts, some of them actually consisting of dilapidated houseboats.

Mesner said river rats were worse rebs even than hillbillies. They drifted up and down the rivers. You staged a raid and they dissolved away into the river like rodents. Many of them skipped quarterly brain-checks, but no one knew how many. Birth and death records weren't kept by river rats.

I walked ahead of Mesner down a winding gravel path into rotting reeds by the river, then we followed another muddy path toward the shanties. Frogs and insects hummed. A path of moonlight moved across the water. A ribby hound dog slunk away from me. A ragged kid looking wilder than the hound, ran across the path and slipped soundlessly into the muddy water.

Mesner pointed out the blind man's shack. Then he looked at me and smiled with that absurd little cupid bow mouth. "This isn't the time either, Fred. If you think we're not covered, you're wrong. You couldn't run fifty feet before they burned you down."

We walked nearer the loosely boarded and sagging shack.

"You take the back, Fred. Just remember, better later than now. And be careful. When these river rats get stirred up, they can cause a hell of a row. The entire goon squad would have to move in and there would be a mass bipping spree."

Mesner crept nearer, then whispered. "No light. You can't even tell if one of them's at home after dark. Why do they need a light? Go on, watch the back door, Fred. And don't let this one slip by."

I heard the front door crash inward. A man wearing only tattered pants ran out. He was thin and ribby like the dog, and I could see the moonlight shining on the opaque whiteness of his eyes.

He ran directly at me. And I knew I wasn't going to try to stop him. But I didn't know why. Then Mesner came out and fired a small gun, smaller than the one under his coat. It wasn't the same. This was a nerve-gun and it curled the synaptic connections between neurons.

The blind man collapsed and lay like a corpse at my feet. I knelt down and felt of him. Mesner whispered for me to drag the old man inside. I hooked my hands under his shoulders and pulled him into the shack. It didn't matter to me now, nor to the blind man, I thought.

He hardly weighed anything. His eyes were fixed in a white silence as Mesner shone a small flashlight into them. Then Mesner shut both doors and pulled a ragged cloth across the single window.

He opened his case. He put the stroboscope on the blind man's head. The bluish light began to flicker over the staring opaque eyes. I saw the nerve-gun lying on the floor beside Mesner's hand.

"You're too late," I said. "He's dead. I wouldn't have dragged him in here if I hadn't known he was dead."

Mesner was breathing thickly. His fat round face was pale and shiny with sweat. "I know he's dead. He must have gulped a fast-action poison soon as I came in the door. Maybe even the blind boys are deciding things are getting too hot."

Mesner worked the stroboscope.

"But he's dead," I said.

"Brain cells are the last to die," Mesner said. "Maybe I can pick up a little info yet."

It burst out of me then as from an abscess. The bottle cracked into a thousand fragments. I lunged at Mesner. He seemed to roll away from me, and then he squatted there in the flickering light. He leveled the gun at me.

"So you're beginning to wake up, Fred!"

Probing a dead man. Questioning the dead. Even a corpse was sacred no longer. The vile and horrible bastards, all of them.

"I don't care what happens to me," I said.

"That's noble of you."

"I'm going to kill you."

"Why?"

"You wouldn't understand."

"Maybe I wouldn't agree, but I'll understand, Fred. I know what you're thinking. What I'm doing now is just too much. Right? The final indignity one human being could inflict on another, right? A human mind should be sacred, even if it's dumb. Even if it's dead. Especially if it's dead. Right, Fred?"

I started around the rickety table toward him.

"Now it's set off, Fred. You're fired up now. That's what I've been waiting for. You were planted to sabotage Security itself, Fred, and I always knew that. Now we're going to find out all the rest of it. Now it's squeezing out of your unconscious, and we can drain it, empty it all out. They put a lid on your mind, Fred, and I've taken it off. Put on the ethical pressure, put it heavy on your idealistic Egghead morality, steam it up hot, blow the lid off. It's working, Fred."

"Is it?" I said. "I don't remember anything that would do you any good. I just know that it's wrong, the final horrible fraud. It isn't intelligence you guys want to wipe out, Mesner. Not your own, not the big wheels in power. It's only certain kinds of thinking, undesirable thoughts, attitudes you don't like. Those are what you have to purge."

"Right, Fred. Only the wrong kind of Eggheads. Me, hell I'm an

Egghead too. Remember the prize pupil in your psych class at Drake University, Fred?" Mesner laughed. "That was me."

"You can kill people," I said. "You can't burn a sense of what's right or wrong out of people. That old dead blind man there has preserved something you can't touch."

"Too bad you won't be around to see how wrong you are, Fred. We can make people whatever we damn well want them to be. Your old ethical pals worked out the methods. We're using it for a different end."

The front door squeaked. I felt a moist draft on my face, and a whisper in my brain. A few words. I don't remember what they were. But they were a key that opened floodgates of self-understanding and awareness. I remembered a lot then, a lot of things and feelings that warmed me. I had a wonderful sense of wholeness and I was no longer afraid of being bipped, or afraid to die.

There was an expression of complete triumph on Mesner's face, and he knew what had happened to me and he wanted it, all of it, sucked away into his briefcase. Just the same, the whisper from the doorway distracted his attention and I went for him.

In that second of time, I saw the little blind girl who had whispered that triggering phrase for my release, and behind her, the seeing-eye dog. She was utterly unafraid and smiling at me. Courage she was saying. And I could share it with her.

She had sealed her own death in order to make me whole again.

I smashed the flashlight off the table into the wall and my weight drove Mesner onto the floor. I managed to grab his arm and we lay there in the dark straining for the nerve-gun. I began to hear the whir of heliocars. I twisted Mesner's arm up and around and released the nerve-gun's full charge directly into his face. A stammering scream came out of him. It was the scream of something not human. A full charge of that into the brain, it must have curled up the intricate connections and short circuited his brain into an irreparable hash.

I took the blind girl's hand and we ran toward the river. The sky was crossed with search beams. And in the deep darkness by the river I was suddenly as blind as the girl who held my hand. We kept running and stumbling through the reeds. I felt her hand slip from mine. Then something hit me.

It wasn't a localized impact, but something seemed to have hit me all over and moved through me as though my blood suddenly turned to lead.

I tried to find the girl. I tried to crawl to the river, into the river. And near me I heard the girl say softly, "Goodbye now, Mr. Fredricks. Don't worry, because you'll be brave."

"Thanks," I said. "Little girl, what's your name?"

She didn't answer. I tried to call out to her again in the darkness, but I couldn't move my lips. Paralysis gripped me, and after that blackness, with the lights sometime later beginning to flicker against my tearing eyes, and then the horror.

CHAPTER NINE

The inquisition ended sooner than I thought it would. After the awful intrusion, there isn't any farther awareness of time. After you are thoroughly invaded, after your private soul, every naked cell of your brain is peeled open, exposed to the raw glaring light, after that you no longer care. What is you has been obliterated the way a shadow is eaten by the burn of cold light.

Your identity is gone. They take it. You are theirs, all of you belongs to them. You feel them pouring out your mind down to the pitiful dregs as though they are pouring cups of coffee.

The pain is a shredding, ripping, raveling horror. After that there is no feeling at all, and this is worse.

I told them everything I knew. What I couldn't tell, they tapped, tearing chunks out the way you would rip pages and chapters out of a book.

The responsible humanists, scientists, intellectuals had known what was coming. They prepared for it, and set up the plan before the last days of the Egghead purge. They set up the future saboteurs by a long intricate process of psychodynamic conditioning. They did it in the

Universities before the schools were purged. Promising students were selected, worked on.

Fredricks, a psychology student, was subjected to repeated hypnotic experiments. A blind Professor named O'Hara did most of it. It was all there finally in Fredrick's head, but then it was all suppressed and finally Fredricks himself forgot that he knew. A delayed hypnotic response pattern, an analogue, is set up. Later it will be triggered off by a phrase, a word, a series of words repeated at conditioned response intervals.

Ten years later he was working inside, inside Security itself. When circumstances were right, a blind courier was to have triggered off Fredrick's suppressed knowledge allowing him to sabotage the entire Department of Records and Scientific Method. So many scientists and intellectuals had already been purged that few remained among the available personnel of Security who could have repaired a simple gasoline motor without a step-by-step chart taken from the Department of Records.

It would have been a master coup for the underground.

But Mesner had traced Fredrick's identity back to Drake University, back to O'Hara. He had gotten suspicious, and removed Fredricks from Security.

The blind girl had whispered the key phrase just the same, in order that Fredricks might face the ordeal of the inquisition with as much pride, strength, and courage as possible.

"Only a free man, a man who fully respects himself as an individual and a human being," Fredricks told his inquisitors, "only a man who has learned why he is living, can die like a man."

Then they killed me.

They tried to get more out of me, but what they wanted to know, I knew nothing whatever about. I knew nothing about the underground, or the headquarters of the Eggheads.

But by then I was dead, and what they did was of no importance. I was no longer me. There was no awareness of being me. I had joined Dirkson and the renegade bio-chemist and all the others.

I was hopping up and down in a cage before the Tevee cameras, and a reporter was talking to millions of smiling, care-free citizens and telling them how another vicious crackpot had been captured just in time to avert some terrible disaster which would have disturbed the status quo.

Then I was taken away.

"Are you awake now, Mr. Fredricks?"

I opened my eyes. I was in a clean white room lying near a barred window. An attractive nurse smiled at me. She was holding a clipboard and making notations on a report pad.

"How do you feel now, Fred?" Painfully, I turned and saw several ghosts standing and sitting on the other side of the bed. I could see a door behind them, partly opened onto a softly lit corridor.

There was Dr. Malden, a famous anthropologist whom I had last seen in a newspaper headline during the purge. And Dr. Marquand, Nobel Prize winner in electrobiology. And Dr. Martinson, one time head of the UN Research Foundation. Dr. Rothberg, social psychologist. All dead, all purged, bipped and confined years ago. All ghosts.

Only they were there. And they were alive, and they seemed glad to see me. All I knew was that I was alive again. I was aware of being me. And somehow I knew that these forgotten names were also alive again.

Rothberg handed me a cigarette and the nurse lit it for me. I remembered that once I had liked cigarettes.

"So what's happened," I said. My voice was weak. My insides felt as though they were filled with grinding pieces of broken razor blades.

"You're in Zany-Ward No. 104," Dr. Rothberg said.

"I don't believe I quite understand," I said carefully.

"You will," Dr. Rothberg said. "Let's just say for a starter that when a man is bipped and brought here, we try to put him back together again. It's a long painful process. Sometimes he's not quite the same, but we've done pretty good work. We rebuild burned-out circuits. We have to know exactly what you were before you were bipped, and we try to duplicate the pattern. Regeneration is slow and rough. You'll be all right."

They shook hands with me and smiled down at me and went out. The pretty nurse gave me a pill and I lay back and thought about it. It was logical enough, and I started to laugh. During the months after that while the slow process of re-learning and regeneration continued, I learned more about the Zany-Wards. Serious as it was, and as much as there was yet to be done, it was always amusing.

As Eggheads were apprehended and confined, they were rehabilitated, put back together again, in a way you could say fissioned. The Eggheads are the inmates. They run the Zany-Wards which are used also as bases of operation in a continuing attempt to disrupt the Era of Normalcy. Great scientific labs are concealed underground.

When Security inspection committees appear on the scene, we all put on our acts. We dance, make faces, act like monkeys and giggle.

Doctor Rothberg told me yesterday that if our sabotage work doesn't soon cause people to rebel against the Era of Normalcy, it won't be long before we'll be the only sane people left in the world.

DREAMER'S WORLD

Dreamer's World by Bryce Walton

First published in 1952

This Edition Copyright @2020 by Eli Jayne

All rights reserved.

Cover art by Eli Jayne

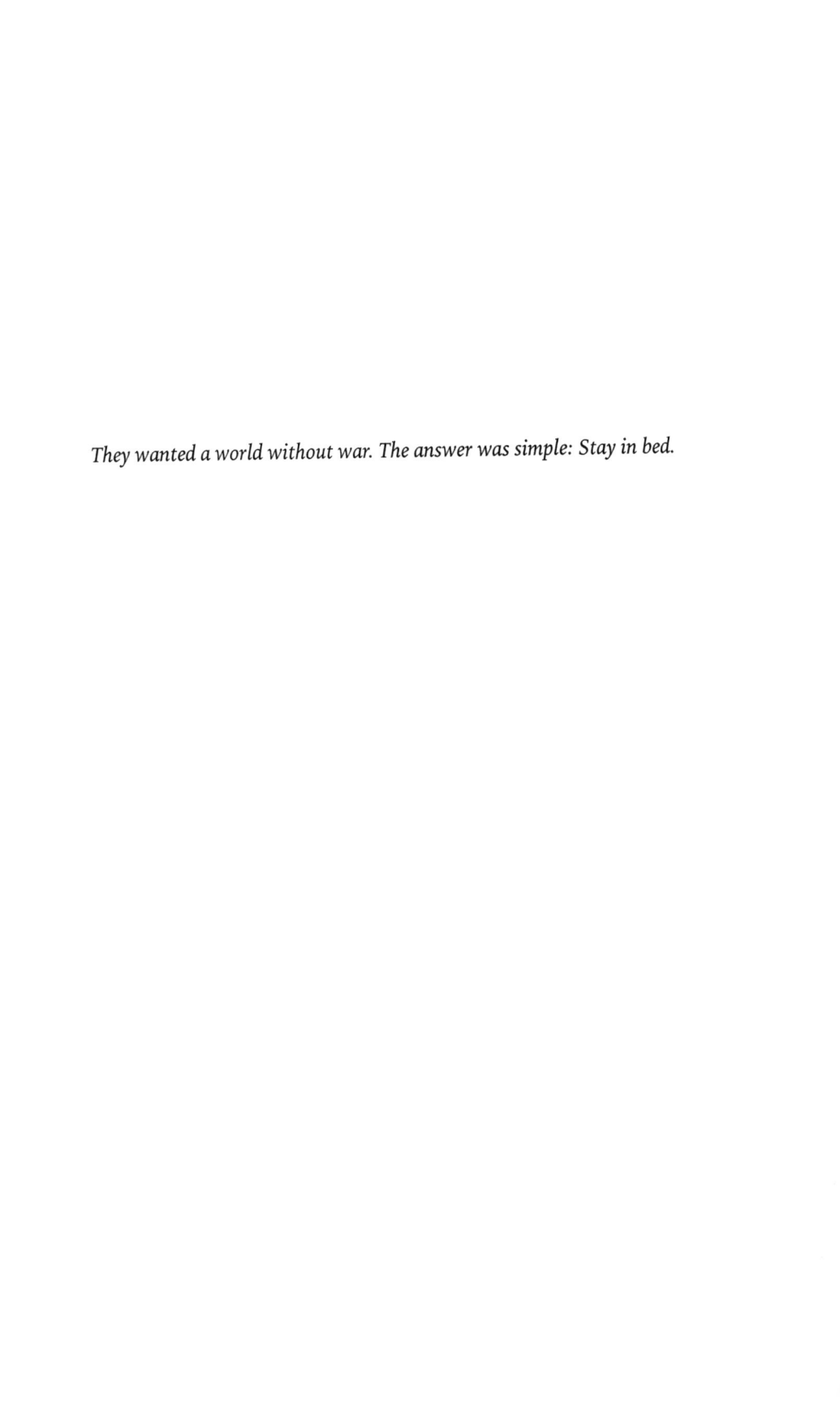

They wanted a world without war. The answer was simple: Stay in bed.

CHAPTER ONE

A warning hum started somewhere down in the audoviso.

Greg stared. Perspiration crawled down his face. This was it. This was the end of the nightmare. This had to be Pat Nichols.

After seventy-two hours in which Greg had had to do without anesthesia! Seventy-two hours of reality! Seventy-two hours of *consciousness*! Consciousness. Reality.

Greg didn't know how he'd managed to remain sane.

It seemed incredible that a man who had advanced to Stage Five in the Dream Continuity Scale, and who had been in anesthesia most of the time, could suffer seventy-two hours of boring, drab, dreary and revolting reality. And still be sane.

Pat Nichols was the answer. Her body faded into slim and luscious focus on the three-dim screen. Her brooding eyes and wide mouth that curled so reprovingly.

In his mind was the certainty: This is no dream.

She had gone psycho. Had fled from the Cowl into the dreadful Outside, seventy-two hours ago. Gone to join that fanatical group of

Venusian Colonists, those outlaw schizoids who planned to start over on Venus.

"Pat!" Greg's hand reached as though she weren't just a three-dim image. "Listen, Pat! Thank the Codes, you haven't blasted yet. I've been crazy, waiting for this call. Pat, I can't even go into integrated anesthesia without you around. My dreams don't seem to focus right."

"That's too bad, Greg," she said.

He moistened his lips slowly. He slid his hand toward the warning button beneath the table. Her eyes didn't notice, never left his face. Accusative, sad eyes.

He felt sick. He pushed the button. Now! Now Drakeson up on the apartment roof would trace the point of her call. He'd chart her location with the rhodium tracker beams. Then the two of them would go and pick Pat up and prevent that insane, suicidal, one-way trip to Venus.

She might consider it a very unfair thing, but then she was psycho. She'd be glad of it, after she was brought back, brain-probed, and re-conditioned. The thought made Greg even more ill. Brain-probing and re-conditioning involved months of a kind of mental agony that no one could adequately describe. The words were enough to give anesthetic nightmares to any Citizen. But, it was for the good of the Cowls, and of the psychos.

Her voice was sad too, like her eyes. "I was hoping you would join me, Greg. Anyway, I called to tell you that in about five hours, we're blasting. This is goodby."

He said something. Anything. Keep her talking, listening. Give Drakeson a chance to employ the rhodium tracker, and spot her location.

A kind of panic got loose in Greg's brain. "Pat, don't you have any insight at all? Can't you see that this is advanced psychosis, that—"

She interrupted. "I've tried to explain to you before, Greg. But you've always preferred anesthesia. You loathe reality. But I'm part of reality."

Yes. He had dreams. The anesthetic cubicles, Stage Five where a man was master of thalamic introjection, dream imagery. A stage where any part of reality was supposed to have faded into utter inconsequence. But Pat Nichols had always been a part of his conditioned personality pattern. By taking her out of it, fate had struck him with an unbalance in psyche that disturbed the sole objective of life—to dream.

"But that's a suicide trip, Pat, and you'll never have a chance to be cured of your schizophrenia, even if you do get to Venus—"

Her interruption had weariness in it.

"Goodby, Greg. I'm sorry for you. That silly status quo, and futile dreaming. It will never let you realize what a fine man you are. You'll decay and die in some futile image. So goodby, Greg. And good dreaming."

She was gone from the screen. Maybe from earth, unless he got out there and stopped her before that suicide ship rocketed out from its hidden subterranean blast tube.

CHAPTER TWO

Greg Hurried. He didn't realize he could function so rapidly in the world of physical reality. In seconds he had zipped thin resilient aerosilk about his body, and was running across the wide plastic mesh roof toward the heliocruiser in which Drakeson was waiting.

Greg felt the physical power flow as he ran. It sickened him. The conditioners kept the body in good shape, but only to allow the cortical-thalamic imagery faculties to function better. Actual physical business like this was revolting to any Cowl citizen. Any sort of physical and materialistic activity, divorced from anesthesia, might be a sign of encroaching psychosis.

That was the fear. That fear of psychosis that might lead to violence. To change. The Cowls over the Cities protected them from any physical interference with an absolutely stabile, unchanging and static culture. But the Cowls hadn't been able to protect the Citizenry from insanity. During the past year, psychosis had been striking increasingly, without warning, indiscriminately.

Greg dropped down beside the thin ascetic figure at the controls. He grabbed Drakeson's arm.

"Did you pick it up, Drake?"

"Uh-huh," Drakeson drawled. His mouth was cynical, his gray eyes somber. "Traced it down to a ten meter radius, but it's underground. About five miles out of Old Washington, just inside the big radioactivated forest east of the Ruins. About half an hour's flight as the crow might fly. If there was a crow left."

"Then let's go. Lift this gadget out of here!"

A spot of nausea bounced into Greg's stomach at Drakeson's reference to what the big Chain blow-up had done to almost all high cellular life forms, including crows. Only insects and a few shielded humans had withstood the radiation. Most higher complex cellular organisms had paid for their complexity. But thanks to the establishment of the Cowled Cities and the Codes of non-change, non-violence, they wouldn't have to pay again. No chance for social change now that might lead to another such disaster.

If they could only trace the cause for this psychosis epidemic—

Greg hadn't thought about it at all until Pat had started talking peculiarly, then when she had broken up completely and left the Cowl, then it had hit home, hard.

The heliocruiser lifted slowly under Drakeson's awkward guidance. Only the Controllers, the Control Council Guards, could work the gadgetry of the City with practiced ease. Everybody else, naturally, was conditioned to various anesthesia states, and had no reason to deal with materialistic things.

The cruiser lifted until it was flying directly beneath the opaque stuff of the Cowl, lost in the dazzling rainbows of sunlight shattering through.

Drakeson said. "We'll keep up here. Maybe the Controllers won't see us."

"What?" A peculiar coolness slid along Greg's spine.

"Maybe they won't see us," repeated Drakeson, and then he smiled wryly. "Listen, Greg. You're way ahead of me in the Dream Continuity. You're a lot further away from reality than I am. More impractical. So listen to a word or two before we try to break through the Cowl.

"We've never been Outside, don't forget that. It's dangerous. You haven't considered any of the angles. For example, I picked up a couple of shielding suits which you hadn't thought of. And two small wrist Geigers. If I hadn't thought of them, then we'd probably have been contaminated with hard radiation out there, and would have been thrown into the septic pools for about six months."

Greg shivered. That would have been very bad.

"It's deadly out there; poisonous, Greg. Only the insane have wanted to go Outside for the last few years, and only the Controllers have been out, and then only to try to track down the hiding places of the Colonists. You hadn't considered that, but I did. So I had to steal a couple of heat-blasters, from the Museum...."

"You what?" Greg stared at the two deadly coiled weapons Drakeson dragged from beneath the seat. "Do the Controllers know?"

"They've probably found out by now, or will very soon," Drakeson looked grim. "They'll be after us with sky-cars and para-guns. And they're sure to slap a psycho label on us. They would anyway, probably, for just going Outside. But having destructive forbidden weapons on us, they're sure to, and we couldn't go Outside without weapons, Greg."

That was right, Greg knew. Paralysis guns wouldn't have been enough out there. Drakeson said softly:

"Is she worth it, Greg? We may have to be brain-probed. Is she worth that kind of pain?"

CHAPTER THREE

Greg's stomach seemed to tie up in knots. Brain-probing, psychometry. Greg whispered hoarsely. "She's worth it, Drake. And besides, it's ridiculous to think that we'll be suspected. I'm only interested in preventing Pat from making that suicide trip. The Controllers have the same interest."

"But that's their job. You and I aren't supposed to be concerned with reality. They've gotten very sensitive this last year. They can't take any chances. At the least sign of disintegration, they have to apprehend and send you to psychometry."

Greg said. "You trying to get out of your bargain, Drake? If you don't want that carton of Stage Five dream capsules, then—"

"Oh no, I'll take a chance to get that carton. I never thought I'd get a chance to experience such premature dreams. It's worth the gamble, we might get away without being probed."

Greg's head ached. Reality always gave him a headache. He wasn't used to it. A man who had reached Stage Five had been an anesthesiac too long to find reality comfortable.

"I know the Codes," Greg whispered. "Legally, there's no reason to be apprehended just for leaving the Cowl. And as for the blasters, well—we can drop them off, hide them, if the Controllers get after us."

The cruiser moved down the sloping arc of the Cowl toward the dark patch that Greg recognized as a merging chamber. The plastic spires of the City reached up around them as though reaching for the sun. Only a few human figures could be seen far below, on roofs, and in the streets. A few low stage humans not in anesthesia.

Greg crawled into the shielding suit. He took over the unfamiliar controls while Drakeson got his own shielding suit on. They weren't heavy, but were sluggish material that could throw off ordinary radiation.

Behind him Greg heard Drakeson's harsh yell. "Sky-cars! Ten of them! Shooting up out of the Control Tower and coming right toward us! Merge, and merge fast, Greg, if you still want to go Outside."

Inside the thick sheeting of the suit, Greg's skin was soaked with perspiration. His face was strained as he moved the cruiser into the first lock chamber. The cruiser had to move through a series of locks to the Outside. A precaution to keep bacteria, radiation, other inimical elements from coming in while an exit from the Cowl was being made.

One by one the locks opened and closed as grav-hooks pulled the cruiser through. It was a precariously balanced culture, this one inside the Cowls, Greg thought. Like living inside a gigantic sealed test-tube. Any slightly alien elements introduced into that test-tube could make it a place of sealed death in a short time. A rigidly controlled, non-changing environment. That was fine, except that some humans within it had a habit of changing, and for the worse. Retrogression, psychosis.

Psychometry was trying frantically to find the cause. It seemed obvious that the Venusian Colonists might be causing psychotics to appear in order to swell their ranks of volunteers to go to Venus to start a "new dynamic, progressive order." Madness. Suicide.

Progressive evolutionary philosophies meant change, and change might lead anywhere. But eventually it could only lead to another horrible *Chain*. One Chain had been enough.

The earth had been thoroughly wrecked. The few survivors had set up the anti-reality standards, the Cowls and the Codes—and the Controllers. They established the Dream Continuity that led to the various anesthetic stages.

But people went insane. They disagreed. They fled the Cowls. Venusian Colonial Enterprises resulted. It was organized insanity. A neatly planned psychosis, with grandiose delusions of justification. They would save humanity! Madness. Schizophrenia.

Venusian Colonization had been organized three years before. At least four known spaceships had been constructed, stocked, and blasted. They changed their subterranean hideouts after each blast. It had just never occurred to Greg that Pat could go psycho and join them.

It was even more ridiculous for the Controllers to suspect *him* of being psycho.

He felt a little better as the cruiser broke out beyond the Cowl and into the blazing natural sun of noon. It blinded Greg. Frightened him a little.

He'd never seen the sun before, except dimmed by the Cowl.

He sent the cruiser climbing rapidly above the weird grotesque terrain. Drakeson jumped into the seat beside him. His face was white.

"Open the converter feed valves wide, Greg! Clear open! The Control cars aren't stopping at the merger. They're coming on through. They're right behind us."

Greg looked back. Ten sky-cars, and within neuro-gun range. He jerked the converter wide open. Acceleration slammed him back hard. He knew now what fear was. In dreams you never suffered it.

CHAPTER FOUR

The audio in the control panel cracked out.

"Dalson! Drakeson! Turn around! Re-enter the Cowl. Return immediately. This is a Control Council order. Do so or we fire with full charge neuro-blasts."

Paralysis guns. And full blast. Greg swallowed. They meant business. And without even a formal enquiry!

Drakeson said in a whisper. "What are we going to do?"

Greg didn't know. How could they think he was psycho?

Drakeson licked his lips. "I don't want to go under the brain-probers, Greg. Nobody does. I don't want to be re-conditioned. I want to stay like I am. I'm not psycho. And they'll brain-probe us sure if we don't turn around and go back. And even if we do—"

The audio's cold impersonal voice said:

"This is the last order. The neuro-guns are ready to fire."

Greg's mind ran in mad circles. He tried to think. He felt Drakeson move, and then he saw Drakeson's hand with that infernal injection solution jiggling around in a big hypodermic syringe.

"I've just given myself another shot, Greg. You'd better have another right now. If we land down there we'll need all the adrenolex we can get."

Greg hardly felt the injection as he tried to think, clarify his situation. I'm not psycho, he thought desperately. I'm doing something a little bit different, but it isn't psychosis.

But good integrated citizens would not fight against the orders from Control. All right. He would submit to brain-probing. But he'd get Pat out of that trap she was in first. He might be able to talk her out of it if he could get to her personally, be with her a while. The Controllers certainly couldn't. They'd drive her away into space as soon as she saw them.

The solution. A legality. He knew the Codes didn't he?

He yelled back at the pursuing sky-cars via the audio:

"Don't fire those neuro-guns. This is Greg Dalson speaking. There's a law against any aggressive destructive action on the part of any Citizen."

The audio replied. "The neuro-guns aren't destructive. Temporary paralysis."

Greg said. "This cruiser is at a high altitude and traveling fast. If you paralyze us now, the cruiser will crash. By using the neuro-guns on us, you will be destructive, homicidal."

A dead silence greeted this statement. Greg went on. "I'm a Stage Five citizen. Legally, there's no restriction against going outside the Cowl. I'll report your action and attitudes to the Council if you fire those neuro-guns."

Drakeson choked something unintelligible. His face was deathly pale. "Clever," he whispered. "But that clinches it. When we do go back, it's psychometry for us, Greg."

Finally the audio answered. The voice was not so cold. It had a tinge of emotionalism. It said. "A technicality, but it does prevent us from firing the neuro-guns. However, we feel it our duty to remain with you until you do return to the Cowl. Because of the recent epidemic of psychosis, we find this authorized by the Control Council...."

Greg savagely flipped off the audio. Drakeson said. "If they stay on our trail, we'll lead them right to Pat. They'll scare her away before you get a chance to talk with her, and try to prevent her from going on the ship."

"I know," Greg said. "I know. We've got to figure something—"

He looked down at the fantastic semi-organic flora below. "How far to go yet, Drake?"

"About three minutes."

"All right. We'll set the cruiser down here, and walk to where Pat is."

Drakeson choked. "That's suicide," he said. "We won't have a chance."

CHAPTER FIVE

Greg didn't have time to be surprised at his own actions. He pulled Drakeson's hands away from the controls. Drakeson was trying to stop him from bringing the cruiser down.

Drakeson gasped. "Even with the heat-blasters, we'll never get a hundred meters away from where we land. I figured on landing directly over the place—"

"So will the Controllers," Greg said. He hurled Drakeson back, heard him sprawl on the mesh flooring where he lay, half sobbing.

Greg angled the ship down abruptly. "As soon as we land, I'm running for it," he called back. "The Controllers will be down there swarming all over us, and I don't want to lead them to where Pat is."

Drakeson crawled over to the bunk and sat on it. "All right," he said. "I'm with you. It's too late to get out of it now. For a carton of premature dreams, I've gotten myself stuck with a psycho tag. I'm stuck with it anyway, now. Might as well go on, and stay out of the brain-probers as long as possible."

Greg felt a tingling crawl up his wrists as they dropped down above the gigantic, semi-organic forest. Mutated cells in the process of change had played havoc with the pre-Chain life forms. According to what little he had gotten from info-tapes, there was no longer any distinction or at least very little, between organic and inorganic life, outside the Cowls.

Psycho. He'd still argue with Drakeson about that, but he didn't have time. He wasn't psycho. As soon as he persuaded Pat to abandon the flight, they'd give themselves up, return to the Cowl, and things would return to normal, to anesthesia, Stage Five, then Six, then Seven, on to the final eternal dream.

That's the way it was going to be.

And if they had to suffer the hells of brain-probing and the awful ego-loss of re-conditioning, then they would do that too. It was for the good of the Cowls, the preservation of the Codes. A noble sacrifice. Must be no change. No menace to stability. Any suggestion of change made one suspect.

Greg's eyes misted as he brought the cruiser to a half-crash landing. Even as he tried to bring his blurred vision into focus, he was running to the exit. He had the sliding panel open. He was up to his knees in writhing tendrils. He was running through a crimson twilight.

Behind him, he heard Drakeson tearing through the tendrils, and clutching vines. Overhead he could hear the drone of the sky-car's atomurbinic motors. Whether they would land and continue the search on foot through the deadly forest, Greg couldn't know.

He didn't know anything about the Controllers' methods. "How far, Drake," he yelled through the inter-person audio. Drakeson came running up beside Greg. Severed strings of torn, still living life-stuff writhed from his shoulders and legs.

"I'd say about half a mile straight ahead. That's a long way through this nightmare."

Greg screamed. A broad mushroom-like growth had opened a mouth. A gigantic, sickeningly gray mouth full of deadly, flesh-eating acid.

A flower-bright vine with great tensile strength raked Drakeson in toward that gaping maw.

Drakeson's arms were held tight against his sides. He was straining—helpless. Through the glassine mask of his helmet, Greg saw Drakeson's face turning red with constriction.

His voice came to Greg in a burst of fear. "The gun, Greg! The heat-blaster—quick—"

Greg leaned forward, staring in rigid fascination. Fleshy stocks swayed toward him. Other mouths opened, petal mouths. Gigantic floral traps, and cannibal blooms.

"Greg! Greg!" Drakeson was framed now by that great cannibal maw.

Greg had the heat-blaster up. He had it leveled. But he couldn't depress the firing stud.

"Drake! I can't! I can't!"

How could any integrated man be deliberately destructive? How could any sane person—kill?

"I can't—Drake—" The awful conflict seemed to rip through his body. He felt the sweat, hot and profuse, rolling down his face. He concentrated on that gun, on his finger, on the firing stud.

The cannibal blossom was closing. Sticky juices dripped over Drakeson. He was screaming. Greg's finger lifted. He could not fire.

The Codes said no destruction. No killing. The Codes had been established after the great Chain disaster. Violence begets violence, the Codes said. And once begun, it was accumulative, like the snowball rolling down hill.

Greg sagged. His knees buckled. He sprawled out in the slippery muck. Tendrils swished softly and hungrily around him. He heard a shout. He tried to twist his head. Figures blurred before his eyes, and he heard the deadly *chehowwwwww* of a terrific blast.

The last thing he remembered before the dark wrapped him up softly and warmly, was the cannibal plant exploding in a million fragments of stringy tissue, and Drakeson falling free.

I didn't fire, he was thinking. *Someone else saved Drakeson. But I think I might have done it. My finger—it was moving—bending—or was it? No. I couldn't have been destructive. Couldn't have killed.*

CHAPTER SIX

Consciousness came back to Greg. Painfully. It came back slowly and it took a long time. He lifted his eyelids. He raised himself to a sitting position. He stared down a gloomy, phosphorescent corridor. It was obviously subterranean. It was damp, chill. Cold luciferin light glowed from lichen on walls and low ragged ceiling.

It was long and it finally curved, he decided. But he could look back into a long slow curve of corridor and ahead into the same. Here and there, the mouths of branch corridors came in.

He looked at his hand. It still clutched the butt of the heat-blaster.

He felt strange. The surroundings were very real, yet they seemed somehow not real. The shock of trying to fire that blaster when the sanity in him shrieked "No!" had been too much for him. The shock had blanked him out.

He breathed a deep sigh of temporary relief and triumph. He hadn't killed. He thought of Drakeson. Somebody had saved him. Someone had killed. Not the Controllers. They could employ only the neuro-guns to paralyze. So he decided that Colonists had probably saved Drakeson.

Terror gripped Greg then. He remembered Drakeson yelling at him, the distended eyes, the straining face. And how he himself had almost given in, had almost killed.

Had almost gone psycho.

But he hadn't. That was the important thing. He was still a sane, integrated part of the Cowls and the Codes. And after a test like that, he figured that nothing could break him. Let them send him to psychometry. Let them clamp on the brain-probers and leave them on for months. They'd not find any psycho tendencies in Greg Dalson.

Greg tried to reason. But he had no place, no foundation, for a beginning. He didn't know where he was, or why he had been left here. He knew that someone, the Colonists probably, had saved Drakeson from that plant thing. Some mental pressure had blacked him out, he thought, and then what? He didn't know.

Which way? It didn't seem to matter. He started walking.

He was bone-weary. His head throbbed. His eyes burned. And he was afraid. He had gotten himself into a completely un-Codified situation. He was lost, helpless, outside the protection of the Cowls, the Codes, and anesthesia.

He was surrounded by reality. Reality in all its essential horror. Conflict. Physical danger. Uncertainties. Materialistic barriers. All the old shibboleths that the Cowls and the Codes and the anesthetic dreams had protected him from.

And all because of Pat Nichols.

But he'd stood a big test. And he'd won. He hadn't killed. He wasn't destructive. He—

The cry touched his ears and died. It was too violent and filled with pain and terror to make any definite impression the first time. He crouched. His eyes distended. The scream came again, and this time it chopped through him. His nerves seemed to shrivel and curl beneath the repeated onslaughts of the screams.

Then he was running. He didn't know why, except that he had to run. He ran with fearful, gasping desperation. But he didn't know why.

CHAPTER SEVEN

He ran past the mouth opening into the main corridor. Then came back and ran into the darker, strangely-lighted artery. He ran harder. And yet he wasn't running. Not all of him. As he ran, he was conscious of some undefinable, but terrific conflict.

Beneath the suit, his skin burned with sweat. He felt the rigid pattern of tensed neck and jaw muscles.

I don't feel at all familiar. Something's very wrong. Everything's wrong. I'm displaced, like something that has slipped into an alien dimension.

He stopped, quickly. His heart seemed to swell, burst with terror. Terror and something else. The something else came, and with it came horror of itself. The emotion, and then horror of the emotion. He stood shivering, his teeth clacking like an ancient abacus.

"Pat!" He screamed her name. The cry pounded back into his ears inside the helmet.

This wasn't Drakeson. This was Pat. Pat was going to die now. Not Drakeson.

The walls were—*alive*. They were not like the walls of the corridors.

This was a circular chamber, and the walls were sagging and undulating like part of a giant's flesh. He heard heavy sluggish sounds.

Masses of the gray viscous stuff sagged, changed form, remolded itself into monstrous shapes.

Pat! Only her face and part of her upper body were visible now. The shielding of her suit had been cracked wide open by pressure as the semi-organic thing, whatever it was, had closed around her.

The walls rushed in as Greg stumbled drunkenly. The ceiling sagged lower. Long knobs fell, like globules of paste, then lengthened into shapeless tendrils that snapped out at Greg.

He fell back.

Pat's scream penetrated again. No beauty remained in her face now. Her eyes were sick. Her lips were loose and trembling.

"Greg—help me—help me—see what it does—the others—"

He saw the others then. Maybe he hadn't noticed before, because his mind didn't want him to see.

Husks. Pallid wrinkled husks, sucked dry and shriveled. Several figures not recognizable anymore, hardly recognizable as human. Just vaguely human, broken, sucked dry.

His mind seemed covered by a grotesque shadow. His flesh crawled and his throat turned dry, and perspiration made a stream down his throat. He felt his eyes looking down at his right hand.

It held the heat-blaster. The skin felt tight as though it would split as he gripped the heavy butt of the coiled weapon.

He concentrated on the finger that was frozen on the firing stud. If he could destroy, then he was insane. His experience with Drakeson, that had been no test at all compared with this. This was Pat. Pat, and she was dying—dying unspeakably.

This was the great test of his sanity. He concentrated on the finger. He must keep it frozen. He must back out of here. Get away, get back to the Cowl, back to anesthesia and sleep.

The finger raised slowly from the stud. His feet lifted as his body moved fitfully back, back, back—

"Greg—help me, Greg—"

Her eyes stopped him. They tumbled into terrible clarity. She whispered starkly.

"Greg—help me—kill it, Greg. For me—Kill it."

He felt his lips part in a great and terrible cry of torture. His shoulders began to twitch slightly. His arms and fingers took up the jerky rhythm. Horror and a violent crimson flood of unfamiliar emotions mushroomed like a volcano of madness. Something began crumbling away.

He lurched forward. He felt the heat-blaster heaving, throwing out its deadly load. The gun had weight and power in his hand as he crouched lower and moved in.

The power load swathed in long slicing arcs. Steam and sickening stench fell around him. He moved in. He stumbled forward kicking out to right and left at the quivering slices of stuff that were falling around him.

Destruction. Kill. Death. This was all three, and in a giant, almost inconceivable quantity.

Her face through the steaming cloud. Her throat moving as she swallowed. Brightness, the brightness of disbelief and impossibility coming into her eyes.

He kept moving in until the monstrous mutated gray thing was thoroughly dead. Until every separate tendril and patch was blasted to smoke. Then he lifted her broken body in his arms.

Tears fell on the opaqueness of his helmet. "I'm sorry, Pat," he choked.

"I'm sorry it didn't happen sooner. I'm sorry I waited too long—but it isn't easy—to let yourself go insane."

Something was wrong. Pat! Pat! She seemed to be fading away from him, drifting away, melting into tattered veils of cloud. Her face became only two bright glad eyes, then they also melted together into a radiant pool. He toppled into the pool. He sank down, a wonderful lifelessness spreading through him.

He closed his eyes. Something was beginning to be very funny. In the thickening dark, he laughed a little. And in that laugh was a crazy, climbing note of—triumph.

CHAPTER EIGHT

He opened his eyes. He was laughing, in a kind of soft hysteria. He was on a couch. Not a dream couch, but just a plain hard bed. He sat up stiffly. Pain tingled down his legs. He saw Pat Nichols. And another. A man. He remembered him vaguely, one of the first who had escaped from the Cowl. His name—yes—he remembered now. Merrol.

Pat Nichols, alive, and smiling. Very beautiful too in a brief aerosilk bra and shorts and sandals. Her hair was a dark lovely cloud flowing down over bare shoulders.

"Hello, Greg," she said softly. "Welcome to—the Colonists."

"What?" He swung his legs around. "I don't understand. Not entirely."

Merrol, a gaunt elderly man, nodded from behind a desk. Merrol's hair was gray and sparse. Strange, seeing a man who showed age. Within the Cowls, one never grew physically old.

Pat said, "This is Ralph Merrol, Personnel Director of Venusian Colonization Enterprises."

Greg's numbness was filtering away beneath Pat's warm glad eyes. He raised his hand. The heat-blaster was still gripped in his fingers. It evidently hadn't been fired.

"It was all illusion," he said. "The scene in the cavern. It never happened?"

Merrol's care-lined face nodded. "It happened, but in your mind, Greg. We rescued you and Drakeson from the cannibal plant. We brought you here. You had lost consciousness. We put you under the hypnosene rays, and put you through an experience that was quite real to you. We proved something to ourselves, and to you. Greg—you're sane now."

Greg tried to understand. The thing didn't make sense yet, but the glimmerings of the truth were beginning to solidify in his aching brain.

"Sane? But I killed. I wanted to kill. I wanted to destroy, and I did. That's hardly the actions of a—sane man."

Merrol smiled thinly. "From our point of view it is, Greg. We consider ourselves sane. We consider the Cowled Cities, and the Codes insane. It's relative I supposed, but I think we can convince you, if we haven't already."

Greg looked at Pat. She smiled. He smiled back. "Justified or not," he whispered. "I'm here. Sane or insane, I'm one of the Colonists now I guess. Unless I want to return to the Cowls, be probed and re-conditioned."

Pat whispered. "Do you, Greg?"

He shook his head. "Not now. I'm tired. I don't want to now. Maybe I never will. All I want now, is rest."

Merrol leaned across the desk. "Before you rest, you'd better get a few things straight, Greg. We want you to be convinced that you're doing the right thing. We feel that the big Chain blow-up shocked the whole human race into a mass psychosis, comparable to individual cases of hysteria, schizophrenia, escape from reality. That's why the non-change, non-aggressiveness Codes were established. Also, the anesthesia, the Dream Continuity Scale—nothing but hysteria on a mass and planned basis."

Merrol got up. He walked around and sat down beside Greg.

"Carried out to its inevitable end, this could only lead to mass racial suicide. That's obvious. It was a static dead end. A few people recovered from the psychosis. They escaped, and formed the Colonists. But their own welfare wasn't the most important thing.

"They concerned themselves then with the freeing of the Citizens of the Cowls from their psychosis. The world is untenable on a large scale now, due to radioactive poisoning. It will remain untenable for some time. Meanwhile we decided to Colonize Venus. We've established Colonies there. Thriving communities, but the important thing is this, Greg—it's given new impetus and enthusiasm to those who become sane and escape the Cowls. It presents a big challenge and solidifies the cure.

"It's bigger than Control has any idea that it is. It will take a long time yet, but we'll win. You have noticed the increase in so-called insanity in the Cowls. It really means just the opposite. Our numbers are increasing by leaps and bounds."

Greg said, "The Controllers think you're using some psychological or physical pressure to create these—cures."

Merrol smiled. "We've got a recruiting system. Drakeson, for example, is a spy. We have spies all over the Cowls."

Greg stared. "Drakeson?"

A door opened. The lean cynical man entered, nodded, and stood beside Pat. His eyes shone more brightly as he looked at Greg.

"That's right," Drakeson said. "Remember the two injections. I said they were adrenolex. They weren't. Our spies inside the Cowls are equipped with a supply of a certain aggression factor. It used to be called Kappa, or K, for killer. This factor is handed down through the generations in the general cell protoplasm. It forces aggressive tendencies. It makes a man capable of physical aggressive action, and able to kill, if he has to. High motivation is required though, in most cases. With you, my probable death wasn't enough. It took the vision of Pat here in the clutches of a monster to make the Kappa factor work on you, Greg."

Greg rubbed his eyes. Pat came over and he took her hand, held it tightly. A warmth came out of her and into him, into his mind.

CHAPTER NINE

Drakeson went on. "We isolated the Kappa factor, made it into solution. We all have it, even the anesthetic citizens of the Cowls, but the mass shock psychosis won't let it work. However, a strong overload of Kappa injection will sometimes break the psychosis, force the person back into an aggressive personality, capable of destruction. Each individual carries an armament of between 200 and 800 particles of the Kappa factor after we give an injection. It took 1600 particles to break your suicidal hysteria."

Pat squeezed his hand. Greg looked up. He grinned with a kind of glad embarrassment.

"I don't know yet whether to thank you or not. Frankly though, I do feel better."

He thought of the Cowls. Test-tubes, glass cages, and dreams that led finally to the final anesthesia, death. He shuddered, and tried to push the memory out of his mind. It seemed unhealthy now. Unclean and—yes, it did seem insane.

He raised his eyes to the ceiling. He saw the self-inverting three dimensional mechanism that had given him that starkly real adventure in which he had been able to kill, for Pat. A dream sequence, partly hypnotic, partly created by cathode image activating the multi-phase AC. A high harmonic of multi-phase AC field hanging over him, and a focusing radiator. Dream. Nightmare.

He looked at Pat. "I think I'll take reality now," he said softly. He felt the pull on his arm, and he got up. She led him through a door and into a soft twilight. He held her tightly against him.

She whispered. "The ship's waiting for us, Greg. The next ship. You're already on the passenger list. You see, I knew you'd come with us. I was hoping so desperately, I couldn't think any differently."

He kissed her. He held her more tightly as though—as though—

He felt her warm muscles tense against him. Her eyes widened.

"Greg! What is it?"

He shook his head. "I—I got to wondering if this too, might not be just a dream. I've been in anesthesia too long maybe. How can I know what's real and what isn't real?"

He felt her warm moist fingers on the back of his neck. He felt her lift on her toes, pull his face down. She kissed him. Her voice was husky, and her breath was warm on his lips.

"Do you know now, Greg? Is this a dream?"

He shook his head. His voice was hoarse.

"No—no—this isn't a dream."

She laughed softly. They moved away, down the corridor toward the ship.

FREEWAY

Freeway by Bryce Walton

First published in 1955

This Edition Copyright @2020 by Eli Jayne

All rights reserved.

Cover art by Eli Jayne

The Morrisons didn't lose their freedom. They were merely sentenced to the highways for life, never stopping anywhere, going no place, just driving, driving, driving....

CHAPTER ONE

Some people had disagreed with him. They were influential people. He was put on the road.

Stan wanted to scream at the big sixteen-cylinder Special to go faster. But Salt Lake City, where they would allow him to stop over for the maximum eight hours, was a long way off. And anyway, he couldn't go over a hundred. The Special had an automatic cut-off.

He stared down the super ten-lane Freeway, down the glassy river, plunging straight across the early desert morning—into nowhere. That was Anna's trouble. His wife couldn't just keep travelling, knowing there was no place to go. No one could do that. I can't do it much longer either, Stan thought. The two of us with no place to go but back and forth, across and over, retracing the same throughways, highways, freeways, a thousand times round and round like mobile bugs caught in a gigantic concrete net.

He kept watching his wife's white face in the rear-view mirror. Now there was this bitter veil of resignation painted on it. He didn't know when the hysteria would scream through again, what she would try next, or when.

She had always been highly emotional, vital, active, a fighter. The Special kept moving, but it was still a suffocating cage. She needed to stop over somewhere, longer, much longer than the maximum eight hours. She needed treatment, a good long rest, a doctor's care—

She might need more than that. Complete freedom perhaps. She had always been an all-or-nothing gal. But he couldn't give her that.

Shimmering up ahead he saw the shack about fifty feet off the Freeway, saw the fluttering of colorful hand-woven rugs and blankets covered with ancient Indian symbols.

It wasn't an authorized stop, but he stopped. The car swayed slightly as he pressed the hydraulic.

From the bluish haze of the desert's tranquil breath a jackrabbit hobbled onto the Freeway's fringe. It froze. Then with a squeal it scrambled back into the dust to escape the thing hurtling toward it out of the rising sun.

CHAPTER TWO

Stan jumped out. The dust burned. There was a flat heavy violence to the blast of morning sun on his face. He looked in through the rear window of the car.

"You'll be okay, honey." Her face was feverish. Sweat stood out on her forehead. She didn't look at him.

"It's too late," she said. "We're dead, Stan. Moving all the time. But not alive."

He turned. The pressure, the suppression, the helpless anger was in him meeting the heavy hand of the sun. An old Indian, wearing dirty levis and a denim shirt and a beaded belt, was standing near him. His face was angled, so dark it had a bluish tinge. "Blanket? Rugs? Handmade. Real Indian stuff."

"My wife's sick," Stan said. "She needs a doctor. I want to use your phone to call a doctor. I can't leave the Freeway—"

This was the fourth unauthorized stop he had made since Anna had tried to jump out of the car back there—when it was going a hundred miles an hour.

The Indian saw the Special's license. He shrugged, then shook his head.

"For God's sake don't shake your head," Stan yelled. "Just let me use your phone—"

The Indian kept on shaking his head. There was no emotion, only a fatalistic acceptance of the overly-complex world he and many of his kind had rejected long ago. "You're a Crackpot."

"But what's that to you when I just want to use your phone? If I can get a doctor's affidavit—"

"If I help you, then the Law come down on my neck."

"But I only want to use the phone!"

"I cannot risk it. You drive on now."

He felt it, the thing that was slowly dying in Anna's eyes. This need to strike out, strike out hard and murderously at something real. This suppressed feeling had been growing in him now for too many miles to remember. He started forward. But the Indian slid the knife from his beaded belt. "I am sorry, and that is the honest truth," the Indian said. "But you have to move on now." The Indian stepped back toward the ancient symbols of his kind. "We have stopped moving. We stay here now no matter what. Now, White Doctor, it is your turn to move on."

He put his hand over his eyes as though to push something down. One act of violence, and the questionable "freedom" would be ended. That would be an admission of defeat. His hand still over his eyes, he backed away. Then he turned, choking and half blinded with smoldering rage.

Keep moving. Nothing else to do with them but put them on the road and keep them moving, never letting them stop over long enough to cause trouble, to stir up any wrong ideas. Hit the road, Crackpot. Head on down the super ten-lane Freeway into the second Middle Ages lit with neon.

Then he was running, yelling at Anna. She was past the shack and stumbling through sand toward the mountains. He coaxed her back and into the car, sickness gorging his throat as she kicked and screamed at him and he forced her into the corner of the back seat.

"Stan, we could run to the mountains."

"The Law wouldn't let us get very far. Remember, the Special's remotely controlled. If we leave the Freeway, they'd be on us in no time. They know when we stop, where we stop. They know if we leave the Freeway!"

"But we would have *tried*!"

"They're just waiting for us to do something legally wrong so they can put us away, honey. We can't let ourselves be goaded into doing anything legally wrong!"

"Stan—" she was shaking her head, and her eyes were wet. "Can't you see, can't you *see*? What they do to us doesn't matter now. It's what we do, or don't do—"

When she quieted down a little, he got back under the wheel. Within a hundred feet, the Special was going eighty-five miles an hour.

CHAPTER THREE

The thing he had to hold on to hard, was the fact that they had never really done anything wrong. Anna needed a good long rest so she could regain the proper perspective. The Higher Court itself had said they hadn't done anything wrong. There were thousands now on the Freeways, none of them had any real criminal labels on them. They were risks. They *might* be dangerous. Attitudes not quite right. A little off center one way or another at the wrong time. Some personal indiscretion in the past. A thought not quite orthodox in the present. A possible future threat. A threat to total security.

Be careful, easy does it. Too many black marks on his road record and the "freedom" of the road would go. Then he would be a criminal in fact, instead of a vague criminal possibility, and put behind bars. Or worse.

The hell with them. The hell with them all. He pulled over onto an emergency siding and stopped. Not authorized. A good long rest and talk with Anna—

Then he saw it. Suddenly, frantically, he wanted to move on. But now he couldn't. He kept seeing the light of defiance fading from Anna's eyes.

The Patrolcar was there, the way it always was there, suddenly, materializing out of the desert, or out of a mountain, a side street. Sometimes it was a helio dropping out of the sky. Sometimes it was a light flashing in darkness.

Every official of the law: city, county, state, or federal, had a full record on every Special. They could control them at will. Stop them, start them, keep them moving down the line.

Jails of the open road. Mobility lending to incarceration a mock illusion of freedom. Open sky. Open prairie. The Freeway stretching ahead.

And the Patrolcar coming up behind.

The Patrolcar stopped. The two Patrolmen in black and gold uniforms looked in at Stan. "Well, egghead," the older, beefy one said. "It was nice of you to stop without being asked. A fellow named Ferreti back at Snappy Service No. 7 said you might be a trouble-maker. We thought we ought to check up."

Stan said, "I wanted to use his phone to try to get a doctor to examine my wife. She's ill. She needs help and I've been trying—"

Without turning, the older Patrolman interrupted, "Larry, what you got on the philosopher here?"

The younger Patrolman who had a shy, almost embarrassed air about him looked into his black notebook. "He isn't a philosopher, not officially, Leland. Every Crackpot we stop, you figure him to be a philosopher. You just hate philosophers that's all."

"Well, that's a fact, boy." When he took the cigar out of his mouth, the corners of his mouth were stained brown. "My kid got loused up plenty by a philosopher in High School last year. I raised a squawk and got the Crackpot kicked out. I also got three others booted out for hiring him in the first place. I found out he was a lousy atheist!"

The Patrolman put the cigar back into his mouth. "What have you got on him, Lieutenant?"

"Stanley L. Morrison, B.A. Drake University, Class of '55. Doctor of Philosophy, Drake University, 1957. Federal employee 1957-59. Dropped from Federal employment, January, 1959—"

"What for, Lieutenant?"

"For excessive political enthusiasm for the preceding political party in office." The Lieutenant looked up almost apologetically. "Looks like he was unfortunate enough to have been on the wrong side of the fence when the Independants were elected."

"These guys are dangerous no matter what side they're on. A Crackpot shouldn't be on either side. Well, Lieutenant, what else?"

"Professor of Nuclear Physics, Drake University, 1960-62. Dismissed by Board of Regents May 31, charged with 'private thought inconsistent with the policies of the University'. Special inquiry August 5. Dismissal sustained. Was put on the road as a permanent risk to security February 3, 1963. He's been on the roads for a year and three months."

Stan forced quiet into his voice. "My wife's sick. If I could get a doctor to examine her, I'm sure I could get a permit to lay over somewhere so she can get rest and proper treatment."

"Only eight hours," the beefy one said. "That's the limit. And you're not supposed to have stopped here at all. Or back at the Indian's."

"I know," Stan said. "But this is an emergency. If you could help me—"

The beefy one grinned into the back seat. "That might be all that's bothering the missus, egghead. She ain't getting the proper treatment maybe."

Easy, easy does it. In the rear-view mirror he could see that what the Patrolman said had brought a flush of life to her face. She was rigid now, and then suddenly she screamed. "Stan! For God's sake, Stan, don't take any more from the simian!"

"Let's go," the young Lieutenant said quickly. "We've got the report and we'll forward it. There's no call to bait them."

"Shut up," the beefy one said.

"Don't tell me to shut up," the Lieutenant said. He put his notebook away. "This man's never committed any crime. That's why he's on the road. They didn't know what else to do with him. We're supposed to keep them moving that's all. Not hold them up because of personal vindictiveness."

The beefy one's face was getting red. "Don't use your big words on me, boy. I'll send you back to College."

"He's getting punishment enough. You've got nothing against him, or the woman."

The beefy one took a deep breath. "Okay, Lieutenant. But I'm going to drop a few words in the right place. I guess you know how the Commissioner feels about Crackpots."

"I don't give a damn. Come on, let's get out of here." The Lieutenant looked at Stan a moment. "You'd better move on, Doctor."

"Thanks," Stan said.

"At the next Snappy Service maybe you can phone. That's an hour's authorized stop for Specials. There's a Government Project in the hills nearby. You might be able to contact a Doctor there."

CHAPTER FOUR

The sage spread out to a blur. Heat wavered up from the Freeway. In the rear-view mirror he saw Anna leaning back, her legs stretched out, her arms limp at her sides. She wasn't thinking about this with an historical perspective, that was the trouble. She had lost the saving sense of continuity with generations gone, which stretched like a lifeline across the frightening present.

Keep the perspective. Wait it out. That was the only way. This was an historical phase, part of a cycle. Stan couldn't blame any one. Anxiety, suspicion of intellectuals and men of science—as though they had been any more responsible really than any one else—suspicion and fear. There always had to be whipping boys. In one form or another, he knew, it had happened many times before. Another time of change and danger. There was a quicksand of fear under men's reasoning.

When things were better, they hadn't remained better. When they were bad, they couldn't stay bad. Wait it out. One thing he knew—neither he nor any other scientist could detach himself from life. The frightened policemen of the public conscience had made the mistake of thinking they could detach the scientist.

I'll not withdraw from it. All of it represents a necessary change. If not for the immediate better, then I'll be here for the immediate worst which will someday change into something better than ever.

But Anna's tired voice was whispering in his ear. "First of all, we're individuals, men, women. We've got to fight, fight back!"

"At what? Ourselves?"

A sign said: HAL'S SNAPPY SERVICE. TWENTY-SEVEN MILES.

She's right, he thought, and started slowing down. This is it. He wasn't going any farther until Anna was examined, and he was given an okay to stop somewhere so she could rest.

CHAPTER FIVE

It was a dusty oasis, an arid anachronism on the desert's edge. Beyond it, the mountains blundered up like giants from a purplish haze, brooding and somehow threatening. Groves of cottonwoods could be seen far ahead, and sprinklings of green reaching into the thinning sage.

The old man shuffled out of the shade by the coke machine. Behind him, through dusty glass, Stan saw the blurred faces staring with still curiosity.

The old man hesitated, then came around between the pumps to the driver's side. He was all stooped bone and leathery skin. His face, Stan thought beneath the rising desperation, resembled an African ceremonial mask.

To the left a '62 Fordster was cranked up for a grease job. But the only life around it was a scrawny dog lying out flat to get all the air possible on its ribby body, its tongue hanging out in the black grease.

"The car's okay," Stan said. "I just want to use your telephone."

"Doctor Morrison, you'd better go on to Salt Lake City. That's an eight-hour stopover."

"My wife needs a doctor's okay for a long rest. I can't take a chance on going clear to Salt Lake City."

"But this is only an hour stop."

Stan got out and shoved past the old man. Heat waves shivered up out of the concrete and through the soles of his shoes. The heat seared his dry throat and burned his lungs.

Anna wasn't even looking. She seemed to have forgotten him. Almost everyone had forgotten him by now, he thought, forgotten Doctor Stanley Morrison the man who had never been afraid to speak out and say what he thought, and think what he wanted to think. Fifteen months with never more than an eight hour stopover. Thought and self-regard frozen by perpetual motion, and shriveled by consequent neglect. Only the old man remembered. That was odd.

A man stepped into the doorway. He was lean and powerful with a long gaunt chewing jaw like that of a horse. His eyes were small and black, and he was grinning with anticipation. Stan felt his stomach muscles tighten.

Behind the man, Stan saw the kid. Almost as tall as the man who was obviously his father, but rail-thin, like an emaciated duplicate of the man, a starved, frustrated shadow, grinning and feverishly picking at a pimple under his left ear. He carried a grease-gun cradled in his left arm as though it were a machine gun.

"I'd like to use your phone, please," Stan said. "My wife's ill. I want to phone the Government Project and see if I can get a doctor over here to look at her."

"What seems to be troubling the missus?"

"I don't know!"

"Then how do you know it's a serious sickness, Crackpot?"

"Just let me use the phone? Will you do that?"

"They phoned in ahead, Crackpot. Said you might be a trouble-maker."

"I don't want to make any trouble. I just want to use the phone!"

"Why? Even if the Doc came over, you wouldn't be here. He can't get here inside an hour. And that's all the longer you can stay here. You got to move on."

"I'm coming in to use the phone," Stan heard himself saying. He fought to keep the breathiness out of his voice, the trembling out of his throat.

"I don't guess I'd want to have it said I was coddling a Crackpot."

"I never caused you any trouble."

"You helped build hellbombs," the man said. He took the toothpick out of his mouth. "You crazy bastards got to be kept moving along the road."

"How do you know what I did or didn't do?"

"You're a Crackpot."

"I never helped build any kind of bomb," Stan whispered. "But even if I did—"

"You're one of them nuclear physicists."

"I was an instructor at a University. I taught at a Government school once too—for a while—" He stopped himself, realizing he was defending himself as though somehow he suspected his own guilt.

"You taught other guys how to build hellbombs. Who needs you and your kind, Crackpot? We need your brains like we need a knife in the back."

Stan lunged forward. The kid yelled something in a high cracked voice as Stan lashed out again. He felt his knuckles scrape across hard teeth. Blood leaped from the man's upper lip in a thin crimson slash. His eyes widened with a grudging respect, then he snarled through the blood as he stumbled backward and off balance. He fell against the window and trying to regain his balance, reeled and went down in a welter of empty gallon oil cans.

He gathered himself for an upward lunge. Through the blood staining his teeth, he muttered, "By gawd, Crackpot. I didn't think you had the guts!"

Stan glanced out the window and saw that Anna was gone from the car.

Dimly, he heard the man saying he was going to beat hell out of the Crackpot, going to beat the Crackpot over the head and then the Crackpot wouldn't be able to cook up any more dangerous ideas in it for a long, long time.

Anna may die now, Stan thought as he stood there bent over a little, feeling his wet fists tightening. She may die now, because of a frustrated fool who doesn't know what else to do with himself on a hot and dull and empty afternoon.

Stan suddenly caught the flash of color out of the corner of his eye. He twisted, not thinking at all, and felt his fist sink into the kid's stomach. The kid fell, curled up among the empty oil cans. He writhed and moaned and held his stomach.

"Get up," Stan yelled into the man's face. "Get up—"

The man came up all at once, and his weight hurled Stan clear across the room. He felt the gum machine shatter under him, and the metal grinding into his side as he rolled. Stan felt the grease-gun in his hand as he saw the man lifting the tire tool, and then Stan swung the grease gun into the face, seeing the terrible grin, the blood-stained white smile.

Unrecognizable as it was, the man's face wouldn't go away. Stan swung at it again. Then he heard her voice, Anna's voice, intense and alive, and there was a flash of Anna the way he remembered her a thousand years ago, before they were put on the road. She was tearing at the man's face with her fingernails and kicking him savagely.

Stan had the man's shirt collar and it was ripping under his fingers as he slammed the head against the concrete floor. The thudding rhythm was coming up through his arm and throbbing behind his eyes.

Like drums, he thought as a sickening light flashed on the dusty glass, like primitive war drums beating out a dance of tribal doom.

Suddenly feeling sick and weak, he stood up and walked stiffly out into the sun.

He leaned against the side of the building trying to keep from retching. Anna touched his arm and he looked up, half blinded by the glare of the sun. Her face was flushed and alive. She seemed ten years younger.

"Don't be sorry," she said. "Be glad, Stan."

"They broke us," he whispered. "We've crawled into the cage."

"It doesn't matter, Stan, it doesn't matter what they do to us now! It's something to admit you're human, isn't it?"

She was partly right at least. He felt both glad and sad. But in either case, it was the end of the road.

CHAPTER SIX

He saw the old man lowering the hood of the Special. He ran back between the pumps carrying a metal tool box. "I've fixed it," he said, breathing heavily. "Now get out of here. Push it to the limit. I broke the cut-off too. Hurry it up!"

"But what's the use?" Stan said. "They'll get us sooner or later—"

"They're not going to get you now, not if you stop reasoning everything out as though it were a problem in calculus! I've cut the remote control off, and the radar and radio. They won't know where you are. I've changed the license plate too. But hurry out of here before Hal or his kid start phoning."

"But being on the Freeway," Stan said, "they'll catch up with us! What's the use—"

"Stan!" Anna said sharply. "Can't you *see*? We're getting away!"

"I don't want to run away from it," Stan said.

"You're not running away from anything," the old man said. "You'll find out. Follow my directions and you'll find out. You're not running away. You can get out of the flood water for a while, sit on the bank, until the water drops and clears a little."

Stan looked into the old man's face a long moment. "Who the hell are you anyway?"

"That doesn't matter, Doctor Morrison. Now will you get out of here! Move on down the road!"

Stan finally nodded and took Anna's arm and they started toward the Special. "All right, but what about you?" he asked the old man.

"I'll make out. You just be concerned about yourself, Doctor Morrison. This isn't the first time I've helped someone off the road. It won't be the last time either, I hope."

He waved to them as the Special, without any limit to its speed now except the limitations of a driver's nerve, roared away toward the mountains.

CHAPTER SEVEN

Now the special became anonymous on the Freeway, one of countless cars hurtling down the super ten-lane Freeway, its license changed, its controls and checkers cut off, its sovereignty returned to it by a nameless old man, a box of wrenches, and a roll of wire.

Three hundred miles farther on, the Freeway began a long banked curve; a thick wall of cottonwoods, willows and smaller brush lined the side where a creek rushed out of a cleft in the lower hills and ran along the Freeway's edge.

Stan started to slow down.

"There, that's it!" Anna said, pointing excitedly. "The big rock, the three tall trees. There, between the rock and the tree. Turn, Stan. *Turn!*"

"But there isn't any road. There isn't—"

"*Turn!*"

Stan turned.

He blinked as the Special roared off the Freeway and smashed through a solid wall of leaves, branches and brush. Then they were on a narrow winding dirt road, dipping down into the stream where a foot of water ran over stones to create a fiord. It twisted up the other side, around the creek's edge, over stones and gravel, twisting tortuously upward and out of sight like a coiled rope.

"Go on, Stan, keep going!"

Stan kept going. It demanded all his power of concentration just to stay on the road which was hardly more than a pathway through the rising mountains. He had no time to think, and had very little to say.

Some hundred and fifty miles farther into the mountains, at an altitude that bit into their lungs, they saw the marker almost buried in rocks at the left of the road. The place where the old man had told them to stop and wait.

But they didn't have to wait. A man, lean and healthy for his age—which must have been at least sixty, Stan thought—stepped from behind a rock, and came toward the Special. He was smiling and he extended his hand.

"Doctor and Mrs. Morrison," he said. Anna was already out of the car, shaking his hand. Stan got out. He took a second look, then whispered: "Doctor Bergmann!"

The man wore levis and a mackinaw, and he carried a rifle slung under one arm. "I wasn't expecting you to recognize me," he said as they shook hands. "I've lost about thirty-five pounds." He smiled again. "It's healthier up here."

He walked around to the driver's side and opened the door. The motor was still running. Stan realized then what Bergmann was doing, and for some reason without definition he started to protest. Bergmann was setting the automatic clutch and releasing the brake. The Special started moving up the road, but there was no one inside to turn the wheel when it reached the hairpin turn about fifty feet ahead.

Stan watched the car gaining speed, its left door swinging like the door in a vacant house. He thought of stories he had heard about convicts finally released after many years, stunned, frightened by reality, begging to be returned to the restricted but understandable cell. Then he smiled. Anna smiled.

The Special, once you pushed the right button, could do almost everything by itself, feed itself gas, gain speed, shift its gears; but it didn't know when to turn to avoid self-destruction.

Stan winced slightly as the car lurched a little and then leaped out into space. He felt the black void opening under him as though he were still in the Special. Fifteen months.

His ears were filled with the sudden screeching whine of the wheels against unresisting air, then the world seemed to burst with a thundering series of solid smashing roars which were quickly dissipated in the high mountain air.

Doctor Bergmann went over to the edge and looked down. "That's the tenth one," he said. "We're going to send a work party down there in a few days to cover it all over with rocks. Still, I doubt if we have to worry about them spotting the wreckage."

He turned. "Well, let's start hiking. It's still a few miles."

"Where," Stan asked. "I've gone along this far. I've had no choice. But now what's it all about?"

"Didn't the old man tell you?"

"No."

"Just remember, Morrison. We're not running away. This is an old Mormon trail. A lot of the old pioneers took it. That marker says that the Williams-Conner Party camped here and was massacred by Indians in 1867. There's an old Indian city at about three thousand feet. I guess we're the first ones to use it for maybe a thousand years. We've got an archeologist up there—Michael Hilliard—who's been going slightly crazy. Anyway, we've got books up there, we raise most of our own food, and we've plenty of time to study and try to figure out where we made the big mistakes. We're really doing very well."

"But what about the old man?" Anna asked.

Bergmann chuckled. "Arch has turned into a regular man of a thousand faces. He works along the Freeways and watches for those who are at the breaking point and can't stay on the road any longer. Some of those condemned to the Freeways are criminals, others are fools or misguided zealots; and we've got to be careful not to wise those birds up by mistake. Arch has an unerring instinct, and sending our people to us is his job."

The three of them started walking up the old pioneer trail.

"We made a lot of mistakes," Bergmann said. "All of us, some more than others. You can't blame people for being afraid, suspicious of us. We *did* unleash the potentialities for total destruction without ever thinking about the social implications or ever bothering to wonder about how our contributions would be used and controlled.

"So we're off there waiting now. Waiting and studying. Someday they'll need us again. And we'll be ready."

"But who was the old man?" Anna asked.

Bergmann laughed. "Only the greatest physicist of the age. Remember Arch Hoffenstein?"

Stan put his arm over Anna's shoulders and they walked on, and up. He had almost forgotten. But now he never would. Somewhere, Arch Hoffenstein was hitch-hiking along the Freeway with the ghost of Galileo.

HAS ANYONE HERE SEEN KELLY?

Has Anyone Here Seen Kelly? by Bryce Walton

First published in 1954

This Edition Copyright @2020 by Eli Jayne

All rights reserved.

Cover art by Eli Jayne

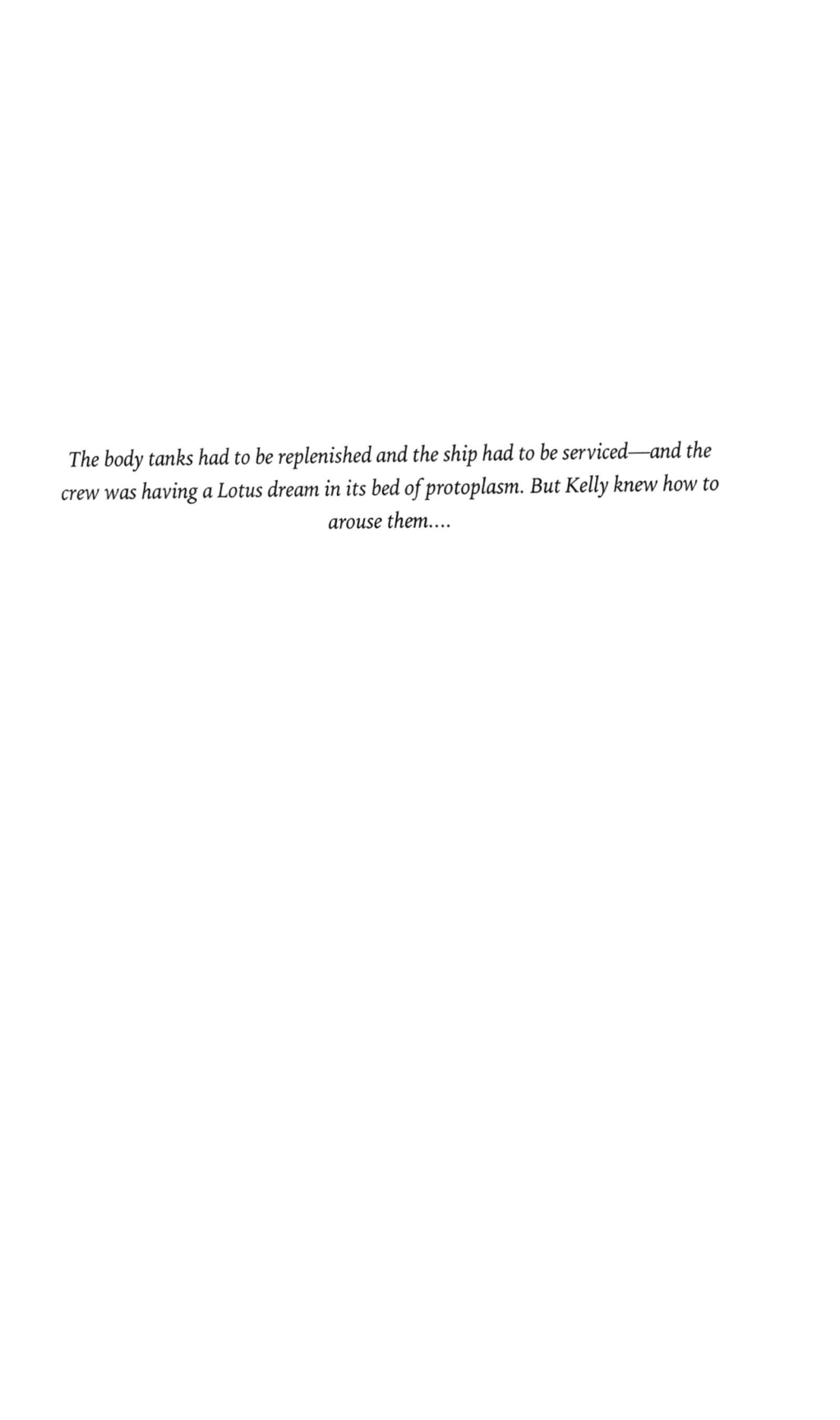

The body tanks had to be replenished and the ship had to be serviced—and the crew was having a Lotus dream in its bed of protoplasm. But Kelly knew how to arouse them....

CHAPTER ONE

THE CREW pulsed with contentment, and its communal singing brought a pleasant kind of glow that throbbed gently in the control room.

"'Has anybody here seen Kelly ... K-E-double-L-Y?'"

"Shut up and dig my thought!" Kelly's stubborn will insisted. "I'm going on out for a while!"

The delicate loom of the Crew's light pattern increased its frequency a little and the song stopped. "Better not," the Crew said.

"But why not?"

"No need."

"We could be running into something bad," Kelly thought.

"No danger now, Kelly. Checking the ship is just a waste of time."

"How can you waste what you have so damn much of?" Kelly thought.

"Do not leave us again, Kelly. We love you and you are the most interesting part of the Crew when you're with it."

"The ship ought to be checked. Our bodies ought to be looked at."

"We know there is no danger any more, Kelly. Do not go. There are so many interesting experiences we have not even begun to share yet. We are only half way through your life and we have not even started to experience your impressions of your colorful and complex Earth culture. And we have not even started on the adult lives of Lakrit or Lljub. Come back with your Crew, Kelly."

"But no one's checked the ship for over a year!"

"Please do not worry about the ship, Kelly. In fifty years nothing has gone wrong. We can trust the ship thoroughly now, it will take care of us."

"*It* will take care of *us*! That's a helluva way to look at it!"

"There can be no danger now, Kelly. In fifty years we have encountered every conceivable danger, every imaginable kind of world or possible menace."

"Have we?" Kelly thought. "Every danger from outside maybe, and I'm not even sure of that. But how about danger from inside?"

"Inside?"

"Us. How about apathy for instance? Apathy's a real danger. You talk about this space-can like it was a big metal mother! Listen, I'm supposed to see that this tub holds together. At least until we get back somewhere near enough to the Solar system so we'll feel we've been somewhere else!"

"But, Kelly—"

"I'm getting out for a while, I tell you!"

"All right," the Crew sighed. The light loom faded a bit, down to a self-indulgent glow. "Hurry back to us, Kelly."

"I'll give some thought to it."

So Kelly concentrated on the increasingly painful and difficult task of tearing his consciousness free of the big glob of protoplasm in the tank, and getting it back into his body that hibernated in the bunkroom.

As usual the switch was too painful. It stretched and stretched and finally snapped in an all too familiar explosion of shocking light.

CHAPTER TWO

HIS BONES creaked. His skin rustled as he sat up and looked around. There was the old feeling that there was dust over everything when there was no dust. There was all that emptiness sweeping away into the endless silence and he thought again, as he always did, how comforting and cozy it was being a part of the Crew.

But someone had to check the ship. It was only machinery after all, and machinery could wear out, sooner or later. And he wasn't at all sure, as he kept insisting, that they had encountered all the possible dangers.

It might seem that in fifty years you could run into everything. But fifty years was no time at all out here where time had no real meaning any more.

His body squeaked as he took a few tentative steps about the bunkroom. One did not actually forget how to walk. It was just awkward as the devil. And the blood, the entire autonomic system, tended to slow down. It seemed reluctant to step up general metabolism.

Apathy. Sure it was a danger. This time, Kelly decided, I'll do something about it. He was the engineer and he had signed on the great odyssey to keep the ship going. But the Crew was part of the ship. Was not there an obligation even greater to keep the Crew going?

The four others lived but almost imperceptibly in some very low state of slowed metabolism there in the bunkroom and Kelly looked at them. The faithful and the wonderful ones. The ones with whom he had shared so many dangers and awful silences that the five of them had been able to evolve the idea of the protoplasm in the tank and merge their consciousness in it.

Kew, the Venusian, in her bowl of self-renewing nitrate. Lakrit from a Jovian satellite, a fluorine fellow of distinction inside a sphere of gaseous sulphur. A crystalline character with a sense of humor named Lljub, whose form gave off a paled glint as it nourished itself on silicates. And a highly intelligent but humble six-foot-long sponge labeled Urdaz stuck in a foundation of chemical sediment at the bottom of a tank of reprocessing salt water.

Each with their own special kind of appendages and sensitivities, each able to move his special closed-system about through the ship by means of clever types of mobility.

But basically, in outward form, they were too alien to have much in common. Only as intelligences, as life forces, could they share a common bed. And it had evolved to that in fifty years. A bed of protoplasm in a shock-absorbent tank.

Kelly looked at them warmly and thought about how it had worked out. The strange thing was that it did have a lot of good things to recommend it. Or had had them. It had solved the problem of intimate communication and driven back the tides of loneliness. It had lessened the dangers of mental and physical illnesses in the material bodies and assured a prolongation of the life of each body, which was important in itself, for this trip had proven to be a lot longer than even the most pessimistic had anticipated.

The Crew, pulsing in its tank, Kelly thought oddly, is a new life form. One that had evolved to meet the exigencies of deep space which had proven to be alien to any adaptability common to any world that rotated through it.

But maybe they were too damn happy, Kelly thought. Too contented. If they ran into a real emergency now, the ship would be finished. The Crew in the tank was, itself, incapable of action of any overt kind. It could not manipulate anything. It could only be happy.

And the bodies here in the bunkroom could not rally fast enough to meet a sudden crisis.

And they had agreed that the first law was survival.

But to survive this way might well mean destruction in another.

So Kelly walked and thought about it, and weighed the precarious balance.

He slipped through the silent ship and to the control room. He peered into the viewscope. Some galaxy or other spun its giant pinwheel outward toward some destiny of its own. The high noon of the endlessness had been unfamiliar for years. He checked the ship's instruments. The Crew in the big tank simmered and throbbed in its introspective bliss, utterly oblivious to Kelly now.

Kelly saw the red dwarf a few hundred million kilos away. Three planets ground their familiar path around it. The second in distance had a breathable oxygen, according to the scopes, but little else to recommend it.

Kelly straightened up. He had no idea when the plan had really started forming, but now it was formed. When Kelly made up his mind to a thing, there was no other course but to conclude it. He knew what he had to do.

Somehow, even as part of the Crew, some part of Kelly had been able to keep that forming plan a secret. Which was a lucky miracle, for if the Crew had known his intentions it would certainly not have let him out this time.

Even if you wanted out, Kelly reasoned, the Crew would keep you in. And maybe after long enough you did not care to get out. But once out, he wondered, could it keep you out if it decided to blackball a man for one reason or another?

Like wrecking the ship?

CHAPTER THREE

IN THE CHROME strip above the control panel, Kelly saw his face grinning strangely back at him, a bearded, hollowed, paled face with an unfamiliar glitter in the eyes. Every time he had left the Crew to enter and reactivate his own body, that body had seemed a little less familiar. This time it seemed to be almost entirely someone else.

He stared at the face in the chrome, then whispered the hell with that and he flipped the controls over to manual. He sat down. Behind him, the Crew whispered in its tank, protoplasm developed in the labs and quivering now with some unified sensation that was purely subjective and blissfully unconcerned with what happened outside itself.

"It's sick," Kelly concluded, with an emphatic clamp of his jaws. "It's not right!"

True, sharing the intimate sensations of alien life forms like Kew, the female Venusian, had been exciting. Especially the sex experiences which, in a flower of Kew's type, was certainly something. There were interesting things to being a part of the Crew all right. But the main purpose, survival, had been forgotten. Now being the Crew was an end in itself. Kelly could imagine the Crew business going on and on until finally even the material bodies in the bunkroom would be forgotten entirely and allowed to rot away to dust about which the Crew would no longer care.

And that was very bad. It should not have worked out this way. But it was not too late to do something, shake them out of the Lotus dream.

He checked the scopes again. Now the second planet revealed plenty of breathable atmosphere settled in the lower valleys. He headed straight for it.

The Crew was soon going to get one devil of a jolt!

He put the ship into a close orbit around the planet. It seemed nothing but a fearsome forest of oxydized spikes rising in corrosive silence, with here and there a lean slash of valley. There was no indication of life, no vegetation visible or revealed by the scopes. One of the valleys had a thin mouth of water stretching down the length of its face. Kelly set the speed and the controls and ran for the bunkroom and the shock-absorbent cushions. He strapped himself in and waited.

It was done. As long as the thing had gone so far, Kelly decided, the truth should never be revealed because that would lessen the therapeutic value of his action. He would wreck the ship. Not too badly. Not so badly that all of the bodies, distinct, separate individual bodies again, couldn't put the ship back together, as in the old days. And that would keep them in their bodies gladly for a while where they belonged! Where the good Lord had intended for them to stay.

They would not be rocked away to apathy in a phony metal mother womb, thinking the ship was going to take care of *them*!

The more Kelly thought about it, the better he felt. He stretched inside the straps. He felt his slightly atrophied muscles luxuriate over the tissues and bones of his big frame.

Any body, no matter what its shape, should be proud of itself. That was Kelly's belief, and this thing that had happened seemed somewhat blasphemous. Without bodies and their complex sensory recording apparatus, the rich consciousness enjoyed by the Crew could not exist, would never have been created at all. The Crew was living off the largesse of experience built up by their bodies. The Crew was just narcotized enough that it did not realize that the body banks had to be replenished.

Metal shrieked.

Kelly yelled feebly. He fought, he grappled with the threatening blackout like a man fighting an invisible opponent on an endless flight of stairs.

The grinding rolling terror of the sound, the ripping, twisting, tearing scream of it cried on and on. Kelly knew one thing then.

He had not figured it right. His calculations were off. *The ship had hit too damn hard.*

CHAPTER FOUR

LATER, when he managed to get the straps off and tried to move, he fell painfully onto the tilted deck. One of his eyes felt sticky. He rubbed at it and his hand was smeared with blood.

He shuffled around in a stumbling circle. Minor damages could have been repaired. But this—the ship was peeled open in glaring strips like a breakfast cannister. A cold wind moaned through the ship that was now nothing but a metal sieve. A hazy light filtered down and ran off the metal like cold flour rust.

Kelly fell to his knees. "Kew," he whispered. "Lljub, Urdaz—Lakrit...."

The Venusian flower lady was sliced down the middle like a cabbage, and the nitrate bowl was shattered and Kew was dead in a pool of fading green blood.

Smashed into the bulkhead was Lakrit's sulphuric bathtub, and his atmosphere had already filtered away with the wind to wherever it was going. Lljub's pale glow was out for good, and his crystalline heart was as opaque as a dead eye. Only a few pieces of Urdaz's tank were visible, and Urdaz himself had already turned to a powdery food that the wind ate slowly in long trailing streamers.

"What—what in the name of God have I done?" Kelly whispered.

All dead—

No! He slammed at the bulkhead until the warped metal gave and he ran to the control room. The Crew—the Crew—

He stared at the tank.

Through a jagged opening in the ship's walls, the wind whined and plucked at Kelly's red hair. The wind was colder now. He kept on looking at the tank. He reached out and touched the big transparent curve of it and then jerked his hand back with a whimper in his breath.

There was nothing in the tank, nothing but a blob of slowly drying slime. He pressed his nose to the tank. "Crew—" he whispered.

There was no life in the slime. When he pounded on the tank, the stuff collapsed in upon itself in withering flatness.

Kelly yelled. The cold wind froze at his teeth. It sucked at his breath and dried at the interior of his mouth. He ran and climbed. The jagged periphery of the opening sliced at his flesh. But he did not feel it, and he fell twenty feet, without feeling that either, down the side of the ship. He started crawling over the hard naked belly of the rock.

He got to his feet. He ran stumbling down an incline of shale worn round and shiny by the wind that had blown here just as it blew now, and would blow for God alone possibly knew how long. He fell and rolled to the edge of the water.

He looked into it. He felt of it. He jerked his hand away. The stuff was icy. But it was worse than icy. It was dead. It was dead water. It was without any bottom, and without any life in it anywhere. You could tell by looking into it. The wind moved over the top of it as though the water were glass, and the water was the color of a slightly transparent naked blue steel.

There was no life here. Maybe there had been once, who knew when, who could guess how long ago. But there was none now and even the water had forgotten it.

Kelly cried out as he stood up. "What have I done?" He raised his arms at the hazy red sun lying over the spires of towering stone and metal like a bloated balloon scraping precariously over rusty spikes. "God, what have I done?"

The cry echoed tinnily on the rocks and fled on the wind.

Kelly ran for a long way, falling and stumbling and getting up again. Kelly had always had one primary drive, and that was to keep going, no matter what. So now he tried to keep going.

But there was no life on this planet. He had known that before. Some strange kinds of intelligence could tolerate some unpleasant worlds. But nothing would live here.

Nothing *could* live here.

"That's your fate," Kelly thought. He sat down and stared at the walls of rock and metal all around. "Your fate, Kelly. Your punishment, your well deserved hell."

That was what it was. Retribution. And knowing that, he tried not to care. He tried to be glad and face what he deserved.

If that were not the answer, then why had only Kelly been spared to face emptiness and silence and no life, all alone?

The irony of it was that he would go on as long as possible keeping himself alive in his own hell. There was food aplenty in the ship, enough to last as long as hell cared to have him.

He turned and started walking back toward the ship that seemed some five miles away. At that instant, the ship disappeared in an abrupt explosion that twisted the rocks, and a mushroom cloud flowered gently above the lake as Kelly fell trembling on his belly and hugged the ground and pushed his face into the shale, while the wind tore and screamed around him and particles of flint ripped his clothes and slashed at his flesh.

CHAPTER FIVE

HE DID NOT bother walking much farther toward where the ship had been. There was only a crater there now which would offer him nothing in the way of sustaining his very personal and thoroughly private hell.

He walked. The effort became more difficult and finally he was on his hands and knees, crawling. The wind sucked at his ripped clothes, and felt like cold sharp steel in his raw wounds. But slowly and deliberately he continued to crawl.

Kelly had always had the idea that a man should keep going and so now he kept on going. Even if there was no place to go, and you could not remember particularly where you had been, you kept on moving and fighting and slugging along until you could no longer move.

He lay there looking up at the hazy rust of the sky with the naked spires pointing up into it for no reason at all, because there was nothing up there.

He had been there and he knew. Nothing up there but space, black and without a beginning or end. He had not even checked the records of the ship so that now, lying here, he did not even know how far away from Earth he was. At the speed they had traveled, a ship went a long way in fifty years. But the ship, the records, everything was lost.

And no one would ever know now how far they had come.

Or gone. What was the difference, anyway?

But Kelly had no difficulty in remembering *why* they had come.

They had come into space because that was how it was with those who fought their way up to being the dominate life form of whatever world they had lived on and grown and died on. If you were the kind who went into space, you went because space was there.

Who needed a better reason than that?

"Kew," he whispered. "Lakrit, Lljub, Urdaz, listen now—I thought I was doing the right thing—maybe my idea was right—but I just made a mistake in the calculations. I just made a helluva mistake—"

The wind sighed over the naked rock and the rusted metal and the rock and the dead blue water.

He turned and pushed his head against the rock, and his body curled up against the bitter wind. "You've got to forgive me," he said.

"'*Has anybody here seen Kelly? K-E-double-L-Y?*'"

He shivered and kept his eyes closed. It was part of the wind. He did not want to go out that way, hearing crazy voices in the wind.

"'Has anybody here seen Kelly—?'"

He raised his head and blinked and the wind drove tears down his cheeks.

"Am I just hearing something that's going crazy inside my head?" He peered around. There was nothing, nothing anywhere of course, nothing where nothing had ever been, and nothing else but nothing could ever be.

"You're wrong, Kelly. Your Crew's here."

Kelly raised himself painfully to an elbow. "Where—*where?*"

"Right here, Kelly. We had a difficult time locating you. Sure, we forgive you. You were trying to do what was right. We know that."

"There's nothing—nothing—" Kelly said.

"You're wrong. The Crew's here and we're waiting."

He stared at the rock. He put his face against it and pushed his hands to it. There was a kind of dull glow in it, a faint hint of warmth in the rock.

"How can this be?" Kelly said.

"This is the life here, Kelly. Perhaps there is life everywhere in the most impossible seeming places. And where life is, Kelly, we can live with it and be welcomed by it. Here, this rock is life, and it has taken us in. It has been here a long time. And it will be here for a much longer time."

"Rock," Kelly said.

"But hurry and come back."

"But no one will ever know. How long—how long can we wait?"

"Who can answer that, Kelly? But maybe they will find the Crew someday."

Kelly looked up once at the completely unfamiliar distances growing darker. Sometime, he thought, they'll come from wherever Earth is and find the Crew of the ship, find a rock here waiting the ages out.

"Hurry, Kelly!"

His head dropped against the rock. His hands slid down it, and a smile moved over his lips and froze there as the wind whispered over it.

SECURITY

Security by Bryce Walton

First published in 1957

This Edition Copyright @2020 by Eli Jayne

All rights reserved.

Cover art by Eli Jayne

*If secrecy can be carried to the brink of madness, what can happen when imprisonment and time are added to **super** secrecy?*

CHAPTER ONE

We, Sam Lewis thought as he lay in the dark trying to sober up, are the living dead.

It was a death without honor. It was a death of dusty, sterile stupidity. It was wretched, shameful, a human waste, and far too ridiculous a business to bear any longer.

The hell with the war. The hell with the government. The hell with Secret Project X, Y, Z, or D, or whatever infantile code letter identified the legalized tomb in which Sam and the others had been incarcerated too long.

He flung his hand around in the dark in a gesture of self-contempt. And his hand found the soft contours of a woman's breast. Her warm body moved, sighed beside him as he turned his head and stared at the dim outline of Professor Betty Seton's oval face, soft and unharried in sleep. Unharried, and unmarried, he thought.

Good God. He detached his hand, slipped out of bed and stood in the middle of the floor, found his nylon coverall and sandals, dressed silently, and opened the door to get out of Betty's apartment, but fast.

He glanced back, his face hot with bitterness and his mouth twisting with disgust. She moved slightly, and he knew she was awake and looking at him.

"Darling," she said thickly, "don't go."

She was awake but still drifting in the euphoria of Vat 69.

He felt both sad and very mean. Then he shut the door behind him, ran out into the desert night. The line of camouflaged barracks on one side, the grounds including the lab buildings, all loomed up darkly under the starlight. He took a deep breath.

Now, he asked himself, have you the guts to get out, tell them off, make the gesture? It won't do any good. Nobody else will care or understand. They're too numb and resigned. You'll never get past the fence. The Guards will haul you in to the Wards and work you over. They'll work over what's left until what's left won't be worth carrying over to the incinerator with the other garbage in the morning. You'll be brainwashed and cleared until you're on mental rock bottom and won't even know what direction up is, and you won't give a damn.

But don't you have the guts even to make the gesture, just for the sake of what's left of your integrity, before they dim down your futile brain cells to a faint glow of final and perpetual mediocrity?

Betty and he had clung to some integrity, had made a point of not getting too intimate, a kind of challenge, a hold-out against the decadence of the Project. What was left now of any self-respect?

A security Guard with his white helmet and his white leather harness and his stungun, sauntered by and Lewis ducked into the shadows beside the barracks. His heart skipped several thumps as the Guard paused, looked at the entrance to Betty's apartment. Maybe someone had reported his liaison with Betty.

Beautiful and desirable as she was, and as much as he wanted to marry her, he had not been able to marry Betty Seton. If the war ever ended, if the security curtain was ever lifted, if they were ever let out of compulsive Government employment, then they would get married.

That was what they had kept telling one another during quick secret meetings.

If, if, if——

Somewhere along the trail of this last alcoholic binge, one or both of them had abandoned what they had both considered an important tradition. It wasn't much, but they had clung to it against temptation, knowing that once they gave in, it wasn't much further to the bottom of skidhill.

Betty Seton had been a world famous physicist. Sam Lewis had been a top-rate atomics engineer. And what are we now, he thought, watching the Guard, except just a couple of alky bums looking for a few extra kicks to keep us from admitting we're dead?

A request for a marriage license had never been answered. Betty Seton did not have "Q" clearance for some reason. Sam had full clearance and worked in The Pit, the highest "Q" security section in the Project. And never the twain could meet. If their little tryst was discovered, Betty Seton would be taken to the mental wards and 'cleared', a polite term for having any security info you might have picked up cleaned out of your brain along with a great many other characteristics that made you a distinct personality. It was just one of those necessary evils. It had to be done. For security. Psychological murder in the name of Security.

The Guard walked on and disappeared around the corner of the end barracks building.

Lewis started walking aimlessly in the dark, up and down in front of the barracks, past the blacked out windows and doors and the shadowy hulks of the lab buildings, and beyond that the camouflaged entrances to other subterranean labs, the synthetic food plants, the stores, and supplies. The Project was self-sustaining; in complete, secure and sterile isolation from the world, from all of humanity.

He headed for Professor Melvin Lanier's apartment. Tonight the big party was at Lanier's. There was a drunken brawl going on all the time at someone's apartment. There was nothing else to do.

Liquor, tranquillizing drugs, wife-swapping, dope addiction, dream-pills, sleeping tablets, and that was it. That was what the Project had come to. Experimental work at the Project had wobbled to a dead end.

Only the pathetic and meaningless motions remained.

Still, he thought, as he walked in through the open door of Lanier's apartment, there *is* a war on. H-bombs and A-bombs outlawed, but anything less than that was sporting.

He wanted to do what he could, but he was squelched; just as everyone else here was smothered and rendered useless by regulations and a Government of complete and absolute secrecy carried to its ultimate stupid denominator in the hands of political and military incompetents.

Still, there is a war on, he thought again as he walked into the big living room filled with artificial light and even more artificial laughter. Was it possible to do something, just some little thing, to shake loose this caged brain?

A few more drinks, he thought, will help me reach another completely indecisive decision.

In another two hours he would have to report back to the Pit. No reason for it now. It was just his job, his patriotic duty. Progress in nuclear developments and reactor technology in the Pit had ground to a dismal halt for him over seven months ago.

Yes, no doubt about it, he needed a few more shots to make palatable for a while longer his standing membership in the walking dead.

CHAPTER TWO

Through shadows in the garden, shapes wavered about drunkenly to the throb of hi-fi. Lewis went to the robotic barkeep and started drinking. This time, however, he didn't feel any effects. He stood looking around, ashamed, made sicker by what he saw: some of the world's finest minds, top scientists, reduced to shallow burbling buffoons.

Dave Nemerov, Nobel Prize Winner in physics, weaved up to Sam and looked at him out of bleary eyes. "Hi, Sammy. All full of gloom again, boy?"

Nemerov, a chubby little man dressed in shorts and nothing else, frowned with drunken exaggeration. "Easy does it, Sammy. You might find the security boys giving you a lobotomy rap."

A drop of sweat ran down the side of Lewis' high-boned cheek.

"Well, what's the great physicist been doing for his country?" Lewis asked. He knew that Nemerov hadn't even been in his lab for over a month. He even remembered when Nemerov had griped about the shortage of technically trained personnel, the policy of secrecy that clouded, divided and obstructed his work, hampered his research until it finally was no longer worth the struggle. His story was the story of everyone in the Project. He couldn't get information from other departments and projects, because of secrecy. They were all cut off from one another. No information was ever released from the restricted list. Most important documents were secret, and had remained out of reach.

The only declassified documents available in the project were grade-school stuff that everybody had known twenty years ago.

For an instant, Nemerov appeared almost sober, and completely saddened.

"I've forgotten what I was working on," Nemerov said.

"Have another drink then," Lewis said, "and you'll forget that you've forgotten."

They clinked glasses. "Smile, Sammy," Nemerov said. "It can't last forever. We'll soon get the word. The war will be over."

"What war?" Lewis whispered.

"Ssshhh, Sammy, for God's sake!" Nemerov moistened his lips and looked around, but there weren't any Guards at the party. There never were. The Guards had a barracks of their own in the Commander's private sector. They never talked to civilians. They never attended parties. They kept strictly to themselves. So did the Commander. For almost a year now, as far as Lewis knew, no civilian in the Project had seen the Commander. His reports were issued daily. Occasionally his voice was heard on the intercom.

"Wonder who is winning the war out there?" Lewis said, to no one in particular. He thought of Betty. Some whiskey spilled from the shot glass.

"I wish you would shut up," Nemerov said hoarsely.

It still seemed incredible to Lewis, that the military psychologists had decided among themselves that, for the sake of security, all intercommunication between the Project and the outside was to be cut off. No news, no television, no radio, no nothing. For security, and also on the theory that scientists could work better completely cloistered up like medieval monks. Not even a phone-call. Absolute, one-hundred percent isolation. Legalized catatonia.

They had choked this Project to death, and he wondered how many others were dead, and where they were. He didn't know where this Project was, except that it was on the desert. He didn't even know for sure what desert. He had been drugged when he was brought here two years ago, for security you know.

Nemerov never mentioned his wife and kids any more. From the behavior of Nemerov and most of the others, you would think the outside no longer existed.

Cardoza, the cybernetic genius, came up, his eyes glazed with the effects of some new narcotic that Oliver Dutton, world renowned biochemist, had cooked up for want of anything better to do.

The wives of two other scientists hung on Cardoza's arms, their bodies mostly bare, their eyes dulled as they wandered about the room like radar for the promise of some emotional oasis in the wasteland.

"How you fellas like my robotic barkeep?" Cardoza yelled.

"It pours a nice glass of whiskey," Lewis said.

"This is only the beginning," Cardoza said, his mouth glistening and wet under his hopped-up eyes. "That barkeep's a perfect servant and can never make a mistake. Spent the last year building it. It can mix anything."

"It'll practically win the war for us," Lewis said. Nemerov wiped at his sweating face. The two straying wives stared dumbly.

Cardoza winced. "Don't be cutting, my friend," he said to Lewis. His mouth turned down at the corners. "I tried, just as the rest of us tried. To go on and develop what I was sent here to develop, I need "Q" clearance. I can't get it because when the war started I wasn't a citizen. Is that clear, Lewis?"

"Forget it," Lewis said.

"That's what I intend to keep on doing," Cardoza said. "Meanwhile, my little robotic barkeep is only the beginning. I'm working on other even more ingenious automata. One will do card tricks. Another is a tight-wire artist. And one can even tell fortunes."

"How about one that can drag humans out of a hat?" Lewis asked.

"Come on, ladies," Cardoza said as he moved away. "Let's go play Dr. McWilliams' new Q-X game."

"Ohhh," one of the wives said, giggling. "Something *new*?"

"Yeah," Lewis said to her, thinking of the fact that at one time, long ago and far away, McWilliams had been working on a theory supposed to have been aimed far beyond Einstein. "McWilliams' new mathmatical game. This one's also played in the dark. Mixed couples of course. Q-X, the big mathmatical discovery of the age. People get lost in pairs and later in the dark they add up to bigger numbers."

CHAPTER THREE

Lewis shoved off from the bar, and walked toward the far corner of the garden where he saw old Shelby Stenger, the great atomics expert, flat on his belly, lying in the moonlight with fountain water misting his face, snoring like a tired old dog, with a little thread of drool hanging out of the corner of his mouth.

Mac Brogarth, nuclear physicist, came waltzing grotesquely across the garden and toppled backward into the pool under the fountain and lay there too weak even to raise his head out of the water. He would have drowned if Lewis hadn't lifted it out for him.

The old man in Lewis' arms looked up at Lewis with a passing light of tragic sobriety.

"Sam Lewis," he said. "That's you, isn't it, Sam? I had a cabin up near Lake Michigan and I was going up there to finish important work. I'll never get back there, Sam. I know now that I never will. I never will."

Lewis stood up. Without seeing or hearing anyone, he walked out into the dry coolness of the starlit desert night.

He walked between the barracks, past the messhall toward the labs, turned down the length of that ominous looking hulk which concealed

The Pit, and the Monster with which Lewis had worked until there was no use working any more. Beyond that, he saw the electric fence, and the white helmeted Guards standing at rigid attention.

He walked over there, his shoes crunching on sand and gravel, and looked into the Guard's face. It was a mask, expressionless, and rigid. Its eyes were hardly human, Lewis thought. It had many of the characteristics of Cardoza's robotic barkeep.

Lewis knew that the security Guards had been worked over in the Wards until there was no possibility of their being security risks. Any classified thought, even if it penetrated one side of their heads, quickly drained through the sieved brain and out the other side.

"Carry on, soldier," Lewis said. The Guard didn't seem to hear.

Lewis walked back toward the lab building covering The Pit.

The conflict was like a knife slicing him apart inside. What if he made a grandstand gesture now? It would be much worse perhaps than merely being sent into the Wards for a little mental working over. He would be found guilty of sabotage, tried by the Commander's kangaroo court martial, found guilty of being a traitor to his country, a foreign agent probably. He would be placed inside a gas chamber on a stool and a little gas pellet would be dropped on his lap.

And anyway, aside from his own punishment, would it be morally right? Maybe I'm the one who is crazy, he thought. Maybe it's hell out there, reduced to God knew what kind of social chaos. Maybe we're about to win. Maybe we're about to lose. Maybe as bad as it is, it's the best one could expect during the greatest crisis.

He went inside, and took the elevator down one floor into the lead-lined Pit.

He walked up to the control panel and looked through the thick layers of shielding transparent teflo-nite into the Pit, watching the Monster indirectly through the big lenticular screen disc above the control panel.

CHAPTER FOUR

The Monster stood in the lead-lined Pit, inactive, as it had been inactive for months. And even before that, during the months when Lewis was learning to control the Monster until it seemed an extension of his own nervous system, its work had become useless, due to unobtainable documents and personnel, not to mention lack of communication with other research centers.

The Monster was part of a general plan to compensate for the outlawing of A- and H-bombs. The most deadly conceivable compromise. The Pit was a deadly sea of radioactivity in which only a mechanical robot monster could work. Outside the Pit, Lewis directed the Monster whose duty was the construction of drone planes. A few had been built, but they weren't quite effective, and now it was impossible to go on with the experimentation. The parts were all there. Everything was there except certain vital classified documents that could not be cleared into this particular Project.

Thousands of drone planes were to have been built, and perhaps were being built in some other Project, but not in this one. Thousands of drone planes with raw, un-shielded atomic engines, light and inordinately powerful with an indefinite cruising range, remote controlled, free of fallible human agency, loaded with bacteriological bombs, the terrible gas known as the G-agent, and in addition, loaded 'spray' tanks that would spew deadly gamma rays and neutrons over limitless areas of atmosphere.

Lewis moved his hands over the sensitive controls, and through the lenticular disc, watched The Monster respond with the delicate gestures of a gigantic violinist. The Monster was a robot, ten times bigger than Cardoza's barkeep, and when Lewis moved his hands, the Monster moved its own huge mandibles as its electro-magnum, colloid brain, picked up Lewis' mental directions.

The Monster was immune to radiation, and bacteriological horrors. It swam in death as unconcerned as a lovely lady wallowed in a pink bubble-bath.

Lewis sat in the twilight of the Pit making the monster move about in its futile rounds. Lewis loved the Monster and felt the wasteful tragedy of its magnificent potential. A wonder of the world, a reaffirmation of man's imagination and his powers of reason, the Monster was built for what might seem horribly destructive ends, but its potential was for limitless achievement of the best and most far-reaching in man. Yet here it was, doing nothing at all. Standing in a sea of radioactive poison, a gigantic symbol of man's stupidity to man.

Could a man know the truth and continue to deny it, and still remain sane? You could go on living that way. You could take happy pills, sleeping pills, dream-pills and stay lushed-up on government liquor. But sooner or later you would have to face the horrible empty waste. After that loomed the face of madness.

And yet, Lewis thought, how do I know that I know the truth? I'm cut off. No info, no communication. For all I know we're the only people left in the world. An oasis of secrecy surrounded by desert.

Lewis walked back up to the first floor, and out into the night, heading for Betty Seton's apartment. Maybe she was sober enough now to talk this thing over. The hell with security regulations. Just the same, he walked along in the shadow next to the building to avoid any eye-witness of his proposed rendezvous.

Science, he thought, was really another name for freedom. It couldn't function without freedom of thought, freedom of inquiry. You couldn't mix it up with security and cut off communication, because communication is the essence of science. An idea is universal, and how can you go on thinking when you're no longer a part of the world?

Whatever the decision arrived at in Lewis' own heart might otherwise have been, he was never to know. His decision was made for him by an hysterical laugh, the sound of scuffling on boards, and another laugh. He came around the corner of the barracks and saw the Guard manhandling Betty Seton down the steps of her apartment building.

CHAPTER FIVE

The guard was big, built like a wedge, with a flat bulldog face bunched up under his white helmet. The Guard's brain had been carefully honed down to an efficient, completely unintelligent but precise fighting machine level. He neither knew nor cared why he did anything. But he was handicapped by having Betty Seton in one hand. He was whirling, raising his stungun with the other hand, when Lewis hit him.

Lewis drove in with his weight behind first a solid long blow that broke a rigid wall of muscle in the Guard's belly, turned it to soft clay. Betty fell free and lay laughing on the gravel. Her face was a white smear in the starlight.

Lewis brought his knee up into the Guard's face as he bent over, sank another one into the soft belly, kicked the Guard in the crotch, stamped on his booted foot, came back and ran forward again, driving his shoulder again into the Guard's belly. The Guard's feet hit the bottom step, he smashed into the boards, and his helmet flew off as his head thudded on the stanchion.

The Guard just shook his shaven head, started to get up heavily, reaching again for his stungun, his face expressionless. Lewis heard footsteps pounding around the corner, slashing on gravel.

More Guards. Dehumanized and insensitive, they were almost as invulnerable as so many robots—

He turned, ran past Betty Seton, stilly lying there with only a thin housecoat around her, not laughing now, but looking suddenly sober and horrified.

"Betty!"

She stared up at him. A block away he could hear the Guards coming and he kept on running. He yelled back.

"Get a jeep. Get Brogarth, Cardoza, Nemerov, anybody. We're breaking out of here."

"Where?" he heard her yelling after him as he went around the corner.

He glanced back around the corner and saw the herd of mechanized human beings slogging toward him.

"Near the gate," Lewis said.

He ran toward the Pit.

He ran down the steps, into the console room and looked into the lenticular disc where a ghostly blue radiance shadowed the walls.

"We're going to do ourselves some good after all, Monster," Lewis said tightly.

He gripped the controls and sent the Monster its last set of orders. It hurled tons of drone plane motors into the shielding walls, and its huge mandibles ripped open the shielding and peeled it away like a food canister. Smoke began to boil. Flames crackled in blue arcs. Steel beams crumbled like wax. Globs of concrete fell in a cloud of dust swirling debris.

Lewis grabbed the intercom, dialed the Commander's office. No answer. He got through the exchange and got the Commander's apartment. He heard a drunken whine and behind that the drunken depraved laughter of officers and their wives and the sound of bongo drums.

"The Monster's breaking out of the Pit," Lewis said. "It's shooting out more than enough deadly radioactivity to kill all of you if you don't get the hell out and get out fast."

"What, what's that?"

"If you think I'm having a nightmare," Lewis continued, "take a look out the window, Commander."

Lewis dropped the intercom. The Monster could go quite a distance before it stopped, its remote control radius probably not exceeding three miles.

The Monster went out of the Pit, taking walls and flooring with it. The entire structure trembled, beams fell, ceilings crumbled, and the Monster went through the smoking debris like a juggernaut.

A Guard lay crushed under a steel beam. Lewis took the stungun from his hand and went up the debris choked stairs. Outside, he saw figures streaming out into the starlight, and the lab buildings bursting into flames. He also saw the Monster, glowing with bluish radiance, moving straight ahead toward the electric fence.

The siren was screaming and howling. Shadows seemed to be streaming toward air-raid shelters. That was all right. The security curtain was torn down. They could come back up later into the light and wonder what had happened and find out where they really were.

Guards were running about like ugly toys out of control, looking, listening for commands.

Lewis ran through thickening smoke, and saw the jeep by the South Gate. Betty was in it, together with Brogarth and Nemerov.

"Hurry, hurry, run," he heard Betty scream.

The Guard was cutting at an angle toward Lewis, between him and the jeep. Beyond the Guard was a gaping hole in the fence and on the other side of that he could see the gigantic flickering nimbus of the Monster still walking toward the East.

Lewis kept running. Five feet away he brought up the stungun and shot the Guard in the face. Lewis jumped under the wheel of the jeep, slammed it into gear and they headed down the concrete strip and straight for the gap in the fence.

"What happened to Cardoza?" Lewis asked.

Brogarth said from the back seat, "He said he didn't want to be labeled a security risk and be executed for sabotage."

Nemerov was drunk and he kept mumbling incoherently, and sometimes giving out with bits and pieces of half remembered poetry.

CHAPTER SIX

About a mile out in the sand and next to a wall of sandstone, they waited for any signs of pursuit. There were none. They rested there until morning, only an hour and a half away, and when they looked back toward the location of the Project, they could see nothing that looked any different from sand, brush, rocks and red sandstone.

"Perfect camouflage," Nemerov said as the jeep started up again. "You could walk within fifty feet of that fence and never know there was any Project there."

Later a hot wind came up and they ran into the Monster lying dead on its face with dust devils dancing over it.

An old prospector leading a burro came around the wall of sandstone and looked at the Monster, then at the occupants of the jeep.

"Howdy, folks," he said.

"Hello," Lewis said. "We're lost. Where are we and which way do we go to get to civilization?"

"What's that thing?" the prospector asked, looking at the Monster.

"A scientific experiment that was never finished," Lewis said.

"What I figured," the prospector said. "You scientists out here always up to something." He pointed to the right. "Keep going that way and you'll find a narrow road. Follow it and you'll hit the middle of the valley and a highway right into the Chocolate Mountains."

Lewis knew where he was. The Chocolate Mountains walled off the rushing Colorado River from the Imperial Valley and Los Angeles farther on.

"Thanks," Lewis said.

"How's the war going these days?" Betty asked.

The prospector scratched his head and replaced his felt hat. He looked at them oddly.

"You must have been holed up in the hills a long time, Miss. There ain't been any war for two years. They started one, but the first couple of days scared everybody too much and they called the whole thing off. Where you folks been anyways, to the Moon?"

"Practically," Lewis said.

As the jeep moved away, Nemerov turned and looked back at the Monster and the old prospector who still stood there gazing at it.

"'My name,'" Nemerov said, "'is Ozymandias, King of Kings. Look on my works, ye Mighty, and despair. Round the decay of that colossal wreck, boundless and bare the lone and level sands stretch far away.'"

STRANGE ALLIANCE

Strange Alliance by Bryce Walton

First published in 1947

This Edition Copyright @2020 by Eli Jayne

All rights reserved.

Cover art by Eli Jayne

Haunted by their dark heritage, a medieval fate awaited them....

CHAPTER ONE

DOCTOR SPECHAUG stopped running, breathing deeply and easily where he paused in the middle of the narrow winding road. He glanced at his watch. Nine a.m. He was vaguely perplexed because he did not react more emotionally to the blood staining his slender hands.

It was fresh blood, though just beginning to coagulate; it was dabbled over his brown serge suit, splotching the neatly starched white cuffs of his shirt. His wife always did them up so nicely with the peasant's love for trivial detail.

He had always hated the silent ignorance of the peasants who surrounded the little college where he taught psychology. He supposed that he had begun to hate his wife, too, when he realized, after taking her from a local barnyard and marrying her, that she could never be anything but a sloe-eyed, shuffling peasant.

He walked on with brisk health down the narrow dirt road that led toward Glen Oaks. Elm trees lined the road. The morning air was damp and cool. Dew kept the yellow dust settled where spots of sunlight came through leaves and speckled it. Birds darted freshly through thickly hung branches.

He had given perennial lectures on hysterical episodes. Now he realized that he was the victim of such an episode. He had lost a number of minutes from his own memory. He remembered the yellow staring eyes of the breakfast eggs gazing up at him from a sea of grease. He remembered his wife screaming—after that only blankness.

He stopped on a small bridge crossing Calvert's Creek, wiped the blood carefully from his hands with a green silk handkerchief. He dropped the stained silk into the clear water. Silver flashes darted up, nibbled the cloth as it floated down. He watched it for a moment, then went on along the shaded road.

This was his chance to escape from Glen Oaks. That was what he had wanted to do ever since he had come here five years ago to teach. He had a good excuse now to get away from the shambling peasants whom he hated and who returned the attitude wholeheartedly—the typical provincial's hatred of culture and learning.

Then he entered the damp, chilled shadows of the thick wood that separated his house from the college grounds. It was thick, dense, dark. One small corner of it seemed almost ordinary, the rest was superstition haunted, mysterious and brooding. This forest had provided Doctor Spechaug many hours of escape.

He had attempted to introspect, but had never found satisfactory causes for his having found himself running through these woods at night in his bare feet. Nor why he sometimes hated the sunlight.

CHAPTER TWO

HE TENSED in the dank shadows. Someone else was in this forest with him. It did not disturb him. Whatever was here was not alien to him or the forest. His eyes probed the mist that slithered through the ancient mossy trees and hanging vines. He listened, looked, but found nothing. Birds chittered, but that was all. He sat down, his back against a spongy tree trunk, fondled dark green moss.

As he sat there, he knew that he was waiting for someone. He shrugged. Mysticism was not even interesting to him, ordinarily. Still, though a behaviorist, he upheld certain instinctual motivation theories. And, though reluctantly, he granted Freud contributory significance. He could be an atavist, a victim of unconscious regression. Or a prey of some insidious influence, some phenomena a rather childish science had not yet become aware of. But it was of no importance. He was happier now than he had ever been. He felt free—young and new. Life seemed worth living.

Abruptly, with a lithe liquid ease, he was on his feet, body tense, alert. Her form was vaguely familiar as she ran toward him. She dodged from his sight, then re-appeared as the winding path cut behind screens of foliage.

She ran with long smooth grace, and he had never seen a woman run like that. A plain skirt was drawn high to allow long bronzed legs free movement. Her hair streamed out, a cloud of red-gold. She kept looking backwards and it was obvious someone was chasing her.

He began sprinting easily toward her, and as the distance shortened, he recognized her. Edith Bailey, a second-year psychology major who had been attending his classes two semesters. Very intelligent, reclusive, not a local-grown product. Her work had a grimness about it, as though psychology was a dire obsession, especially abnormal psychology. One of her theme papers had been an exhaustive, mature but somehow overly determined, treatise on self-induced hallucination and auto-suggestion. He had not been too impressed because of an unjustified emphasis on supernatural myth and legend, including werewolves, vampires, and the like.

She sprang to a stop like a cornered deer as she saw him suddenly blocking the path. She turned, then stopped and turned back slowly. Her eyes were wide, cheeks flushed. Taut breasts rose and fell deeply, and her hands were poised for flight.

But she wasn't looking at his face. Her gaze was on the blood splattering his clothes.

He was breathing deeply too. His heart was swelling with exhilaration. His blood flowed hotly. Something of the whirling ecstasy he had known back in his student days as a track champion returned to him —the mad bursting of the wind against him, the wild passion of the dash.

A burly figure came lurching after her down the path. A tramp, evidently, from his filthy, smoke-sodden clothes and thick stubble of beard. He recalled the trestle west of the forest where the bindlestiffs from the Pacific Fruit line jungled up at nights, or during long layovers. Sometimes they came into the forest.

He was big, fat and awkward. He was puffing and blowing, and he began to groan as Doctor Spechaug's fists thudded into his flesh. The degenerate fell to his knees, his broken face blowing out bloody air. Finally he rolled over onto his side with a long sighing moan, lay limply, very still. Doctor Spechaug's lips were thin, white, as he kicked savagely. He heard a popping. The bum flopped sidewise into a pile of dripping leaves.

He stepped back, looked at Edith Bailey. Her full red lips were moist and gleaming. Her oddly opaque eyes glowed strangely at him. Her voice was low, yet somehow, very intense.

"Wonderful laboratory demonstration, Doctor. But I don't think many of your student embryos would appreciate it."

CHAPTER THREE

D OCTOR SPECHAUG nodded, smiled gently. "No. An unorthodox case." He lit a cigarette, and she took one. Their smoke mingled with the dissipating morning mist. And he kept on staring at her. A pronounced sweater girl with an intellect. This—he could have loved. He wondered if it were too late.

Doctor Spechaug had never been in love. He wondered if he were now with this fundamental archetypal beauty. "By the way," he was saying, "what are you doing in this evil wood?"

Then she took his arm, very naturally, easily. They began walking slowly along the cool, dim path.

"Two principal reasons. One, I like it here; I come here often. Two, I knew you always walk along this path, always late for your eight o'clock class. I've often watched you walking here. You walk beautifully."

He did not comment. It seemed unnecessary now.

"The morning's almost gone," she observed. "The sun will be out very warm in a little while. I hate the sun."

On an impulse he said: "I'm going away. I've wanted to get out of this obscene nest of provincial stupidity from the day I first came here. And now I've decided to leave."

"What are you escaping from?"

He answered softly. "I don't know. Something Freudian, no doubt. Something buried, buried deep. Something too distasteful to recognize."

She laughed. "I knew you were human and not the cynical pseudo-intellectual you pretended to be. Disgusting, isn't it?"

"What?"

"Being human, I mean."

"I suppose so. I'm afraid we're getting an extraordinarily prejudiced view. I can't help being a snob here. I despise and loathe peasants."

"And I," she admitted. "Which is merely to say, probably, that we loathe all humanity."

"Tell me about yourself," he said finally.

"Gladly. I like doing that—to one who will understand. I'm nineteen. My parents died in Hungary during the War. I came here to America to live with my uncle. But by the time I got here he was dead, too. And he left me no money, so there was no sense being grateful for his death. I got a part-time job and finished high school in Chicago. I got a scholarship to—this place." Her voice trailed off. She was staring at him.

"Hungary!" he said and repeated it. "Why—I came from Hungary!"

Her grip on his arm tightened. "I knew—somehow. I remember Hungary—its ancient horror. My father inherited an ancient castle. I remember long cold corridors and sticky dungeons, and cobwebbed rooms thick with dust. My real name is Burhmann. I changed it because I thought Bailey more American."

"Both from Hungary," mused Doctor Spechaug. "I remember very little of Hungary. I came here when I was three. All I remember are the ignorant peasants. Their dumb, blind superstition—their hatred for——"

"You're afraid of them, aren't you?" she said.

He started. "The peasants. I——" He shook his head. "Perhaps."

"You're afraid," she said. "Would you mind telling me, Doctor, how these fears of yours manifest themselves?"

He hesitated; they walked. Finally he answered. "I've never told anyone but you. There are hidden fears. And they reveal themselves consciously in the absurd fear of seeing my own reflection. Of not seeing my shadow. Of——"

She breathed sharply. She stopped walking, turned, stared at him. "Not—not seeing your—reflection!"

He nodded.

"Not seeing your—shadow—!"

"Yes."

"And the full moon. A fear of the full moon, too?"

"But how did you know?"

"And you're allergic to certain metals, too. For instance—silver?"

He could only nod.

"And you go out in the night sometimes—and do things—but you don't remember what?"

He nodded again.

Her eyes glowed brightly. "I know. I know. I've known those same obsessions ever since I can remember."

Doctor Spechaug felt strangely uneasy then, a kind of dreadful loneliness.

"Superstition," he said. "Our Old World background, where

superstition is the rule, old, very old superstition. Frightened by them when we were young. Now those childhood fixations reveal themselves in crazy symptoms."

He took off his coat, threw it into the brush. He rolled up his shirt sleeves. No blood visible now. He should be able to catch the little local passenger train out of Glen Oaks without any trouble. But why should there be any trouble? The blood——

He thought too that he might have killed the tramp, that popping sound.

She seemed to sense his thoughts. She said quickly: "I'm going with you, Doctor."

He said nothing. It seemed part of the inevitable pattern.

CHAPTER FOUR

THEY ENTERED the town. Even for mid-morning the place was strangely silent, damply hot, and still. The 'town' consisted of five blocks of main street from which cow paths wound off aimlessly into fields, woods, meadows and hills. There was always a few shuffling, dull-eyed people lolling about in the dusty heat. Now there were no people at all.

As they crossed over toward the shady side, two freshly clothed kids ran out of Davis' Filling Station, stared at them like vacant-eyed lambs, then turned and spurted inside Ken Wanger's Shoe Hospital.

Doctor Spechaug turned his dark head. His companion apparently hadn't noticed anything ominous or peculiar. But to him, the whole scene was morose, fetid and brooding.

They walked down the cracked concrete walk, passed the big plate-glass windows of Murphy's General Store which were a kind of fetish in Glen Oaks. But Doctor Spechaug wasn't concerned with the cultural significance of the windows. He was concerned with *not* looking into it.

And oddly, he never did look at himself in the glass, neither did he look across the street. Though the glass did pull his gaze into it with an implacable somewhat terrible insistence. And he stared. He stared at that portion of the glass which was supposed to reflect Edith Bailey's material self—*but didn't reflect anything. Not even a shadow.*

They stopped. They turned slowly toward each other. He swallowed hard, trembled slightly. And then he knew deep and dismal horror. He studied that section of glass where her image was supposed to be. *It still wasn't.*

He turned. And she was still standing there. "Well?"

And then she said in a hoarse whisper: *"Your reflection—where is it?"*

And all he could say was: "And yours?"

Little bits of chuckling laughter echoed in the inchoate madness of his suddenly whirling brain. Echoing years of lecture on—cause and effect, logic. Little bits of chuckling laughter. He grabbed her arm.

"We—we can see our own reflections, but we can't see each other's!"

She shivered. Her face was terribly white. "What—what is the answer?"

No. He didn't have it figured out. Let the witches figure it out. Let some old forbidden books do it. Bring the problem to some warlock. But not to him. He was only a Doctor of Philosophy in Psychology. But maybe—

"Hallucinations," he muttered faintly. "Negative hallucinations."

"Doctor. Did you ever hear the little joke about the two psychiatrists who met one morning and one said, 'You're feeling excellent today. How am I feeling?'"

He shrugged. "We have insight into each other's abnormality, but are unaware of the same in ourselves."

"That's the whole basis for psychiatry, isn't it?"

"In a way. But this is physical—functional—when psychiatry presents situation where—" His voice trailed off.

"I have it figured this way." How eager she was. Somehow, it didn't matter much now, to him. "We're conditioned to react to reality in certain accepted ways. For instance that we're supposed to see our shadows. So we see them. But in our case they were never really there to see. Our sanity or 'normalcy' is maintained that way. But the constant auto-illusion must always lead to neuroticism and pathology —the hidden fears. But these fears must express themselves. So they do so in more socially acceptable ways."

Her voice suddenly dropped as her odd eyes flickered across the street. "But we see each other as we really are," she whispered tensely. "Though we could never have recognized the truth in ourselves."

She pointed stiffly. Her mouth gaped, quivered slightly.

He turned slowly. His mouth twitched with a growing terrible hatred. They were coming for him now.

CHAPTER FIVE

FOUR MEN WITH RIFLES were coming toward him. Stealthily creeping, they were, as though it were some pristine scene with caves in the background. They were bent slightly, stalking. Hunters and hunted, and the law of the wild and two of them stopping in the middle of the street. The other two branched, circled, came at him from either side, clumping down the walk. George recognized them all. The town marshal, Bill Conway, and Mike Lash, Harry Hutchinson, and Dwight Farrigon.

Edith Bailey was backed up against the window. Her eyes were strangely dilated. But the faces of the four men exuded cold animal hate, and blood-lust.

Edith Bailey's lips said faintly, "What—what are we going to do?"

He felt so calm. He felt his lips writhe back in a snarl. The wind tingled on his teeth. "I know now," he said. "I know about the minutes I lost. I know why they're after me. You'd better get away."

"But why the—the guns?"

"I murdered my wife. She served me greasy eggs. God—she was an animal—just a dumb beast!"

Conway called, his rifle crooked in easy promising grace. "All right, Doc. Come on along without any trouble. Though I'd just as soon you made a break. I'd like to shoot you dead, Doctor."

"And what have I done, exactly," said Doctor Spechaug.

"He's hog-wild," yelled Mike Lash. "Cuttin' her all up that way! Let's string 'em up!" Conway yelled something about a "fair trial," though not with much enthusiasm.

Edith screamed as they charged toward them. A wild, inhuman cry.

Doctor Spechaug's eyes flashed up the narrow street.

"Let's go!" he said to Edith Bailey. "They'll see running they've never seen before. They can't touch us."

They ran. They heard the sharp crack of rifles. They saw the dust spurting up. Doctor Spechaug heard himself howling as he became aware of peculiar stings in his body. Queer, painless, deeply penetrating sensations that made themselves felt all over his body—as though he was awakening from a long paralysis.

Then the mad yelling faded rapidly behind them. They were running, streaking out of the town with inhuman speed. They struck out in long easy strides across the meadow toward the dense woods that brooded beyond the college.

Her voice gasped exultingly. "They couldn't hurt us! They couldn't! They tried!"

He nodded, straining eagerly toward he knew not what, nosing into the fresh wind. How swiftly and gracefully they could run. Soon they lost themselves in the thick dark forest. Shadows hid them.

CHAPTER SIX

DAYS LATER the moon was full. It edged over the low hill flanking Glen Oaks on the east. June bugs buzzed ponderously like armor-plated dragons toward the lights glowing faintly from the town. Frogs croaked from the swampy meadows and the creek.

They came up slowly to stand silhouetted against the glowing moon, nosing hungrily into the steady, aromatic breeze blowing from the Conway farm below.

They glided effortlessly down, then across the sharp-bladed marsh grass, leaping high with each bound. As they came disdainfully close to the silent farm house, a column of pale light from a coal oil lamp came through the living room window and haloed a neglected flower bed. Sorrow and fear clung to the house.

The shivering shadow of a gaunt woman was etched against the half drawn shade. The two standing outside the window called. The woman's shadow trembled.

Then a long rigid finger of steel projected itself beneath the partially raised window. The rifle cracked almost against the faces of the two. He screamed hideously as his companion dropped without a sound, twitching, twitching—he screamed again and began dragging himself away toward the sheltering forest. Intently and desperately the rifle cracked again.

He gave up then.

He sprawled out flatly on the cool, damp, moon-bathed path. His hot tongue lapped feverishly at the wet grass. He felt the persistent impact of the rifle's breath against him, and now there was a wave of pain. The full moon was fading into black mental clouds as he feebly attempted to lift his bleeding head.

He thought with agonized irony:

"Provincial fools. Stupid, superstitious idiots ... and that damned Mrs. Conway—the most stupid of all. *Only she would have thought to load her dead husband's rifle with silver bullets!* Damned peasants——"

Total darkness blotted out futile revery.

ELI JAYNE
SCI FI CLASSICS

Eli Jayne is pleased to present reformatted science fiction classics.

elijayne.com

facebook.com/Eli.Jayne.Scifi.Originals
twitter.com/jayne_eli
instagram.com/eli.jayne.scifi

THE CHASM

The Chasm by Bryce Walton

First published in 1956

This Edition Copyright @2020 by Eli Jayne

All rights reserved.

Cover art by Eli Jayne

It was a war of survival. Children against old men. And not a chance in the world to bridge——

CHAPTER ONE

The old man's face was turning gray with fatigue under the wrinkled brown. He was beginning to get that deadly catching pain in his left chest. But he forced himself to move again, his ragged dusty uniform of the old Home Guard blending into the rubble the way a lizard merges with sand.

He hobbled behind a pile of masonry and peered through the crack. He angled his bald head, listening. His hands never really stopped quivering these days and the automatic rifle barrel made a fluttering crackle on the concrete. He lowered the barrel, then wiped his face with a bandanna.

He'd thought he heard a creeping rustle over there. But he didn't see any sign of the Children.

He'd been picked to reconnoiter because his eyes were only comparatively good. The truth was he couldn't see too well, especially when the sun reflecting on the flat naked angles of the ruined town made his eyes smart and water and now his head was beginning to throb.

A dust devil danced away whirling a funnel of dust. Sal Lemmon looked at it, and then he slid from behind the rubble and moved along down the shattered block, keeping to the wall of jagged holes and broken walls that had once been the Main Street of a town.

He remembered with a wry expression on his face that he had passed his ninety-fourth birthday eight days back. He had never thought he could be concerned with whether he lived to see his ninety-fifth, because there had always been the feeling that by the time he was ninety-four he would have made his peace with himself and with whatever was outside.

He moved warily, like a dusty rabbit, in and out of the ruins, shrinking through the sun's dead noon glare.

He stopped, and crouched in the shade behind a pile of slag that had once been the iron statue of some important historical figure. He contacted Captain Murphy on the walkie-talkie.

"Don't see any signs of Children."

"Max said he saw some around there," Murphy yelled.

"Max's getting too old. Guess he's seeing things."

"He saw them right around there somewhere."

"Haven't seen him either."

"We haven't heard another word from Max here, Sal."

The old man shrugged. "How could the Children have gotten through our post defenses?" He looked away down the white glare of the street.

"You're supposed to be finding out," Murphy yelled. He had a good voice for a man two months short of being a hundred. He liked to show it off.

Then Sal thought he saw an odd fluttery movement down the block.

"I'll report in a few minutes," he said, and then he edged along next to the angled wall. A disturbed stream of plaster whispered down and ran off his shoulder.

Near the corner, he stopped. "Max," he said. He whispered it several times. "Max ... that you, Max?"

He moved nearer to the blob on the concrete. Heat waves radiated up around it and it seemed to quiver and dance. He dropped the walkie-talkie. There wasn't even enough left of Max to take back in or put under the ground.

He heard the metallic clank and the manhole cover moved and then he saw them coming up over the edge. He ran and behind him he could hear their screams and cries and their feet striking hard over the blisters, cracks, and dried out holes in the dead town's skin.

He dodged into rubble and fell and got up and kept on running. The pain was like something squeezing in his belly, and he kept on running because he wanted to live and because he had to tell the others that the Children were indeed inside the post defenses.

He knew now how they had come in. Through the sewers, under the defenses. He began to feel and hear them crawling, digging, moving all over beneath the ruins, waiting to come out in a filthy screaming stream.

CHAPTER TWO

Sal was still resting in the corner of the old warehouse by the river. A lantern hung on a beam and the dank floor was covered with deep moving shadows.

Captain Murphy was pacing in a circle, looking like something sewn quickly together by a nervous seamstress. Doctor Cartley sat on a canvas chair, elbows on knees, chin in his hands. He kept looking at the floor. He was in his early eighties and sometimes seemed like a young man to Sal. His ideas maybe. He thought differently about the Children and where things were going.

"We're going to get out tonight," Captain Murphy said again. "We'll get that barge loaded and we'll get out."

Sal sat up. The pills had made his heart settle down a bit, and his hands were comparatively calm.

"Is the barge almost loaded now? It better be," Sal said. "They'll attack any minute now. I know that much."

"Another hour's all we need. If they attack before then we can hold them off long enough to get that barge into the river. Once we get into the river with it, we'll be safe. We can float her down and into the sea.

Somewhere along the coast we'll land and wherever it is will be fine for us. We'll have licked the Children. They know we've found the only eatable food stores in God knows how many thousands of miles in this goddamned wasteland. They can't live another month without this stuff, and we're taking it all down the river. That's right isn't it, Doc?"

Cartley looked up. "But as I said before, squeezing a little more life out of ourselves doesn't mean anything to me. What do we want to get away and live a little longer for? It doesn't make sense, except in a ridiculous selfish way. So we live another month, maybe six months, or a year longer? What for?"

Sal glanced at Murphy who finally sat down.

"We want to live," Murphy said thickly, and he gripped his hands together. "Survival. It's a natural law."

"What about the survival of the species?" Cartley asked. "By running out and taking the food, we're killing ourselves anyway. So I don't think I'll be with you, Murphy."

"What are you going to do? Stay here? They'll torture you to death. They'll do to you what they did to Donaldson, and all the others they've caught. You want to stay for that kind of treatment?"

"We ought to try. Running off, taking all this food, that means they're sure to die inside a few weeks. They might catch a few rats or birds, but there aren't even enough of those around to sustain life beyond a few days. So we kill the future just so we can go on living for a little longer. We've got no reason to live when we know the race will die. My wife refused to fight them. They killed her, that's true, but I still think she was right. We've got to make one more attempt to establish some kind of truce with the Children. If we had that, then we might be able to start building up some kind of relationship. The only way they can survive, even if they had food, is to absorb our knowledge. You know that. Without our knowledge and experience, they'll die anyway, even if they had a thousand years of food supplies."

"It can't be done," Murphy said.

Cartley looked at the shadows for a long time. Finally he shook his head. "I don't have any idea how to do it. But we should try. We can't use discipline and power because we're too weak. And too outnumbered. We'd have to do that first in order to teach them, and we can't. So there has to be some other way."

"Faith?" Sal said. He shook his head. "They don't believe in anything. You can't make any appeal to them through faith, or ethics, any kind of code of honor, nothing like that. They're worse than animals."

Cartley stood up wearily and started to walk away. "They hate us," he said. "That's the one thing we're sure of. We're the means and they're the ends. We made them what they are. They're brutalized and motivated almost completely by hatred. And what's underneath hatred?" He fumed back toward Murphy. "Fear."

Sal stood up. "I never thought of them as being afraid," he said.

"That doesn't matter," Murphy said. "It's the hate and vicious brutality we have to deal with. You do whatever you want to do, Cartley. We've voted, and we've voted to move the stuff out tonight on the barge. The world we helped make is dead, Cartley. The Children grew up in a world we killed. We've all got bad consciences, but we can't do anything about it. The chasm between them and us is too wide. It was wide even before the bombs fell. And the bombs made it a hell of a lot wider. Too wide to put any kind of bridge across now."

"Just the same, we ought to die trying," Cartley said. When he went outside, Sal followed him.

The barge was about loaded. All outer defense units had been pulled in and were concentrated on the head of the pier behind walls of sandbags. Burp guns and machine guns were ready, and the barge lay along the side of the pier in the moonlight like a dead whale. There were several sewer openings near the head of the pier. Men were stationed around these sewers with automatic rifles, hand grenades and flame throwers.

Sal walked to where Cartley stood leaning against the partly closed door of the rotting warehouse. Jagged splinters of steel and wood angled out against the sky.

After a while, Sal said softly, "Well, what could we try to do, Doc?"

Cartley turned quickly. Some of the anguish in his eyes had gone away, and he gripped Sal's shoulders in hands surprisingly strong for so old a man. "You want to help me try?"

"Guess I do. Like you said, we only have a little time left anyway. And if we can't help the Children, what's the good of it?"

They stood there in the shadows a while, not saying anything.

"This way," Cartley said. He led Sal down away from the pier and along the water's edge. Dry reed rustled, and mud squished under their shoes.

"Here," Cartley said. There was a small flat-bottomed rowboat, and in it were several cartons of food supplies, all in cans. There were also several large tins of water.

"We'll need a little time," Cartley said. "We'll have to wait. I figure we'll row upstream maybe a few hundred yards, and hole up in one of those caves. We can watch, Sal. We can watch and wait and try to figure it out."

"Sure," Sal said. "That seems the only way to start."

Cartley sat down on the bank near the boat, and Sal sat down too.

"The Children," Cartley said, "never had a chance to be any other way. But we're the oldsters, and we've got this obligation, Sal. Man's a cultural animal. He isn't born with any inherent concepts of right, or wrong, or good or bad, or even an ability to survive on an animal level. We have to be taught to survive by the elders, Sal. And we're the elders." He hesitated, "We're the only ones left."

A flare of horrid light exploded over the warehouse down river and it lit up Cartley's face and turned it a shimmering crimson. His hands widened to perfect roundness and he raised his hands in a voiceless scream to stop the sudden explosions of burp guns, grenades, machine guns, and rifles.

Looking down river then, Sal could see the flames eating up through the warehouse. The pier, the barge, everything for a hundred square yards was lit up as bright as day, and the flare spread out over the river and made a black ominous shadow of the opposite bank.

"They're getting away," Cartley said.

Sal watched the barge move out. The Children came screaming out of the blazing warehouse, overran the pier, streamed into the water. But a steady blast of fire from the barge drove them back, and in a few more minutes the barge dissolved downriver into darkness.

Cartley's hands were shaking as he gripped Sal's arm. "Let's go now. We need time. Time may help us a lot, Sal. We can wait and watch. We can figure something out."

Sal heard the screams and mocking savage cries coming up over the water, and then the jagged cries of some oldsters who hadn't managed to get away.

Still looking downstream toward the blazing pier, Sal pushed Cartley into the rowboat, and they shoved off. Sal started rowing, but he kept looking back.

"They should have put them in the same shelters with us," Sal said, "that would have made a difference. But they put us in separate shelters."

Only the oldest and the youngest had been saved. The old out of pity and because they were helpless, had been granted the safety of shelters. The young because they were the symbols of hope had been granted shelters, too.

"No," Cartley said. "It started long before that. The chasm was building up long before the war. This alienation between the young and the old. Between the sun and the seed. That's what we've got to bring back, Sal. Between us, we have stored up a hundred and seventy-nine years of human culture. There isn't a kid back there, Sal, more than twelve years old."

"We'll find a way," Sal said.

The rowboat was about fifteen feet away from the thick reeds growing in the marshy ooze of the bank.

Cartley heard the sound first and turned, his face white. When Sal looked toward the bank, he saw the girl. She came on out from the curtain of reeds and looked at them. She was perfectly clear in the moonlight standing there. She wore a short ragged print dress and she had long hair that seemed silken and soft and golden in the moonlight even though it, her dress, her little legs and her face were streaked with mud.

Sal hesitated, then pulled heavily on his left oar and the boat nosed toward her. Up close, Sal could see her face, the clear blue eyes wet, and the tears running down her cheeks.

The girl reached out and asked in a sobbing breath,

"Granpa? Is that you, Granpa?"

"Oh God, Oh God," Cartley said. He was crying as he picked her up and got her into the boat. He was rocking her in his arms and half crying and half laughing as Sal rowed the boat upstream.

"Yes, yes, honey," Sal heard Cartley say over and over. "I'm your granpa, honey. Don't cry. Go to sleep now. I'm your granpa and I've been looking for you, honey, and now everything's going to be all right."

It's funny, Sal thought, as he kept on rowing upstream. It's a funny thing how one little girl remembered her granpa, and how maybe that was the beginning of the bridge across the chasm.

THE HAPPY HERD

The Happy Herd by Bryce Walton

First published in 1956

This Edition Copyright @2020 by Eli Jayne

All rights reserved.

Cover art by Eli Jayne

Everyone was thoughtful, considerate, kind and very happy. But where was the right of dignity or individuality? It was like being dropped into the middle of a nightmare. The kind that finds you running naked in a crowd.

CHAPTER ONE

The Captain told Kane to take his cushion pills, that they were contacting the pits at La Guardia within half an hour.

"I still can't figure you," the Captain said. "Up there, just you and your wife for sixteen years. That's a hell of a long time."

Kane smiled. He had been almost completely out of touch with the world for sixteen years, and it surprised him a little that anyone thought it remarkable in any way. Particularly the Captain who spent most of his time, too, alone.

But the Captain was genuinely perturbed about it. The authorities had abandoned the space-station project. Abandoned the Martian project. They had taken away the other three ships from the Moon-run, and there was no explanation for it at all.

The rest of the Captain's crew, except an old atomics man, had drifted away and never come back, and the Captain had been unable to find out anything whatsoever about what had happened to them. He had never heard from them again. They had never been replaced.

But the Captain couldn't seem to define what it was he was warning Kane to be wary of down there.

"I haven't left my ship for years, Professor Kane, and that's the truth. I take on supplies and see to the ore getting into the holds but when those machines up there that do the digging and loading wear out, they won't be replaced. Just no interest in space any more. I can tell.

"I stay on the ship, with my wife, see. And the few guys down there around the field at La Guardia I have to rub up against—why, sir, they treat me as if I had some kind of contagious disease!

"But they need this ore I'm bringing back here now, so they leave me alone."

"Who leaves you alone?"

"Whoever didn't leave the rest of my crew alone. Whoever sang 'em the old siren song, that's who. Once a spaceman, always a spaceman, sir. And not a one of those men pulled out because he wanted to do it! That's what I'm saying. And I'm telling you to watch out. I'm blasting off for the Moon again on the 25th. I hope you're aboard."

Kane shrugged as the Captain bowed out, making disgruntled noises in his throat. He was getting along in years, Kane reasoned, and was probably just expressing that fact, externalizing some way or another. Still, what he had said was odd—

The truth was, Kane had been inexcusably out of contact with the world.

The pills dulled his senses and he began to fall asleep on the pneumatic couch. He thought of the years of work on his theories concerning the unified fields in the formulation of spatial matter. He thought of Helen, the good years together before her sudden death, sharing love and work, how complete and full and good it had been. During all those sixteen years he couldn't recall a moment of real boredom.

He hadn't missed life on Earth. When a man has one full love and his work, he's isolated no matter where he is, even in the middle of New York City.

He had ten notebooks full of notes in his briefcase. It would open their eyes, a really basic new theory that would defy the pessimistic theory of entropy, and its assurance of an inevitable death of all things.

Finding another wife to replace Helen wouldn't be easy of course. A new relationship would be different, but it should be as good. It might require some difficulties which he had anticipated and was prepared for. He was only forty-six. He had a long time to look. He was in excellent physical condition and was not unattractive, though of course that wasn't the real issue either way.

He wanted love, a companion, someone who could truly share in his work. Who would love that observatory in Albetagnius crater as a home for the rest of her life.

He woke up, and prepared to leave the ship. He carried his briefcase with his notes in it. The rest of his luggage would follow later. According to Phil Nordson, there was a suite reserved for him at the Midtown Hotel at 50th and Madison Avenue.

He climbed down the ladder to the exit. The door was open and a heavy fog drifted past the opening, but a small dark car with two drivers waited outside.

As Kane stepped down the gangplank, one of the figures, a woman in a light blue uniform, jumped out and opened the door for him.

Interest and excitement rose in Kane as the car moved through the mist toward the terminal where he was to meet Phil. It would probably do him good, get away from his work, different surroundings, just rest up a little. Even live it up a little perhaps. There would be parties, and he wanted to see a little of the country. Maybe visit some of Helen's relatives in the Middle West, and he certainly wanted to have some long bull sessions with Professors Martinson and Legmann over at the University.

Then there was the question of meeting the right kind of woman. That was something only the fates could decide, Kane thought. He was no romantic, but that sort of thing wasn't something you could figure out in advance, plot out like an equation. It wasn't anything you could handle with personality charts, though they had been trying that when he'd left. The personality you could measure with gadgets was such a small part of it really....

But Phil would arrange for the social activities. As he recalled his old schoolmate, he remembered that Phil was a very social kind of fellow. Phil had thought it was absurd, Kane's volunteering for that job in Albetagnius. Phil hadn't even gone on to post-graduate work in electronics, his chosen field. Phil had gone right out to accept a position with Isotopics Unlimited, somewhere in New Jersey.

They had corresponded for a while; and the cablegram from Phil had expressed Phil's delight at Kane's decision to return to Earth.

The car stopped before the well-lighted entrance to terminal building No. 214 and the woman hopped out, opened the door for Kane. He went inside the building, feeling the abnormally heavy pull of gravity. He had grown accustomed to the gravity on the Moon, and though his body was already starting to adapt itself, it would take time, and he was beginning to feel the drag.

Phil was there waiting. He hadn't mentioned anyone else being there, and Kane certainly didn't expect anyone else. He didn't know anyone really, no one other than Phil except Martin and Legmann. But there was Phil, and a number of people around him, and they were all rushing toward Kane, smiling, shouting, waving their arms. Phil looked much the same, tall and flashily dressed, thin and good looking as always, but with hair slightly greying.

The others, men, women, various ages and sizes, waving scarfs and circling eagerly around Kane, broke out in a happy chorus of mixed voices:

Greetings! Welcome, Old Friend Kane!

Welcome home to Earth again.

Kane felt a brief compulsion to retreat, but that was absurd.

"Good to see you, Prof!" Phil shouted.

"Hello, Phil." Someone grabbed his briefcase. Kane tried to get it back but it was gone among the frothing arms and milling bodies.

"We'll take care of it, Kane boy," Phil said. His arm was over Kane's shoulders. Several women were hanging onto Kane's arms. Healthy, tanned, lovely women.

"Sure glad to see you, Prof. Aren't we?"

A chorus enthusiastically shrieked, "Yes!"

Kane felt some embarrassment. He was being crowded out an exit toward a line of cabs. Several shiny ten-foot saucers with railings around them whirred past and disappeared in the fog. All of them had two or more people on them, and from the sound, there were quite a number of them up in the fog somewhere.

"We've all got a saucer now," Phil said. "Only we have to take cabs over to Lucie's house. This way we can all ride together. We can all get into two cabs, can't we, gang?"

"Yes!"

"Lucie?" Kane asked as they crowded around the two cabs. Who were these people? Friends of Phil's of course.

"We're Lucie," the woman said softly. Kane caught a glimpse of a mature face and a lovely figure. The face was odd, Kane thought, the maturity seeming to be disguised by an insincere smile. What a peculiar way of introducing oneself....

"We're having a little party at the house," Lucille said. "Aren't we?"

"Yes!"

"We've got lots of fun planned for us, Kane boy," Phil said.

Kane remembered a look of sardonic mockery in Lucille's eyes as her face disappeared and was replaced by several others.

Somehow, Kane couldn't figure out how, five of them were jammed into the back seat of one of the cabs and then they were moving away through the fog.

Someone who said "We're Laura," with a tight tanned body was wriggling on Kane's lap and her arm was around Kane's neck. She had bright teeth and she breathed scentedly into Kane's face.

"Nothing to worry about, Kane boy," he heard Phil say in a muffled joy. "We're the gang."

"'It's always fair weather, the Sunhill Gang is always together,'" Laura was crooning. The red-faced fat man next to Kane laughed and then Kane saw that the red-faced man whose name seemed to be Ben and the woman on his lap whom he called Jenny, were kissing one another. There was something embarrassingly intimate about the way they did it. It was suddenly much more than a mere spontaneous show of affection.

Kane looked away. Beyond a certain point, he felt that love-making was something that should be reserved for privacy.

That sort of thing might be expected to change, of course. Customs changed, and as Kane recalled, one could say the trend had been somewhat in that direction.

There were two drivers up front. That was a change too. Every cab had had two drivers, a man and a woman.

It was all a bit overdone, Kane thought. Still, they were friends of Phil's. A friend of yours is a friend of mine.

But it affected Kane adversely. He felt uneasy. He didn't really know them at all. In fact, he scarcely even knew Phil.

"We're so glad with you," the girl on Kane's lap said. She crushed her lips over his mouth and pressed her body against him. Kane couldn't say that was affecting him adversely. In fact, if there weren't all these other people around—

"We're nice together," Laura breathed against his lips.

Everyone was so damn glad to see him. All they needed were banners, little pins. Official Welcoming Party to Greet the Arrival of Professor Larry Kane.

Kane managed to look out the window as they crossed the Tri-Borough Bridge at 125th Street and started up the East River Drive.

"Things haven't changed much," Kane said. "Not nearly so much traffic though."

"The saucers," Phil said. "Most of the traffic's up in the air."

"We're looking at things," Laura said.

"Great old town," Ben said and laughed, on and on. Jenny laughed too, then said. "It looks just the same almost as when we left."

They're all speaking for me. Kane thought. Funny, a damned funny custom. It was a reflection of something else. What did it really mean? His feeling of unease seemed exaggerated. But then their efforts to make him welcome seemed pretty exaggerated too....

"Everybody happy?" the fat man yelled.

"Yes!"

"We're happy aren't we, honey," Laura said.

"Sure," Kane said.

Why not?

Kane noticed the amazing dearth of traffic on Madison Avenue.

No traffic cops either. That had changed too. One thing you had always been sure of seeing and that was a cop in New York.

When Kane asked about it, the smiles almost fled from every face, and the moment of silence seemed like a form of shock. Kane realized then that there hadn't been even a second of silence before then.

"It's hard to realize we've been away so long," Phil finally said.

"I'm really tired," Kane said to Phil as they went on past the Midtown Hotel toward Lucille's apartment. "I was intending to go directly to the hotel and rest up a while—"

"We'll relax at Lucie's," Jenny said. "We got music, we got music, we got music, who could ask for anything more?"

"But—" Kane started to protest at least mildly, but the rest of the sentence was blotted out by a long kiss from Laura.

CHAPTER TWO

They had all crowded into an elevator, and then rushed into Lucille's apartment on a high level of The Sunny Hill building near Washington Square. The apartment consisted of one huge room with a circular couch in the middle upon which everyone immediately sat.

Laura sat beside Kane who was getting more tired every minute. There was just enough room for the gang to squeeze up tight to one another in a circle around a table supporting some kind of machine with wires that were immediately run from it and attached to everyone's wrist, and to a narrow metal headband with which everyone's head was crowned.

Kane was listening to music. It was like being dropped unexpectedly into the middle of a large symphony orchestra. The sound seemed to pulse and vibrate gigantically all around him. It was more than merely listening. He was in it. He felt himself a part of it, swimming in it, and almost fighting to keep from being carried away by what seemed to be perfectly recorded music that was now being delivered by some final form of hi-fi.

The music itself was familiar enough. Instrumentalized opera arias orchestrated on a fantastic scale. The quantity was so great that sensitivity as to quality was dulled. Kane, shocked by thunderous sweeps of sheer volume gave way before the sound. It wasn't sleep. He could hardly say he rested, but he was in a semi-stupor. When he glanced at his watch sometime later, two hours and some minutes had passed.

The wires were being removed from wrists, headbands from heads. Kane's head ached slightly. Everyone was reaching as cards fell out of the machine in the middle.

Laura handed one to Kane. It was covered with symbols in the form of some kind of graph, but he couldn't decipher it.

There was a great deal of chatter, musical jargon, colloquial in both space and time, most of it eluding comprehension. Kane stood there holding his card as everyone milled around one another.

Phil said, "Let's see how we liked it, Prof?"

That seemed to have been the general idea—how much everyone liked the music. And each one looked at his card, and they were all comparing cards and exclaiming over them.

Phil was looking at Kane's card, comparing it with his own and with some other cards.

"Well, not bad," Phil was saying, "Is it, gang?"

"Not bad at all!" they chorused.

"What isn't bad?" Kane asked.

"Our taste, man," Laura said. "You'll fit so good."

The odd one, Lucille, raised an eyebrow, with some mockery in it still, at Kane.

"You'll sure belong, Professor. Don't worry," Lucille said. She held up her card. "We liked it."

"Of course it'll take a little time," Phil said as he threw his arm over Kane's shoulder. "A few sessions and you'll match up just right."

"I really don't believe I understand," Kane said vaguely.

"You will," Lucille said as she moved away from him. "You sure will, Professor." She was tall, and with long lithe legs. She was a handsome woman, Kane thought.

As Phil explained casually on the way toward the Midtown Hotel, they had just had a music session. Everything was done in sessions, in groups that is. Everyone had his group, and his group did everything together.

Anyway, they had had a music session. The machine in the middle was a Reacto. The cards were Reacto Cards. It was really a kind of taste tester, and the point was that the Reacto tested everyone's reaction to the music.

The cards enabled everyone to check their reactions, check them against the reactions of all the others. It involved conformity ratings, and tendencies to stray from the group norm.

The important thing about the taste rate cards was that they enabled you to find out just how much group spirit you had. The closer your card resembled that of all the others in your group, the more GS you had.

"My GS rating's gone up," Laura kept burbling all the way to the Midtown Hotel. "It's gone up!"

The same process applied to reading, movies, television, eating, anything involving the elements of reacting. The important thing was not how you yourself felt, but how you felt in relation to the feelings of the group. The problem seemed to be that of reducing deviation tendencies to a minimum.

On the way to the Midtown Hotel, Jenny asked Phil how he liked the new best-seller, *Love Is Forever,* and Phil took a small card out of his wallet and they all compared Reacto Cards in order to determine relative reactions to *Love Is Forever*.

Good God! *You had to look at a card to find out how you liked something!* It was frightening as hell.

Kane wondered how wide-spread, how universal, it really was, this incredible conformity, this collective thinking.

This appalling sacrifice of individuality.

Kane was too tired to give much thought to it right then. He was anxious to get to the Hotel, and he was beginning to fantasize a bed, cool sheets, his body stretching and sinking down into blissful slumber.

But as appalling as the situation seemed at the time, Kane soon found that he had only circled on the fringes of it. This was only the beginning.

CHAPTER THREE

"Here we are, here were are, gang!" someone shouted as they piled out of the cabs and Kane was being hustled toward the suddenly formidable glint of a revolving door.

So here we are, Kane thought. It was nice being here all right. He was glad, very glad. But it sounded as though someone might swoon over the fact.

There was some difficulty with the revolving door. No one seemed able to move first, and there were spontaneous group lunges ending in jamming chaos in which someone hurt their arm. Kane thought it was the fat man, Ben.

"We're hurt!" Jenny screamed.

"Oh—it's not bad," Ben said, laughing all the time he was groaning. "Just bruised a little, gang. We're just bruised a little."

Kane grabbed his advantage and ventured alone through the revolving doors into the lobby. A pair of desk clerks nodded across the lobby. A group was emerging from behind drapes and beyond them Kane saw an ornate, subtly lighted, cocktail lounge.

Kane was heading for the elevator when the gang overtook him.

Laura had hold of one of his arms, and Phil the other.

"We're having cocktails," Laura said.

Phil repeated it, and Ben and Jenny joined in. The young man, Clarence, was singing as he herded the others toward the drapes of the cocktail lounge, and they were all whisking Kane away before he could voice any protest.

"What'll the gang have?" the waiter asked, smiling. Only he wasn't really smiling at any of them, Kane thought. He had picked out a center point of focus and was smiling at that so as not to appear to be smiling at any one, but at everyone.

"Martinis!" several voices said.

The waiter nodded, whirled away.

"Ah, waiter," Kane said. "I'll have a double shot of Scotch. No ice."

The waiter seemed shocked, unable to come to grips with Kane's seemingly simple order. "But—but I thought you said Martini."

The gang was still smiling, but faintly. The waiter was backing away.

"No," Kane insisted. "He said Martinis, and she said Martinis, and so did several others. But I didn't say Martinis. I said Scotch, no ice."

"But Martinis—"

Ben forced a pained laugh. "But we ordered Martinis."

"Martinis," Laura said.

"The ayes always have it," Kane heard Lucille whisper near him.

Phil said, with a kind of shaky joviality. "Martinis—"

"Gin makes me ill," Kane said. "For me, it has to be Scotch."

Phil whispered. "Scotch."

"Scotch," the waiter said.

A jukebox in a far corner blasted out from a sea of bubbling, multicolored light.

We're all pals togetherrrrrrrr.

The Gang knows no bad weatherrrrrr.

We're all for us all for us,

And we're rolling do-own life's highway,

On our crowded busssssss!

Laura whispered huskily in his ear. "Don't worry about any little old thing. We're one together, man."

CHAPTER FOUR

God, he was tired. He was so tired he could hardly sit there. He felt numb, and there was desperation under the numbness. Kane wanted to get off somewhere by himself so he could rest, sleep, and think. He wanted to think....

Bits of information drifted haphazardly into Kane's consciousness from the conversation. He had ordered another double Scotch and was almost through with it. He was passing out, but held to conscious awareness by the unceasing banter, laughter and the jukebox—like a marionette held up with wires.

If he suddenly found himself alone in silence, he knew he would collapse instantly.

It seemed that this was a group with a certain common Reacto level, and they all worked in the same place, and lived in the same section of a big housing project, a place called Sunny Hill.

Phil was their Integrator, and he was also an Official in the Isotopic Corporation where the Group worked. Phil was an Integrator for the Isotopic Corporation, a sort of personnel man whose main duty was the integration of the employees' private lives.

When Kane tried to find out about the work itself, no one seemed interested enough to respond. The work was relatively unimportant. The emphasis seemed to be centered almost completely on how people got along together. If your Reacto cards reported a general reaction that strayed too far from your Group norm, you were either sent to another group, or sent to a Staff.

A Staff was a rather vague term for specialists in Integration on a clinical level.

The job was always referred to as "our job", and the Gang seemed to do practically everything together.

Someone mentioned that a friend hadn't been competent in group relations at school and had been Processed. Kane didn't like the words they were so casually throwing around. In fact Kane didn't like any of it, and he was liking it less all the time.

Another term that referred to some sort of adjustment process was the word homogenized. Someone had been "homogenized".

Once Kane tried to find out about his old friends, Professors Legmann, and Martin over at New York University. Phil avoided the question for a time, then finally admitted that Martin was still there in the archeology department, but that Legmann had quit the profession years ago. "He quit teaching and became a plumber."

"A plumber?" Kane whispered. "Legmann?"

"That's right," Phil grinned.

"We're all plumbing together," Laura lisped.

"But—that's preposterous!" Kane almost yelled. "Legmann—why he was the finest research chemist—"

"But he wasn't really happy in his profession," Phil said. "As I recall—he just wasn't well adjusted as a research chemist and teacher."

"Who said he wasn't?"

"Why the Staff."

"What Staff—?"

"Anyway, he's a plumber now somewhere," Phil said. "He's happy now."

Kane felt a coldness on his neck. His stomach seemed to turn completely over. The devil with this, he thought. His eyeballs felt as though they were covered with sand, and his lids seemed leaded weights. He pushed back his chair.

"You'll excuse me," he said. "But I'm really tired out. I'm going to get some rest—"

"But the night's young for us, man," Laura shrieked.

"We're having more Scotch," Lucille said, watching him carefully.

"Fun time's only starting for us," the young man protested, and the fat man and Jenny and all of them protested loudly together, laughing all the while.

Kane was backing away. The hell with them. He turned and ran for the elevator. Then he remembered that he didn't know what room he was supposed to be checked into. He didn't have a key either. He—

Two smiling men, were on either side of him. In a mirror he could see the half smiling, half concerned faces of Phil and Laura, and the slightly sardonic eyes of Lucille.

"Don't worry, Gang," he heard Phil say. "We're taking a Special room. We'll be together again soon."

"This way," the two young smiling men said. They wore uniforms and appeared to be bellhops. "We'll show you to our room."

The two bellhops started to back out of the room. "What's special about it?" Kane asked. "Only thing I can see about it that could be considered special is that it's about big enough to be someone's closet! I reserved a suite. What kind of a run-around is this anyway?"

It was hardly bigger than a large closet. A white room, with only a single bed in it, and a bureau. Through a narrow, partly open door, he could see a bathroom, and that was it.

"Well," the bellhop said, smiling. "It's our Single."

"You mean you call it special because it's a single," Kane asked.

The bellhops nodded.

"Why?" Kane insisted. "What's special about a single?"

"We only have one single here," the bellhops said. "We hope you are comfortable with us, Professor Kane."

"Look here! Why should you only have one single in this entire hotel? And what's so special about it?"

"This single is seldom demanded by guests," the bellhop said.

"I didn't demand it. I reserved a suite, or at least I understood that my friend, Phil Nordson, reserved a suite. I certainly didn't demand this!"

"But—but of course you did. We have to have a single when we're—not getting along well with ourselves."

Kane started for the door, but the two men backed out and shut it in his face. He tried the knob. The door was locked. He turned quickly and scanned the room, but there was no key visible. Then one of the curtains moved as he walked toward it, and he saw that the narrow window was barred.

As he swept the curtains aside to look out through the bars, and grabbed at the bars in a kind of instinctual gesture, a metal panel slid noiselessly across and shut out a flash of neon light.

He was alone, locked up like a dangerous madman!

CHAPTER FIVE

By the head of the narrow bed that resembled something antiseptic in a barracks, Kane saw the black eye of a phone peeking out of a niche in the wall.

He pulled it out and jabbed at a button. His throat felt tight and he could feel the pounding of his heart as he leaned against the wall.

"This is Professor Kane, room 2004."

"Yes, we're here."

"And I'm here! In this ridiculous closet. I'm locked in. There must be some sort of mistake. The window—"

"We'll be all right. We'll be fine in a little while."

"Look here—connect me with the cocktail lounge. I want to speak with Phil Nordson. Yes, he's there—"

He heard nothing, absolutely nothing, except his own heart. No clock in the room either. The walls and ceiling had a peculiar grained look.

"Hello, Prof!"

"Phil! Phil, listen, what in the name of God goes on here? I'm locked in! You said you reserved a suite for me, and this room—"

"We aren't going to worry," Phil said. Kane heard laughter in the background and the high-pitched choral voices from the jukebox. "We'll be all right. We figured there would be a little trouble here and there, at first."

"I don't give a damn about a little trouble there! Phil, I'm talking about me, here! I'm locked in. And my luggage. Where is it? And—"

Kane's stomach jumped. A kind of terror hit him like a cold breath. "Phil! My briefcase. Where's my briefcase?"

"We have it somewhere—" Phil was saying. "Just don't let us worry."

Kane heard a clicking sound somewhere and he yelled into the phone but nothing came back. He released the phone and it was sucked back into the wall.

He sank down on the bed and fumbled absently at his coat and then at his necktie. The walls had a blurred quality and he felt on the edge of passing out. He kept thinking of the briefcase, with years of work in it, the equations, more than could be preserved entirely in a man's head.

It was too sickening to think about, the possibility of them losing his briefcase. Phil didn't seem concerned. No one was concerned with his briefcase, that was obvious. The only thing they were concerned about was that he didn't get along with the Gang.

The hell with the Gang, every last one of the Gang. If he never heard of the Gang or saw the Gang again, he would consider himself extremely fortunate.

He felt numb, too tired to think about anything. He fumbled at one shoe, got it off, then worked vaguely at the other one. He would rest, sleep, sleep for a long time, then he would be able to think. He might find this all exaggerated, unreal, once he slept, rested, woke up again.

A man certainly had rights. There was some authority he could contact of course. He was just too upset to think about it anymore.

He had his shirt, his undershirt off. He had his shoes and socks off and he flexed his feet in ecstasy. He unzipped his fly and as he started to stand up to take his pants off, he groaned with fright and fell backward onto the bed.

A chair fused with the bed. Laura was there, sitting on the chair, but also practically sitting in Kane's lap.

He blinked rapidly and reached out, and his hand moved through the image of Laura, only Laura seemed solid, three-dimensional, very real indeed. Too real.

"Get out," he whispered. "What—"

Glass clinked loudly right in the room with him. The jukebox blared.

Kane couldn't move. He sat rigidly, and the table was there, and all the Gang around it, and Phil there smiling and they were all around Kane drinking Scotch, double shots of Scotch, no ice.

Lucille looked across the table and shook her lovely head slightly. There was concern, genuine concern, a kind of sadness, behind the false smile. The smile, he knew, was for the others. But the concern was for him.

Phil raised his glass. Nine glasses were in the air.

"Here's to us, happy Gang, Prof," Phil shouted.

"Here's to us! Here's to Sunny Hill!" they shouted.

Kane slowly moistened his lips. The three walls and the ceiling had come alive. They were actually huge TV screens, and the effect was startlingly three-dimensional. Only the absence of touch could break the illusion. But the visual and the audial made up for the absence of touch. Kane didn't want to touch them anyway. He wanted them to go away, altogether.

His room was crammed with phantoms from the cocktail lounge. In fact, his room was fused with the cocktail lounge. It was all there somehow.

"Go to sleepy-bye," Laura whispered and made a very suggestive gesture. Her cheeks were flushed as she leaned into and through him.

"Take ourselves a good long snooze," Phil grinned. "Don't worry. The Gang's all here."

Lucille said, hardly smiling at all. "No, don't worry, Professor. We'll all sleep with you."

He zipped his pants back up and slid back through several phantom shapes and pressed against the wall.

"Phil," he finally said. "Phil!"

"Aren't you sleepy now?" Phil asked.

"He's sleepy," Laura said. "We're sleeping with you, Professor man."

"Yes, yes I am sleepy. Goodnight now," Kane said. "Goodnight."

He waited. They didn't take the hint. To them it was no hint at all. He knew they weren't going away. He knew that no matter what he said or did, they wouldn't go away. That was the thing he understood, incredible as it was, he knew now that no matter what he said or did, they wouldn't go away.

They only understood that he was somehow ill. He knew that too. They were right, so he was wrong. They thought they were doing what was best for him. That was obvious. It was all over their faces and actions. If they had any idea how he felt, they still considered his feelings only symptoms of some kind, and they seemed confident that Kane would soon be all right.

But his being all right had nothing to do with their going away.

Kane decided not to give way, not to scream or anything absurd like that. It wouldn't do any good. Calm, be calm and—well maybe just try pretending they're not there at all.

Then he remembered the bathroom and ran through several chairs, a table, and three people, and into the bathroom. He slammed the door and leaned against it and let out a long relieved breath.

He was taking off his shorts when the bathroom walls and the ceiling came alive.

What had been labeled "Boy's Room" down in the cocktail lounge was being projected into the bathroom of room 2004.

It wasn't false modesty that prompted Kane's moan. It wasn't any form of prudishness that moved Kane to clutch his undershorts to his body and leap into the shower stall.

It was a panicky realization of the absolutely involuntary nature of the way things were. Strangers, with friendly smiles, everywhere around him all the time, and he, Larry Kane, had nothing—*absolutely nothing to say about it.*

The shower stall with the pulled curtain was no refuge either. There was a superimposed sink in there on the wall with a phantom shape using an electric razor.

Phil and Ben were leaning through the shower curtain. They weren't there for anything specific. They were just there, chatting, smiling, bantering.

Others came in and out of the "Boy's Room" of the cocktail lounge. Everyone said hello, or directed some sort of friendly comment casually at Kane as though superimposed washrooms were the quintessence of social normalcy. And, Kane thought pushing hard at panic, they probably were.

Phil and Ben were there for no other reason than to keep Kane company. To help him. He could see that. No matter how tortured he seemed, their attitude remained that of beneficence. The trouble was all his, and they gave no indication of seeing his side of anything.

Evidently, to them, being alone was the worst thing that could happen to anybody. If he wanted to be alone then he was wrong, he was sick, he was put in a special room. A single. But they wouldn't go away.

He managed to turn on the shower, and he turned his face up to the icy water and closed his eyes and imagined he was back in blessed isolation in the study of the observatory on the Moon. But it was a long long way back to the Moon.

It worked both ways. He could see and hear them. They could hear and see him too, but he determined to do his best to ignore them. The idea of social amenities no longer bothered Kane. Being impolite was an absurdity. Social decency was a mutual thing, and these people weren't considering his rights at all.

He finished his shower and draped the towel around his waist and went back out into the closet they had given him. He walked toward the bed, sidestepping people, chairs, tables still unable to realize fully that these things weren't really here.

CHAPTER SIX

The jukebox got louder. A couple danced through him. Suddenly, Kane stood shivering, a raw panic taking hold. Control fled before the rising jukebox clangor, the laughter, the waving and shouting and hideous unwelcome demons of camaraderie.

He felt himself wildly waving his arms about and shouting at the walls.

"Get out! For God's sake get out and let me sleep!"

Ben was staring at Kane from only a few inches away.

"You," Kane pointed a finger at the three dimensional ghost. "You—fade out, go away somewhere. No—no, Phil, not you. Get these other people out. I want to talk to you—Phil—"

"Easy now," Phil said soothingly. "We'll be all right. In a little while now—"

"I am all right, but I won't be if I can't sleep. Phil—can't all this just—just be tuned out or something?"

Kane tried to imagine none of the others were there. Just the small room, himself, and Phil. But the others were all looking at Kane, all of them looking, all of them smiling. Lucille was looking too, but somehow he was sure he could see a reflection of his own feelings in her eyes, hidden, but there.

"We'll be with you all the way," Phil said.

"But how can I sleep with a cocktail lounge full of people all over my bed? Tell me. I'm listening. Tell me how!"

Phil's smile disappeared completely for a brief second. He whispered, close to Kane's ear. "Try to do it, Larry. Please—*try*!"

Kane ran to the wall, clicked the light switch. He knew that the lights in his room went out, but the slightly dimmer lights projected from the cocktail lounge remained. Somehow, that was even worse. It seemed to resemble the implacable characters of a persisting nightmare. Subdued, with the coruscating bubbling play of multicolored light from the jukebox turning a rainbow over and over the ceiling and the bed, and the Gang, the Gang all there like ghosts with greenish faces smiling, sitting, whispering round the bed.

Kane threw himself on the bed and covered his eyes with his arms.

He was going mad with fatigue, and yet he knew he could never sleep, never rest, under these circumstances. It wasn't just the figures there, the lights, the laughter and whispering and the chorus breaking from the jukebox. It was what their being there really meant, the suggestion of the bigger cause behind what was happening to Kane.

A man who fears to sleep in the dark is not really afraid of the dark. But of what is hiding in it.

CHAPTER SEVEN

Shadows moved above his closed lids. Glass tinkled with ice cubes. Under his sweating forearm, his eyes throbbed and his body felt as though the skin had been scraped all over until it was raw.

Kane propped himself on an elbow, and looked to one side at Phil. Phil grinned sympathetically. Laura was in the same cushioned chair, but she seemed to be sitting beside Kane on the bed. Lucille was avoiding looking at Kane.

"Phil."

"Well, Prof, we thought we were getting our sleep!"

"No," Kane whispered. "I can't sleep. I'm asking you, you Phil, and all the rest of you, to let me sleep. I'm asking you to help me in that way, just for a while. I'm imploring you really to just tune yourselves out for a while and let me sleep."

There was something blank, uncomprehending in the way they smiled at him. Kane knew then that they could never allow themselves to try to understand his situation, because then they might question their own. For example, if they've taken refuge in one another from a terrible fear of insecurity, anxiety, and aloneness, then Kane could only represent the threat of reawakened fear.

What was the use?

"We'll turn the lights down low, how would that be, Prof?" Phil asked.

"We'd like that," Laura whispered.

"Don't be afraid, we're with you," Ben said.

"We'll sing you into dreamland," Jenny said.

"Don't be afraid. We're all together and our Gang is with you," someone else said. It didn't matter who really, Kane thought, because they all spoke not as individuals but as the Gang.

"Through sunshine and in shadow," Lucille said.

The lights dimmed slowly as Kane curled up on the bed and clenched his eyes shut. He pulled the sheet up over his face. He pressed his fingers into his ears. But it wouldn't work. Nothing like that would do any good. You couldn't shut off indignity such as this. You couldn't block out such an intrusion of spirit and human dignity by burying your head, or pressing your ears.

You could try, but not very long, not when you knew it wouldn't do any good.

He had no idea now what time it was, how long he had been here. He had tried to spot a wall clock somewhere in the cocktail lounge, but none was within view. That didn't help either, this timeless feeling. That only enhanced the similarity it all had to a persisting nightmare.

It was a gnawing murmur all around him. It was like a hollow tooth. The softened sounds of their voices going on and on was maddening because they were softened. Softened for him, yet they were still there. He felt like an irritated baby sleeping while adults talked, pretending to soften their voices.

His body was slimy with sweat, and his head pounded with a dull ache. He jumped out of bed and ran straight through Laura to the wall and jerked the phone from its slot.

He yelled into it.

"This is Professor Larry Kane. Room 2004. I'm checking out. Send someone up here with a key! I said send someone up here...."

"We understand, Professor Kane."

"Then you'll send someone up immediately with a key!"

"Please don't get upset. The Staff has been busy, but now the Staff will soon be with you."

The Staff....

"I just want a key, I want to get the hell out of here!"

Kane yelled several times into the phone after the click, but no voice came back. He had grabbed up the table, the metal table at the head of the bed, and flung it into the wall before he realized what he was doing.

The shadows moved toward him. Phil, Laura, Ben, Jenny, Lawrence, Lucille, all the others, nameless, what did it matter anyway, their names?

They were smiling, holding out their arms to him. Compassionate, sympathy, they had it all. All they wanted to do was help him.

He ran through them back toward the bathroom. It was still full of men from the downstairs john. "What time is it?" Kane yelled at someone with a paper towel pressed to his eyes.

"'Bout three I'd say, what a night!"

"Three—"

Three o'clock in the morning, but the fact was Kane wasn't sure about the day. He backed out of the bathroom, slammed the door.

"The Staff is ready, Prof," Phil said.

"We're all with you, aren't we?" Laura giggled.

The closet.

Kane ran into the closet and slammed the door. There was something immediately cozy in the narrow black confines of the closet. Either closet walls weren't TV screens, or they had decided to let him sleep at last. Probably the former. Better convert closets to Television. In case kiddies misbehave and get locked in the closet, they'll not be alone in there....

He curled up on the floor in the pitch blackness and almost immediately began to drift off into sleep. The narrow darkness tightened around him like a thick comforting blanket on a cold night....

Sometime later—he had no idea how much time had passed—a light was blinking at his lids. He opened them slowly and stared into a flickering yellow eye.

A doorhinge creaked. Up there somewhere a voice said pleasantly:

"Professor Kane, your Staff is here."

"Staff?" he whispered, trying to see above the blinking light.

"We're here."

CHAPTER EIGHT

The TV walls were dead now, but that was hardly consoling. The overhead light was glaring with an intense whiteness. The three members of the Staff were busy, and Kane was being Tested.

Kane had emerged from the closet determined to remain as rational as possible, to control his emotions, and find out what he could about his human rights as an individual.

That was easy to find out and only required a few questions honestly and frankly answered.

As a minority, Kane had no rights whatsoever.

He had one big right, the right to think as the majority did. But that didn't count for much yet because Kane was ill, maladjusted and had anti-group feeling.

The Staff was going to test him, find out what was wrong with Kane. And this of course implied that when they found out what was wrong, the difficulty would be taken care of.

The Staff was kind, considerate, almost excessively polite considering the circumstances. They were young efficient men with crewcuts, briefcases, and wearing tight conservative dark suits. Only slight differences in build distinguished them one from another, but this superficial outward difference only seemed to emphasize the Staff's basic unity, its Group Spirit, its Staff Consciousness.

Every public institution, every business establishment, every school, club, hotel, factory, office building—in short, everywhere that people congregated in official Groups, there was a regular Staff on duty twenty-four hours a day.

They were Integrators. Glorified personnel men.

Electrodes were clamped on Kane's head and wrists. Something was strapped around his chest. Wires ran into a miniature Reacto. A stylus began to make jagged lines on a strip of moving tape.

"We're getting a complete personality checkup," the Staff said.

It was indeed complete. It was as complete as a personality checkup could be short of an actual dissection.

Kane looked at countless ink-blots. He was shown a great many pictures and whether he answered verbally or not was of no concern of the Staff.

Whatever his reactions were, they were all analyzed by the machines. Words weren't necessary. The Staff had a shortcut to personality checkups. From the mind right into the machine.

The Staff only interpreted the results, or maybe they didn't even do that. It was more likely that machines did that too.

Kane protested for a while, but he was too tired to protest very long. He asked them a great many questions, and they answered them willingly enough—up to a point. They were interested in his questions too. He was an interesting symptom, but actually he knew that they already had him pretty well tabbed.

They answered his questions the way big-hearted adults answered inquisitive children.

"We must," the Staff said, "determine why you don't fit in."

Kane talked about his work, his theories, his years of devotion to what he had always considered to be a contribution to society. They hardly seemed interested. What good was all that—astronomy and such—when a man was not happy with others?

"What about this aversion to people?" the Staff said, in a kindly way. "This—well—clinically, this de-grouping syndrome. This antagonism to the group spirit."

"You mean my reaction to Phil and his friends?"

"Your friends. Your Group," The Staff said.

"But I don't dislike those people," Kane insisted. "Certainly, I have no aversion to them! Hell, I don't even *know* them."

"But they're people," the Staff said. "Part of the family of man."

"I know that. But I was tired and wanted to sleep!"

"You'll find the true group Spirit," the Staff said. "Let us ask you this, Professor Kane. If you really had no aversion to people generally, why would you object to them being with you? Why should the presence of people disturb your sleep? Wouldn't a healthy person enjoy sleeping with others merely because they were there? Doesn't one sleep best among friends, knowing he isn't alone, knowing even his sleep is shared—"

There was a great deal more, but it all boiled down to the same thing.

Kane was wrong.

And he didn't have the right to be wrong.

CHAPTER NINE

They, or rather it, the Staff, seemed to concentrate on the whole question of why Kane had ever volunteered for a job demanding extreme isolation in the first place. The point was that apparently Kane had been anti-social, a Group Spirit deviant from the beginning.

Kane tried to explain it, calmly at first, then more emotionally. Either way, he knew that whatever he said was only additional grist to their syndrome recording mill. Being alone in order to do certain kinds of work demanding isolation seemed to be beside the point.

The point was that being on the Moon deprived a man of Groups. It was a kind of psychological suicide. Now that he was back home they would straighten him out. The question of returning to the Moon was ignored. To them, this was an absurdity. What did Kane want?

Kane was in no position to know what he really wanted—yet. They were going to help him decide what he really wanted. But they already knew that. It only remained for Kane to agree with them.

The majority was always right.

He explained his values to them. They listened. He told them that as far as he was concerned the social setup was now deadly, a kind of self-garrisoned mental concentration camp in which free thought was impossible. A stagnate, in fact a regressive state of affairs. Proficiency in skills would go, science would die. A herd state. Individuality lost. Depersonalized. Tyranny of the Majority. Integration mania. Collective thinking. Mass media. Lilliput against Leviathan....

But Kane wasn't happy, that was the important thing wasn't it?

Could a knowledge of how rapidly the Universe was expanding contribute to the happiness of a human being living on Madison Avenue in Manhattan?

Obviously the answer to that was no.

Kane was going to be happy. He wouldn't concern himself with the stars any more. He wouldn't practice a self-imposed barren isolation of himself any more. Kane was going to be happy. He was going to be one of the Group.

Time went by. He was given sedatives. He slept at last. He awoke and was tested and went to sleep again, many times. He was fed too, given injections with needles of energy and vitamins and proteins and glucose and carbohydrates, because he refused to eat any other way.

Vaguely he remembered episodes of babbling under the influence of hypnotic drugs.

He kept remembering the briefcase. In a dream the Group had it, throwing it around among them like a basketball. The clasp broke. The papers, thousands of papers spilled out and drifted away over New York and Kane was running through a maze looking up at them and then he was lost.

Now he knew what had happened to the other Moon ships, and to the rest of the Captain's crew, where they had gone to and never come back from.

Space was lonely and dark. Space was empty. Space was frightening.

They had gone back to the closeness and warmth and security of their Group.

How many were there left such as the Captain, and Kane—Kane for a while yet perhaps? How many were there?

Could he escape?

At some unrelated point on the Testing chart, the Staff closed up their briefcases, politely said good-bye, and left.

The data would be run through more machines.

Kane would be happy.

All he had to do was wait.

CHAPTER TEN

Kane awoke with a galvanic start and stared at the prison of his room.

The walls began coming alive. Phil, Laura, Lucille, Herby, Clarence, Jenny, Ben, the happy happy Group, always there, always waiting, always reliable, sharing everything, pleasure and pain.

"How we feeling now, Prof," Phil yelled. He was stark naked.

"You look so cuddly," Laura giggled, and for an instant there, Kane could almost feel her snuggling in beside him.

Kane lay there in a dim superimposed puzzle of furniture, moving forms, corners of rooms jutting out of the wrong walls, bodies walking through beds and one another, and then a naked figure curving into the air, falling toward him in a graceful arc, down, getting larger and larger, plunging right for Kane's face.

Kane rolled frantically. And then somewhere under him he heard a splash and there was the vague ripple of unreal water as Phil swam away across his cool blue pool.

There—that was Laura, only in a boudoir, standing before a mirror wearing only a pair of very brief panties, and nothing else. Her reflection in the mirror smiled at Kane as she brushed her hair.

"Morning, Prof honey. How we feeling this morning?"

It was morning. Some morning on some day during some year.

There was Lucille on this morning lying in a sunchair, her black hair shining in the sunlight somewhere. Probably in the Group house at Sunny Hill. In a while now, Kane knew, the Group would all go away together to their office, and they would do their work, concentrating on getting along together until they could return to Sunny Hill together.

Lucille was reading a newspaper, and she glanced up at Kane. There was a pale line around her mouth and she pulled her eyes quickly away as though she didn't want to look at him. She wasn't like the others. She was different. Of course. It had to be a matter of degree. Nothing was black and white. There had to be differences of opinion, some degree of individuality—somehow. Somewhere. Perhaps Lucille—

"Good morning, good morning to all of us!" Kane shouted suddenly.

"Did we have a good rest, Prof?"

Phil was yelling from his pool. He seemed greatly pleased with Kane's enthusiastic social response. Not that Kane was really trying to fool anybody. He was pretty sure the Staff wouldn't be fooled. Somewhere the machines were scanning the data. Soon, the Staff would have a full analysis of Kane, what was wrong, and what would make it right. What he should have done, and what he should be.

Jenny and Ben were making love on a couch. Kane tried to keep on watching them as though he suffered no embarrassment, but it was impossible.

"I've a full schedule planned for today," Phil yelled up. "Soon we'll all be going to the Office. You'll be going with us soon too, Prof!"

He would belong to the happy Group. Sharing everything. But maybe it wouldn't be this happy Group. Maybe the machines would decide that he belonged in some other Group. Whatever Group it was it would be happy. That was a fact.

Could he escape? Could he, perhaps, get back to the La Guardia Pits, and the Captain of the Moonship?

The windows still barred, paneled in metal. The door locked. If he managed to get out of this Single, say, and out of the Midtown Hotel, and into the street, then what?

That didn't matter. If he could only get that far—

Laura was standing there naked, close to Kane. "We're having our wedding at five," she whispered.

"Who?" Kane said, startled.

"Ben and Jenny. They're right for all of us together."

From a number of rooms, people were watching Ben and Jenny being right for all of us together, but Kane couldn't look.

"See us all," Laura shouted and dived through the floor. A spray of water spilled up and fell unfelt through Kane's flinching torso. Ben and Jenny ran away.

Kane was practically alone with Lucille. It was the first time in he had no idea now how long that he had been this much alone with any one other person.

She glanced rather sadly at Kane above the paper she was reading.

"You know how I feel, Lucie?"

She nodded, almost imperceptibly.

"How can you stand it, all the time this way?" he asked.

"Some of us learn to be in it, with a part of us out of it. A kind of self-hypnosis, a retreat of some kind. Into fantasy, that's what it really is. But—but I don't think any of us can keep on doing it forever. We will all give way completely—sooner or later."

"I've got to get out," Kane said. "Do you want to get out?"

"It's impossible to get out."

"I've got to try."

"What's the use of trying if you know you can't get away? Where can anyone go?"

"There must be people who break away," Kane said. "There have to be."

"There's supposed to be an underground, some secret group of some kind that helps people get out."

"Get out—where? Out of the country?"

"It's pretty much like this everywhere. But there are supposed to be areas where it isn't. Islands somewhere. Hidden places right here in the country. Supposed to be places in the Kentucky Mountains, and in New Mexico, places like that."

"The Moon," Kane said. "That's a place I know of. I've been there."

Her eyes were bright for a moment. "I know. It must have been wonderful. Why on Earth did you ever leave?"

"I didn't know what it was like here. And—my wife died. I wanted and needed another wife. More than a wife really. Someone who could share that kind of a life with me, someone who would be interested in the work too."

She turned quickly back to the paper.

"You might be able to get out of the hotel," she said. "But you would be too conspicuous."

"Because I would be traveling alone?"

"Yes."

"If you came with me, there would be two of us. We wouldn't be conspicuous that way."

He saw the flush move up through her face. "Is that the only reason?"

"You know it isn't."

She knew it. They both knew it and had probably known it for a long time. They had a lot in common, a minority of two.

And then he remembered. She wasn't really there in the Midtown with him. She was in Sunny Hill, wherever that was. They couldn't leave inconspicuously together because they weren't together now, and they couldn't get together without the Gang being together too.

The rooms, furniture, sounds, everything began to fade.

"Goodbye," Lucille said.

"Get sick or something," Kane said quickly. "Don't go with the Group to work. Stay there, wherever you are! *Stay there—*"

Faintly, her voice came to him out of a kind of melting mask of a face. "I'll try—"

Kane was alone in the single room and the door opened. The smiling Staff came in and shut the door.

The three of them stood there happily holding their briefcases.

"We're happy to report that we have completed your personality breakdown."

The word was a bit premature, Kane thought. "What is it?" he asked.

"Excellent," the Staff beamed. "You should never have been an astronomer. You took up that profession as a way of escaping from people. Actually, of course, you love people and hate your profession.

"Have you determined what I should be if not an astronomer?"

"Naturally, it's all in the breakdown."

"What is it?"

"Generally, you prefer physical work, not mental work. Mental work is a constant strain on your psychological balance. You have done it neurotically to reinforce your need to avoid people."

"Physical work? What kind?"

"Specifically, it seems that you are best suited for the profession of plumbing."

"Plumbing?" Kane said. "Plumbing what?"

"Plumbing, the art of pipe-fitting, the study of water mains, sewage lines, and so forth."

"Plumbing." Kane said.

"Of course, you react antagonistically to it now. But that will be changed."

Kane had nothing against plumbers or plumbing. Once, as a kid, he remembered having a long interesting talk with a plumber who was unstopping the kitchen sink. He had fascinating tools, and at that time, Kane had said he would be a plumber when he grew up. But he had also wanted to be any number of other things when he grew up, including an astronomer.

Now he had no desire whatsoever to be a plumber.

Kane drew the metal bedside table up hard and the edge of it caught number one of the Staff under the chin. Kane attacked, violently. He did it knowing that something more was at stake than his life—his identity.

CHAPTER ELEVEN

Number one fell down on his knees and whimpered. He wasn't hit hard. But he squatted there blubbering as though he had suffered some horrible shock. Numbers two and three gaped as though equally shocked without ever having been hit at all.

That was Kane's initial advantage. The Staff seemed incapable of understanding that anyone would do what Kane was doing. Kane hit number two four times before number two covered up his face with his hands and started to cry. Kane ran him into the closet and locked the door.

Number three swung his briefcase at Kane's head, fluttering his other hand wildly. Kane was heavier than he should have been because he was accustomed to the Moon. But he was desperate and that was some compensation. He had some experience, a very little, as a boxer in college, but that had been years ago. But as little experience as he had at this sort of thing, he was way ahead of number three. Number three kept swinging his briefcase, and Kane hit him on the chin and then in the stomach and then on the back of the neck. Number three lay unconscious on the floor.

Kane stared at his bleeding knuckles a moment, then dragged Number one up onto his feet.

"You're going to help me," Kane said. "We're getting a saucer and then we're going to Sunny Hill. You know where Sunny Hill is?"

Number one ran his hand nervously through his dark brushcut. He had a boyish face that seemed deeply insulted by what Kane had done. Insulted and shocked as though he had been a good boy all his life and then someone had slapped his hand—for no reason at all.

Kane doubled his fists. Number one winced and looked shocked again, and very frightened. A great deal more frightened than anyone would be who was afraid only of physical injury.

"Yes, that's part of a big Group Housing Project downtown."

"Where can we get a saucer?"

"The roof."

"Unlock the door," Kane said. "And just pretend everything is happy and that we're relating beautifully to one another. Now listen—I'll kill you if you try anything else. I hope you believe it because I really will. What you fellows intend doing with me, as far as I'm concerned, is worse than murder."

They stepped onto one of several saucers decorating the roof of the Midtown Hotel. The rotary blades in the ten foot platform whirred under them, and Kane felt the saucer rise up to a thousand feet, then dip downtown. The air was full of them and only some kind of sixth-sense seemed to keep them from jamming into one another.

There was never less than two on a saucer. And Kane noticed that most of the saucers were flying in Groups like aimless geese.

Kane jumped from the saucer and ran across the roof landing of the Sunny Hill project building. There were a number of them like huge blocks arranged in some incomprehensible plan.

Kane glanced back to see number one leaping from the saucer and running in the opposite direction. Kane ran on toward the elevator. He knew he didn't have much time, but what bothered him was the authority he was running against. Public opinion was a general attitude, not a cop car, or a squad of officers with guns. Getting out of line, Kane figured, was usually its own punishment—isolation, loneliness, social ostracism.

But what about the exception? The guy who fought conformity and the majority opinion.

Who would they put on Kane? Or what? It would help to know what he was running from. What concrete force or power would try to stop him.

Then he saw her running toward him.

Her face was flushed and the wind blew her dress tightly against her slim body as she stopped and looked at him.

He took hold of her arm.

"We've got to hurry," she said. "The Group knows I've run away. The Staff will be after me."

Kane glanced at the elevator, then they ran back toward the saucer.

"You'll have to pilot this thing," Kane said. "It's a little crowded up there for me."

She started the motor and the saucer lifted abruptly. "The terminal at La Guardia?" she said.

"No. The ship's at least two miles from the Terminal. We'll go directly to the ship." He hesitated. "The only thing is—it isn't due to blast out of here until the 25th."

"That doesn't matter," she said.

"Why doesn't it? We're flaunting the law. They're after us. They won't let us just hide away on that ship until the 25th."

"They?"

He stared at her. "You said yourself we had to hurry, because the Staff—"

"But don't you see, there's no one to stop us now. The Staff at Sunny Hills could have, but here there isn't any Staff. There's none at the ship either, is there?"

"No."

"Well then, we'll just wait on the ship until—we go to the Moon."

"But you were afraid, Lucie. You talked about undergrounds, and how it was impossible—"

She touched his arm and then took hold of his hand. "You don't understand I guess. Maybe you never will."

"Understand what?"

"What it is to try to get away, be alone, be by yourself, when you can't. When no matter what you do you're with the Group, night and day, even in your dreams. You knew it for a while, but imagine it for years, not days. There's no place to hide. Wherever you go the Group goes with you. That's why I said you couldn't get away—"

"Then there isn't any law to prevent us from going to the Moon?"

"Only the law of the majority, of Public Opinion," she said. "But you can't stay here and fight it, not for very long. Finally you have to give in to it. You become what they are or go mad. And there are Groups even for them."

The saucer dropped down to the fog draped earth and they were walking toward the pits where the Moonship waited.

It looked like such a wonderful world, he thought. Everyone happy, everyone smiling all the time. No wars. No externalized authority.

The Manufacturers of consent. A quasi-totalitarian society in which means of communication had largely replaced force as the apparatus of compulsion. Communication, fear, insecurity. In his isolation and insecurity, man clung to his Group, to the majority, the accepted opinions.

The majority did not need to force a man now. No need for police, or armies.

They *convinced* him.

The only way you could keep from being convinced was to get out.

The hatch slid open.

"Welcome aboard," the Captain said.

THE HIGHEST MOUNTAIN

The Highest Mountain by Bryce Walton

First published in 1952

This Edition Copyright @2020 by Eli Jayne

All rights reserved.

Cover art by Eli Jayne

First one up this tallest summit in the Solar System was a rotten egg ... a very rotten egg!

CHAPTER ONE

Bruce heard their feet on the gravel outside and got up reluctantly to open the door for them. He'd been reading some of Byron's poems he'd sneaked aboard the ship; after that he had been on the point of dozing off, and now one of those strangely realistic dreams would have to be postponed for a while. Funny, those dreams. There were faces in them of human beings, or of ghosts, and other forms that weren't human at all, but seemed real and alive—except that they were also just parts of a last unconscious desire to escape death. Maybe that was it.

"'Oh that my young life were a lasting dream, my spirit not awakening till the beam of an eternity should bring the 'morrow," Bruce said. He smiled without feeling much of anything and added, "Thanks, Mr. Poe."

Jacobs and Anhauser stood outside. The icy wind cut through and into Bruce, but he didn't seem to notice. Anhauser's bulk loomed even larger in the special cold-resisting suiting. Jacobs' thin face frowned slyly at Bruce.

"Come on in, boys, and get warm," Bruce invited.

"Hey, poet, you're still here!" Anhauser said, looking astonished.

"We thought you'd be running off somewhere," Jacobs said.

Bruce reached for the suit on its hook, started climbing into it. "Where?" he asked. "Mars looks alike wherever you go. Where did you think I'd be running to?"

"Any place just so it was away from here and us," Anhauser said.

"I don't have to do that. You are going away from me. That takes care of that, doesn't it?"

"Ah, come on, get the hell out of there," Jacobs said. He pulled the revolver from its holster and pointed it at Bruce. "We got to get some sleep. We're starting up that mountain at five in the morning."

"I know," Bruce said. "I'll be glad to see you climb the mountain."

Outside, in the weird light of the double moons, Bruce looked up at the gigantic overhang of the mountain. It was unbelievable. The mountain didn't seem to belong here. He'd thought so when they'd first hit Mars eight months back and discovered the other four rockets that had never got back to Earth—all lying side by side under the mountain's shadow, like little white chalk marks on a tallyboard.

They'd estimated its height at over 45,000 feet, which was a lot higher than any mountain on Earth. Yet Mars was much older, geologically. The entire face of the planet was smoothed into soft, undulating red hills by erosion. And there in the middle of barren nothingness rose that one incredible mountain. On certain nights when the stars were right, it had seemed to Bruce as though it were pointing an accusing finger at Earth—or a warning one.

CHAPTER TWO

With Jacobs and Anhauser and the remainder of the crew of the ship, *Mars V*, seven judges sat in a semi-circle and Bruce stood there in front of them for the inquest.

In the middle of the half-moon of inquisition, with his long legs stretched out and his hands folded on his belly, sat Captain Terrence. His uniform was black. On his arm was the silver fist insignia of the Conqueror Corps. Marsha Rennels sat on the extreme right and now there was no emotion at all on her trim, neat face.

He remembered her as she had been years ago, but at the moment he wasn't looking very hard to see anything on her face. It was too late. They had gotten her young and it was too late.

Terrence's big, square face frowned a little. Bruce was aware suddenly of the sound of the bleak, never-ending wind against the plastilene shelter. He remembered the strange misty shapes that had come to him in his dreams, the voices that had called to him, and how disappointed he had been when he woke from them.

"This is a mere formality," Terrence finally said, "since we all know you killed Lieutenant Doran a few hours ago. Marsha saw you kill him. Whatever you say goes on the record, of course."

"For whom?" Bruce asked.

"What kind of question is that? For the authorities on Earth when we get back."

"When you get back? Like the crews of those other four ships out there?" Bruce laughed without much humor.

Terrence rubbed a palm across his lips, dropped the hand quickly again to his belly. "You want to make a statement or not? You shot Doran in the head with a rifle. No provocation for the attack. You've wasted enough of my time with your damn arguments and anti-social behavior. This is a democratic group. Everyone has his say. But you've said too much, and done too much. Freedom doesn't allow you to go around killing fellow crew-members!"

"Any idea that there was any democracy or freedom left died on Venus," Bruce said.

"Now we get another lecture!" Terrence exploded. He leaned forward. "You're sick, Bruce. They did a bad psych job on you. They should never have sent you on this trip. We need strength, all the strength we can find. You don't belong here."

"I know," Bruce agreed indifferently. "I was drafted for this trip. I told them I shouldn't be brought along. I said I didn't want any part of it."

"Because you're afraid. You're not Conqueror material. That's why you backed down when we all voted to climb the mountain. And what the devil does Venus—?"

Max Drexel's freckles slipped into the creases across his high forehead. "Haven't you heard him expounding on the injustice done to the Venusian aborigines, Captain? If you haven't, you aren't thoroughly educated to the crackpot idealism still infecting certain people."

"I haven't heard it," Terrence admitted. "What injustice?"

Bruce said, "I guess it couldn't really be considered an injustice any longer. Values have changed too much. Doran and I were part of the crew of that first ship to hit Venus, five years ago. Remember? One of the New Era's more infamous dates. Drexel says the Venusians were aborigines. No one ever got a chance to find out. We ran into this village. No one knows how old it was. There were intelligent beings there. One community left on the whole planet, maybe a few thousand inhabitants. They made their last mistake when they came out to greet us. Without even an attempt at communication, they were wiped out. The village was burned and everything alive in it was destroyed."

Bruce felt the old weakness coming into his knees, the sweat beginning to run down his face. He took a deep breath and stood there before the cold nihilistic stares of fourteen eyes.

"No," Bruce said. "I apologize. None of you know what I'm talking about."

Terrence nodded. "You're psycho. It's as simple as that. They pick the most capable for these conquests. Even the flights are processes of elimination. Eventually we get the very best, the most resilient, the real conquering blood. You just don't pass, Bruce. Listen, what do you think gives you the right to stand here in judgment against the laws of the whole Solar System?"

"There are plenty on Earth who agree with me," Bruce said. "I can say what I think now because you can't do more than kill me and you'll do that regardless...."

He stopped. This was ridiculous, a waste of his time. And theirs. They had established a kind of final totalitarianism since the New Era. The psychologists, the Pavlovian Reflex boys, had done that. If you didn't want to be reconditioned to fit into the social machine like a human vacuum tube, you kept your mouth shut. And for many, when the mouth was kept shut long enough, the mind pretty well forgot what it had wanted to open the mouth for in the first place.

A minority in both segments of a world split into two factions. Both had been warring diplomatically and sometimes physically, for centuries, clung to old ideas of freedom, democracy, self-determinism, individualism. To most, the words had no meaning now. It was a question of which set of conquering heroes could conquer the most space first. So far, only Venus had fallen. They had done a good, thorough job there. Four ships had come to Mars and their crews had disappeared. This was the fifth attempt—

CHAPTER THREE

Terrence said, "why did you shoot Doran?"

"I didn't like him enough to take the nonsense he was handing me, and when he shot the—" Bruce hesitated.

"What? When he shot what?"

Bruce felt an odd tingling in his stomach. The wind's voice seemed to sharpen and rise to a kind of wail.

"All right, I'll tell you. I was sleeping, having a dream. Doran woke me up. Marsha was with him. I'd forgotten about that geological job we were supposed to be working on. I've had these dreams ever since we got here."

"What kind of dreams?"

Someone laughed.

"Just fantastic stuff. Ask your Pavlovian there," Bruce said. "People talk to me, and there are other things in the dreams. Voices and some kind of shapes that aren't what you would call human at all."

Someone coughed. There was obvious embarrassment in the room.

"It's peculiar, but many faces and voices are those of crew members of some of the ships out there, the ones that never got back to Earth."

Terrence grinned. "Ghosts, Bruce?"

"Maybe. This planet may not be a dead ball of clay. I've had a feeling there's something real in the dreams, but I can't figure it out. You're still interested?"

Terrence nodded and glanced to either side.

"We've seen no indication of any kind of life whatsoever," Bruce pointed out. "Not even an insect, or any kind of plant life except some fungi and lichen down in the crevices. That never seemed logical to me from the start. We've covered the planet everywhere except one place—"

"The mountain," Terrence said. "You've been afraid even to talk about scaling it."

"Not afraid," Bruce objected. "I don't see any need to climb it. Coming to Mars, conquering space, isn't that enough? It happens that the crew of the first ship here decided to climb the mountain, and that set a precedent. Every ship that has come here has had to climb it. Why? Because they had to accept the challenge. And what's happened to them? Like you, they all had the necessary equipment to make a successful climb, but no one's ever come back down. No contact with anything up there.

"Captain, I'm not accepting a ridiculous challenge like that. Why should I? I didn't come here to conquer anything, even a mountain. The challenge of coming to Mars, of going on to where ever you guys intend going before something bigger than you are stops you—it doesn't interest me."

"Nothing's bigger than the destiny of Earth!" Terrence said, sitting up straight and rigid.

"I know," Bruce said. "Anyway, I got off the track. As I was saying, I woke up from this dream and Marsha and Doran were there. Doran was shaking me. But I didn't seem to have gotten entirely awake; either that or some part of the dream was real, because I looked out the window—something was out there, looking at me. It was late, and at first I thought it might be a shadow. But it wasn't. It was misty, almost translucent, but I think it was something alive. I had a feeling it was intelligent, maybe very intelligent. I could feel something in my mind. A kind of beauty and softness and warmth. I kept looking—"

His throat was getting tight. He had difficulty talking. "Doran asked me what I was looking at, and I told him. He laughed. But he looked. Then I realized that maybe I wasn't still dreaming. Doran saw it, too, or thought he did. He kept looking and finally he jumped and grabbed up his rifle and ran outside. I yelled at him. I kept on yelling and ran after him. 'It's intelligent, whatever it is!' I kept saying. 'How do you know it means any harm?' But I heard Doran's rifle go off before I could get to him. And whatever it was we saw, I didn't see it any more. Neither did Doran. Maybe he killed it. I don't know. He had to kill it. That's the way you think."

"What? Explain that remark."

"That's the philosophy of conquest—don't take any chances with aliens. They might hinder our advance across the Universe. So we kill everything. Doran acted without thinking at all. Conditioned to kill everything that doesn't look like us. So I hit Doran and took the gun away from him and killed him. I felt sick, crazy with rage. Maybe that's part of it. All I know is that I thought he deserved to die and that I had to kill him, so I did."

"Is that all, Bruce?"

"That's about all. Except that I'd like to kill all of you. And I would if I had the chance."

"That's what I figured." Terrence turned to the psychologist, a small wiry man who sat there constantly fingering his ear. "Stromberg, what do you think of this gobbledegook? We know he's crazy. But what hit him? You said his record was good up until a year ago."

Stromberg's voice was monotonous, like a voice off of a tape. "Schizophrenia with mingled delusions of persecution. The schizophrenia is caused by inner conflict—indecision between the older values and our present ones which he hasn't been able to accept. A complete case history would tell why he can't accept our present attitudes. I would say that he has an incipient fear of personal inadequacy, which is why he fears our desire for conquest. He's rationalized, built up a defense which he's structured with his idealism, foundationed with Old Era values. Retreat into the past, an escape from his own present feelings of inadequacy. Also, he escapes into these dream fantasies."

"Yes," Terrence said. "But how does that account for Doran's action? Doran must have seen something—"

"Doran's charts show high suggestibility under stress. Another weak personality eliminated. Let's regard it that way. He *imagined* he saw something." He glanced at Marsha. "Did *you* see anything?"

She hesitated, avoiding Bruce's eyes. "Nothing at all. There wasn't anything out there to see, except the dust and rocks. That's all there is to see here. We could stay a million years and never see anything else. A shadow maybe—"

"All right," Terrence interrupted. "Now, Bruce, you know the law regulating the treatment of serious psycho cases in space?"

"Yes. Execution."

"No facilities for handling such cases en route back to Earth."

"I understand. No apologies necessary, Captain."

Terrence shifted his position. "However, we've voted to grant you a kind of leniency. In exchange for a little further service from you, you can remain here on Mars after we leave. You'll be left food-concentrates to last a long time."

"What kind of service?"

"Stay by the radio and take down what we report as we go up the mountain."

"Why not?" Bruce said. "You aren't certain you're coming back, then?"

"We might not," Terrence admitted calmly. "Something's happened to the others. We're going to find out what and we want it recorded. None of us want to back down and stay here. You can take our reports as they come in."

"I'll do that," Bruce said. "It should be interesting."

CHAPTER FOUR

Bruce watched them go, away and up and around the immediate face of the mountain in the bleak cold of the Martian morning. He watched them disappear behind a high ledge, tied together with plastic rope like convicts.

He stayed by the radio. He lost track of time and didn't care much if he did. Sometimes he took a heavy sedative and slept. The sedative prevented the dreams. He had an idea that the dreams might be so pleasant that he wouldn't wake up. He wanted to listen to Terrence as long as the captain had anything to say. It was nothing but curiosity.

At fifteen thousand feet, Terrence reported only that they were climbing.

At twenty thousand feet, Terrence said, "We're still climbing, and that's all I can report, Bruce. It's worth coming to Mars for—to accept a challenge like this!"

At twenty-five thousand feet, Terrence reported, "We've put on oxygen masks. Jacobs and Drexel have developed some kind of altitude sickness and we're taking a little time out. It's a magnificent sight up here. I can imagine plenty of tourists coming to Mars one of these days, just to climb this mountain! Mt. Everest is a pimple compared with this! What a feeling of power, Bruce!"

From forty thousand feet, Terrence said, "We gauged this mountain at forty-five thousand. But here we are at forty and there doesn't seem to be any top. We can see up and up and the mountain keeps on going. I don't understand how we could have made such an error in our computations. I talked with Burton. He doesn't see how a mountain this high could still be here when the rest of the planet has been worn so smooth."

And then from fifty-three thousand feet, Terrence said with a voice that seemed slightly strained: "No sign of any of the crew of the other four ships yet. Ten in each crew, that makes fifty. Not a sign of any of them so far, but then we seem to have a long way left to climb—"

Bruce listened and noted and took sedatives and opened cans of food concentrates. He smoked and ate and slept. He had plenty of time. He had only time and the dreams which he knew he could utilize later to take care of the time.

From sixty thousand feet, Terrence reported, "I had to shoot Anhauser a few minutes ago! He was dissenting. Hear that, Bruce? One of my most dependable men. We took a vote. A mere formality, of course, whether we should continue climbing or not. We knew we'd all vote to keep on climbing. And then Anhauser dissented. He was hysterical. He refused to accept the majority decision. 'I'm going back down!' he yelled. So I had to shoot him. Imagine a man of his apparent caliber turning anti-democratic like that! This mountain will be a great tester for us in the future. We'll test everybody, find out quickly who the weaklings are."

Bruce listened to the wind. It seemed to rise higher and higher. Terrence, who had climbed still higher, was calling. "Think of it! What a conquest! No man's ever done a thing like this. Like Stromberg says, it's symbolic! We can build spaceships and reach other planets, but that's not actual physical conquest. We feel like gods up here. We can see what we are now. We can see how it's going to be—"

Once in a while Terrence demanded that Bruce say something to prove he was still there taking down what Terrence said. Bruce obliged. A long time passed, the way time does when no one cares. Bruce stopped taking the sedatives finally. The dreams came back and became, somehow, more real each time. He needed the companionship of the dreams.

It was very lonely sitting there without the dreams, with nothing but Terrence's voice ranting excitedly on and on. Terrence didn't seem real any more; certainly not as real as the dreams.

CHAPTER FIVE

The problem of where to put the line between dream and reality began to worry Bruce. He would wake up and listen and take down what Terrence was saying, and then go to sleep again with increasing expectancy. His dream took on continuity. He could return to the point where he had left it, and it was the same—allowing even for the time difference necessitated by his periods of sleep.

He met people in the dreams, two girls and a man. They had names: Pietro, Marlene, Helene.

Helene he had seen from the beginning, but she became more real to him all the time, until he could talk with her. After that, he could also talk with Marlene and Pietro, and the conversations made sense. Consistently, they made sense.

The Martian landscape was entirely different in the dreams. Green valleys and rivers, or actually wide canals, with odd trees trailing their branches on the slow, peacefully gliding currents. Here and there were pastel-colored cities and there were things drifting through them that were alive and intelligent and soft and warm and wonderful to know.

'... dreams, in their vivid coloring of life, as in that fleeting, shadowy, misty strife of semblance with reality which brings to the delirious eye more lovely things of

paradise and love—and all our own!—than young Hope in his sunniest hour hath known....'

So sometimes he read poetry, but even that was hardly equal to the dreams.

And then he would wake up and listen to Terrence's voice. He would look out the window over the barren frigid land where there was nothing but seams of worn land, like scabs under the brazen sky.

"If I had a choice," he thought, "I wouldn't ever wake up at all again. The dreams may not be more real, but they're preferable."

Dreams were supposed to be wishful thinking, primarily, but he couldn't live in them very long. His body would dry up and he would die. He had to stay awake enough to put a little energy back into himself. Of course, if he died and lost the dreams, there would be one compensation—he would also be free of Terrence and the rest of them who had learned that the only value in life lay in killing one's way across the Cosmos.

But then he had a feeling Terrence's voice wouldn't be annoying him much more anyway. The voice was unreal, coming out of some void. He could switch off Terrence any time now, but he was still curious.

"Bruce—Bruce, you still there? Listen, we're up here at what we figure to be five hundred thousand feet! It *is* impossible. We keep climbing and now we look up and we can see up and up and there the mountain is going up and up—"

And some time later: "Bruce, Marsha's dying! We don't know what's the matter. We can't find any reason for it. She's lying here and she keeps laughing and calling your name. She's a woman, so that's probably it. Women don't have real guts."

Bruce bent toward the radio. Outside the shelter, the wind whistled softly at the door.

"Marsha," he said.

"Bruce—"

She hadn't said his name that way for a long time.

"Marsha, remember how we used to talk about human values? I remember how you seemed to have something maybe different from the others. I never thought you'd really buy this will to conquer, and now it doesn't matter...."

He listened to her voice, first the crazy laughter, and then a whisper. "Bruce, hello down there." Her voice was all mixed up with fear and hysteria and mockery. "Bruce darling, are you lonely down there? I wish I were with you, safe ... free ... warm. I love you. Do you hear that? I really love you, after all. After all...."

Her voice drifted away, came back to him. "We're climbing the highest mountain. What are you doing there, relaxing where it's peaceful and warm and sane? You always were such a calm guy. I remember now. What are you doing—reading poetry while we climb the mountain? What was that, Bruce—that one about the mountain you tried to quote to me last night before you ... I can't remember it now. Darling, what...?"

CHAPTER SIX

He stared at the radio. He hesitated, reached out and switched on the mike. He got through to her.

"Hello, hello, darling," he whispered. "Marsha, can you hear me?"

"Yes, yes. You down there, all warm and cozy, reading poetry, darling. Where you can see both ways instead of just up and down, up and down."

He tried to imagine where she was now as he spoke to her, how she looked. He thought of Earth and how it had been there, years ago, with Marsha. Things had seemed so different then. There was something of that hope in his voice now as he spoke to her, yet not directly to her, as he looked out the window at the naked frigid sky and the barren rocks.

"'... and there is nowhere to go from the top of a mountain,

But down, my dear;

And the springs that flow on the floor of the valley

Will never seem fresh or clear

For thinking of the glitter of the mountain water

In the feathery green of the year...."

The wind stormed over the shelter in a burst of power, buried the sound of his own voice.

"Marsha, are you still there?"

"What the devil's the idea, poetry at a time like this, or any time?" Terrence demanded. "Listen, you taking this down? We haven't run into any signs of the others. Six hundred thousand feet, Bruce! We feel our destiny. We conquer the Solar System. And we'll go out and out, and we'll climb the highest mountain, the highest mountain anywhere. We're going up and up. We've voted on it. Unanimous. We go on. On to the top, Bruce! Nothing can stop us. If it takes ten years, a hundred, a thousand years, we'll find it. We'll find the top! Not the top of this world—the top of *everything*. The top of the UNIVERSE!"

Later, Terrence's voice broke off in the middle of something or other—Bruce couldn't make any sense out of it at all—and turned into crazy yells that faded out and never came back.

Bruce figured the others might still be climbing somewhere, or maybe they were dead. Either way it wouldn't make any difference to him. He knew they would never come back down.

He was switching off the radio for good when he saw the coloration break over the window. It was the same as the dream, but for an instant, dream and reality seemed fused like two superimposed film negatives.

He went to the window and looked out. The comfortable little city was out there, and the canal flowing past through a pleasantly cool yet sunny afternoon. Purple mist blanketed the knees of low hills and there was a valley, green and rich with the trees high and full beside the softly flowing canal water.

The filmy shapes that seemed alive, that were partly translucent, drifted along the water's edge, and birds as delicate as colored glass wavered down the wind.

He opened the shelter door and went out. The shelter looked the same, but useless now. How did the shelter of that bleak world get into this one, where the air was warm and fragrant, where there was no cold, from that world into this one of his dreams?

The girl—Helene—was standing there leaning against a tree, smoking a cigarette.

He walked toward her, and stopped. In the dream it had been easy, but now he was embarrassed, in spite of the intimacy that had grown between them. She wore the same casual slacks and sandals. Her hair was brown. She was not particularly beautiful, but she was comfortable to look at because she seemed so peaceful. Content, happy with what was and only what was.

He turned quickly. The shelter was still there, and behind it the row of spaceships—not like chalk marks on a tallyboard now, but like odd relics that didn't belong there in the thick green grass. Five ships instead of four.

There was his own individual shelter beyond the headquarters building, and the other buildings. He looked up.

There was no mountain.

CHAPTER SEVEN

For one shivery moment he knew fear. And then the fear went away, and he was ashamed of what he had felt. What he had feared was gone now, and he knew it was gone for good and he would never have to fear it again.

"Look here, Bruce. I wondered how long it would take to get it through that thick poetic head of yours!"

"Get what?" He began to suspect what it was all about now, but he wasn't quite sure yet.

"Smoke?" she said.

He took one of the cigarettes and she lighted it for him and put the lighter back into her pocket.

"It's real nice here," she said. "Isn't it?"

"I guess it's about perfect."

"It'll be easy. Staying here, I mean. We won't be going to Earth ever again, you know."

"I didn't *know* that, but I didn't *think* we ever would again."

"We wouldn't want to anyway, would we, Bruce?"

"No."

He kept on looking at the place where the mountain had been. Or maybe it still was; he couldn't make up his mind yet. Which was and which was not? That barren icy world without life, or this?

"*Is all that we see or seem,*" he whispered, half to himself, "*but a dream within a dream?*"

She laughed softly. "Poe was ahead of his time," she said. "You still don't get it, do you? You don't know what's been happening?"

"Maybe I don't."

She shrugged, and looked in the direction of the ships. "Poor guys. I can't feel much hatred toward them now. The Martians give you a lot of understanding of the human mind—after they've accepted you, and after you've lived with them awhile. But the mountain climbers—we can see now—it's just luck, chance, we weren't like them. A deviant is a child of chance."

"Yes," Bruce said. "There's a lot of people like us on Earth, but they'll never get the chance—the chance we seem to have here, to live decently...."

"You're beginning to see now which was the dream," she said and smiled. "But don't be pessimistic. Those people on Earth will get their chance, too, one of these fine days. The Conquerors aren't getting far. Venus, and then Mars, and Mars is where they stop. They'll keep coming here and climbing the mountain and finally there won't be any more. It won't take so long."

She rose to her toes and waved and yelled. Bruce saw Pietro and Marlene walking hand in hand up the other side of the canal. They waved back and called and then pushed off into the water in a small boat, and drifted away and out of sight around a gentle turn.

She took his arm and they walked along the canal toward where the mountain had been, or still was—he didn't know.

A quarter of a mile beyond the canal, he saw the high mound of red, naked hill, corroded and ugly, rising up like a scar of the surrounding green.

She wasn't smiling now. There were shadows on her face as the pressure on his arm stopped him.

"I was on the first ship and Marlene on the second. None like us on the third, and on the fourth ship was Pietro. All the others had to climb the mountain—" She stopped talking for a moment, and then he felt the pressure of her fingers on his arm. "I'm very glad you came on the fifth," she whispered. "Are you glad now?"

"I'm very glad," he said.

"The Martians tested us," she explained. "They're masters of the mind. I guess they've been grinding along through the evolutionary mill a darn long time, longer than we could estimate now. They learned the horror we're capable of from the first ship—the Conquerors, the climbers. The Martians knew more like them would come and go on into space, killing, destroying for no other reason than their own sickness. Being masters of the mind, the Martians are also capable of hypnosis—no, that's not really the word, only the closest our language comes to naming it. Suggestion so deep and strong that it seems real to one human or a million or a billion; there's no limit to the number that can be influenced. What the people who came off those ships saw wasn't real. It was partly what the Martians wanted them to see and feel—but most of it, like the desire to climb the mountain, was as much a part of the Conquerors' own psychic drive as it was the suggestion of the Martians."

She waved her arm slowly to describe a peak. "The Martians made the mountain real. So real that it could be seen from space, measured by instruments ... even photographed and chipped for rock samples. But you'll see how that was done, Bruce, and realize that this and not the mountain of the Conquerors is the reality of Mars. This is the Mars no Conqueror will ever see."

CHAPTER EIGHT

They walked toward the ugly red mound that jutted above the green. When they came close enough, he saw the bodies lying there ... the remains, actually, of what had once been bodies. He felt too sickened to go on walking.

"It may seem cruel now," she said, "but the Martians realized that there is no cure for the will to conquer. There is no safety from it, either, as the people of Earth and Venus discovered, unless it is given an impossible obstacle to overcome. So the Martians provided the Conquerors with a mountain. They themselves wanted to climb. They had to."

He was hardly listening as he walked away from Helene toward the eroded hills. The crew members of the first four ships were skeletons tied together with imperishably strong rope about their waists. Far beyond them were those from *Mars V*, too freshly dead to have decayed much ... Anhauser with his rope cut, a bullet in his head; Jacobs and Marsha and the others ... Terrence much past them all. He had managed to climb higher than anyone else and he lay with his arms stretched out, his fingers still clutching at rock outcroppings.

The trail they left wound over the ground, chipped in places for holds, red elsewhere with blood from torn hands. Terrence was more than twelve miles from the ship—horizontally.

Bruce lifted Marsha and carried her back over the rocky dust, into the fresh fragrance of the high grass, and across it to the shade and peace beside the canal.

He put her down. She looked peaceful enough, more peaceful than that other time, years ago, when the two of them seemed to have shared so much, when the future had not yet destroyed her. He saw the shadow of Helene bend across Marsha's face against the background of the silently flowing water of the cool, green canal.

"You loved her?"

"Once," Bruce said. "She might have been sane. They got her when she was young. Too young to fight. But she would have, I think, if she'd been older when they got her."

He sat looking down at Marsha's face, and then at the water with the leaves floating down it.

"'... And the springs that flow on the floor of the valley will never seem fresh or clear for thinking of the glitter of the mountain water in the feathery green of the year....'"

He stood up, walked back with Helene along the canal toward the calm city. He didn't look back.

"They've all been dead quite a while," Bruce said wonderingly. "Yet I seemed to be hearing from Terrence until only a short time ago. Are—are the climbers still climbing—somewhere, Helene?"

"Who knows?" Helene answered softly. "Maybe. I doubt if even the Martians have the answer to that."

They entered the city.

THE RECRUIT

The Recruit by Bryce Walton

First published in 1962

This Edition Copyright @2020 by Eli Jayne

All rights reserved.

Cover art by Eli Jayne

It was dirty work, but it would make him a man. And kids had a right to grow up—some of them!

CHAPTER ONE

Wayne, unseen, sneered down from the head of the stairs.

The old man with his thick neck, thick cigar, evening highball, potgut and bald head without a brain in it. His slim mother with nervously polite smiles and voice fluttering, assuring the old man by her frailty that he was big in the world. They were squareheads one and all, marking moron time in a gray dream. Man, was he glad to break out.

The old man said, "He'll be okay. Let him alone."

"But he won't eat. Just lies there all the time."

"Hell," the old man said. "Sixteen's a bad time. School over, waiting for the draft and all. He's in between. It's rough."

Mother clasped her forearms and shook her head once slowly.

"We got to let him go, Eva. It's a dangerous time. You got to remember about all these dangerous repressed impulses piling up with nowhere to go, like they say. You read the books."

"But he's unhappy."

"Are we specialists? That's the Youth Board's headache, ain't it? What do we know about adolescent trauma and like that? Now get dressed or we'll be late."

Wayne watched the ritual, grinning. He listened to their purposeless noises, their blabbing and yakking as if they had something to say. Blab-blab about the same old bones, and end up chewing them in the same old ways. Then they begin all over again. A freak sideshow all the way to nowhere. Squareheads going around either unconscious or with eyes looking dead from the millennium in the office waiting to retire into limbo.

How come he'd been stuck with parental images like that? One thing —when he was jockeying a rocket to Mars or maybe firing the pants off Asiatic reds in some steamy gone jungle paradise, he'd forget his punkie origins in teeveeland.

But the old man was right on for once about the dangerous repressed impulses. Wayne had heard about it often enough. Anyway there was no doubt about it when every move he made was a restrained explosion. So he'd waited in his room, and it wasn't easy sweating it out alone waiting for the breakout call from HQ.

"Well, dear, if you say so," Mother said, with the old resigned sigh that must make the old man feel like Superman with a beerbelly.

They heard Wayne slouching loosely down the stairs and looked up.

"Relax," Wayne said. "You're not going anywhere tonight."

"What, son?" his old man said uneasily. "Sure we are. We're going to the movies."

He could feel them watching him, waiting; and yet still he didn't answer. Somewhere out in suburban grayness a dog barked, then was silent.

"Okay, go," Wayne said. "If you wanta walk. I'm taking the family boltbucket."

"But we promised the Clemons, dear," his mother said.

"Hell," Wayne said, grinning straight into the old man. "I just got my draft call."

He saw the old man's Adam's apple move. "Oh, my dear boy," Mother cried out.

"So gimme the keys," Wayne said. The old man handed the keys over. His understanding smile was strained, and fear flicked in his sagging eyes.

"Do be careful, dear," his mother said. She ran toward him as he laughed and shut the door on her. He was still laughing as he whoomed the Olds between the pale dead glow of houses and roared up the ramp onto the Freeway. Ahead was the promising glitter of adventure-calling neon, and he looked up at the high skies of night and his eyes sailed the glaring wonders of escape.

CHAPTER TWO

He burned off some rubber finding a slot in the park-lot. He strode under a sign reading *Public Youth Center No. 947* and walked casually to the reception desk, where a thin man with sergeant's stripes and a pansy haircut looked out of a pile of paperwork.

"Where you think you're going, my pretty lad?"

Wayne grinned down. "Higher I hope than a typewriter jockey."

"Well," the sergeant said. "How tough we are this evening. You have a pass, killer?"

"Wayne Seton. Draft call."

"Oh." The sergeant checked his name off a roster and nodded. He wrote on a slip of paper, handed the pass to Wayne. "Go to the Armory and check out whatever your lusting little heart desires. Then report to Captain Jack, room 307."

"Thanks, sarge dear," Wayne said and took the elevator up to the Armory.

A tired fat corporal with a naked head blinked up at tall Wayne. Finally he said, "So make up your mind, bud. Think you're the only kid breaking out tonight?"

"Hold your teeth, pop," Wayne said, coolly and slowly lighting a cigarette. "I've decided."

The corporal's little eyes studied Wayne with malicious amusement. "Take it from a vet, bud. Sooner you go the better. It's a big city and you're starting late. You can get a cat, not a mouse, and some babes are clever hellcats in a dark alley."

"You must be a genius," Wayne said. "A corporal with no hair and still a counterboy. I'm impressed. I'm all ears, Dad."

The corporal sighed wearily. "You can get that balloon head ventilated, bud, and good."

Wayne's mouth twitched. He leaned across the counter toward the shelves and racks of weapons. "I'll remember that crack when I get my commission." He blew smoke in the corporal's face. "Bring me a Smith and Wesson .38, shoulder holster with spring-clip. And throw in a Skelly switchblade for kicks—the six-inch disguised job with the double springs."

The corporal waddled back with the revolver and the switchblade disguised in a leather comb case. He checked them on a receipt ledger, while Wayne examined the weapons, broke open the revolver, twirled the cylinder and pushed cartridges into the waiting chamber. He slipped the knife from the comb case, flicked open the blade and stared at its gleam in the buttery light as his mouth went dry and the refracted incandescence of it trickled on his brain like melted ice, exciting and scary.

He removed his leather jacket. He slung the holster under his left armpit and tested the spring clip release several times, feeling the way the serrated butt dropped into his wet palm. He put his jacket back on and the switchblade case in his pocket. He walked toward the elevator and didn't look back as the corporal said, "Good luck, tiger."

Captain Jack moved massively. The big stone-walled office, alive with stuffed lion and tiger and gunracks, seemed to grow smaller. Captain Jack crossed black-booted legs and whacked a cane at the floor. It had a head shaped like a grinning bear.

Wayne felt the assured smile die on his face. Something seemed to shrink him. If he didn't watch himself he'd begin feeling like a pea among bowling balls.

Contemptuously amused little eyes glittered at Wayne from a shaggy head. Shoulders hunched like stuffed sea-bags.

"Wayne Seton," said Captain Jack as if he were discussing something in a bug collection. "Well, well, you're really fired up aren't you? Really going out to eat 'em. Right, punk?"

"Yes, sir," Wayne said. He ran wet hands down the sides of his chinos. His legs seemed sheathed in lead as he bit inwardly at shrinking fear the way a dog snaps at a wound. You big overblown son, he thought, I'll show you but good who is a punk. They made a guy wait and sweat until he screamed. They kept a guy on the fire until desire leaped in him, ran and billowed and roared until his brain was filled with it. But that wasn't enough. If this muscle-bound creep was such a big boy, what was he doing holding down a desk?

"Well, this is it, punk. You go the distance or start a butterfly collection."

The cane darted up. A blade snicked from the end and stopped an inch from Wayne's nose. He jerked up a shaky hand involuntarily and clamped a knuckle-ridged gag to his gasping mouth.

Captain Jack chuckled. "All right, superboy." He handed Wayne his passcard. "Curfew's off, punk, for 6 hours. You got 6 hours to make out."

"Yes, sir."

"Your beast is primed and waiting at the Four Aces Club on the West Side. Know where that is, punk?"

"No, sir, but I'll find it fast."

"Sure you will, punk," smiled Captain Jack. "She'll be wearing yellow slacks and a red shirt. Black hair, a cute trick. She's with a hefty psycho who eats punks for breakfast. He's butchered five people. They're both on top of the Undesirable list, Seton. They got to go and they're your key to the stars."

"Yes, sir," Wayne said.

"So run along and make out, punk," grinned Captain Jack.

CHAPTER THREE

A copcar stopped Wayne as he started over the bridge, out of bright respectable neon into the murky westside slum over the river.

Wayne waved the pass card, signed by Captain Jack, under the cop's quivering nose. The cop shivered and stepped back and waved him on. The Olds roared over the bridge as the night's rain blew away.

The air through the open window was chill and damp coming from Slumville, but Wayne felt a cold that wasn't of the night or the wind. He turned off into a rat's warren of the inferiors. Lights turned pale, secretive and sparse, the uncared-for streets became rough with pitted potholes, narrow and winding and humid with wet unpleasant smells. Wayne's fearful exhilaration increased as he cruised with bated breath through the dark mazes of streets and rickety tenements crawling with the shadows of mysterious promise.

He found the alley, dark, a gloom-dripping tunnel. He drove cautiously into it and rolled along, watching. His belly ached with expectancy as he spotted the sick-looking dab of neon wanly sparkling.

FOUR ACES CLUB

He parked across the alley. He got out and stood in shadows, digging the sultry beat of a combo, the wild pulse of drums and spinning brass filtering through windows painted black.

He breathed deep, started over, ducked back. A stewbum weaved out of a bank of garbage cans, humming to himself, pulling at a rainsoaked shirt clinging to a pale stick body. He reminded Wayne of a slim grub balanced on one end.

The stewbum stumbled. His bearded face in dim breaking moonlight had a dirty, greenish tinge as he sensed Wayne there. He turned in a grotesque uncoordinated jiggling and his eyes were wide with terror and doom.

"I gotta hide, kid. They're on me."

Wayne's chest rose and his hands curled.

The bum's fingers drew at the air like white talons.

"Help me, kid."

He turned with a scratchy cry and retreated before the sudden blast of headlights from a Cad bulleting into the alley. The Cad rushed past Wayne and he felt the engine-hot fumes against his legs. Tires squealed. The Cad stopped and a teener in black jacket jumped out and crouched as he began stalking the old rummy.

"This is him! This is him all right," the teener yelled, and one hand came up swinging a baseball bat.

A head bobbed out of the Cad window and giggled.

The fumble-footed rummy tried to run and plopped on wet pavement. The teener moved in, while a faint odor of burnt rubber hovered in the air as the Cad cruised in a slow follow-up.

Wayne's breath quickened as he watched, feeling somehow blank wonder at finding himself there, free and breaking out at last with no curfew and no law but his own. He felt as though he couldn't stop anything. Living seemed directionless, but he still would go with it regardless, until something dropped off or blew to hell like a hot light-bulb. He held his breath, waiting. His body was tensed and rigid as he moved in spirit with the hunting teener, an omniscient shadow with a hunting license and a ghetto jungle twenty miles deep.

The crawling stewbum screamed as the baseball bat whacked. The teener laughed. Wayne wanted to shout. He opened his mouth, but the yell clogged up somewhere, so that he remained soundless yet with his mouth still open as he heard the payoff thuds where the useless wino curled up with stick arms over his rheumy face.

The teener laughed, tossed the bat away and began jumping up and down with his hobnailed, mail-order air force boots. Then he ran into the Cad. A hootch bottle soared out, made a brittle tink-tink of falling glass.

"Go, man!"

The Cad wooshed by. It made a sort of hollow sucking noise as it bounced over the old man twice. Then the finlights diminished like bright wind-blown sparks.

Wayne walked over and sneered down at the human garbage lying in scummed rain pools. The smell of raw violence, the scent of blood, made his heart thump like a trapped rubber ball in a cage.

He hurried into the Four Aces, drawn by an exhilarating vision ... and pursued by the hollow haunting fears of his own desires.

CHAPTER FOUR

He walked through the wavering haze of smoke and liquored dizziness and stood until his eyes learned the dark. He spotted her red shirt and yellow legs over in the corner above a murky lighted table.

He walked toward her, watching her little subhuman pixie face lift. The eyes widened with exciting terror, turned even paler behind a red slash of sensuous mouth. Briefed and waiting, primed and eager for running, she recognized her pursuer at once. He sat at a table near her, watching and grinning and seeing her squirm.

She sat in that slightly baffled, fearful and uncomprehending attitude of being motionless, as though they were all actors performing in a weirdo drama being staged in that smoky thick-aired dive.

Wayne smiled with wry superiority at the redheaded psycho in a dirty T-shirt, a big bruiser with a gorilla face. He was tussling his mouse heavy.

"What's yours, teener?" the slug-faced waiter asked.

"Bring me a Crusher, buddyroo," Wayne said, and flashed his pass card.

"Sure, teener."

Red nuzzled the mouse's neck and made drooly noises. Wayne watched and fed on the promising terror and helplessness of her hunted face. She sat rigid, eyes fixed on Wayne like balls of frozen glass.

Red looked up and stared straight at Wayne with eyes like black buttons imbedded in the waxlike skin of his face. Then he grinned all on one side. One huge hand scratched across the wet table top like a furious cat's.

Wayne returned the challenging move but felt a nervous twitch jerk at his lips. A numbness covered his brain like a film as he concentrated on staring down Red the psycho. But Red kept looking, his eyes bright but dead. Then he began struggling it up again with the scared little mouse.

The waiter sat the Crusher down. Wayne signed a chit; tonight he was in the pay of the state.

"What else, teener?"

"One thing. Fade."

"Sure, teener," the waiter said, his breathy words dripping like syrup.

Wayne drank. Liquored heat dripped into his stomach. Fire tickled his veins, became hot wire twisting in his head.

He drank again and forced out a shaky breath. The jazz beat thumped fast and muted brass moaned. Drumpulse, stabbing trumpet raped the air. Tension mounted as Wayne watched her pale throat convulsing, the white eyelids fluttering. Red fingered at her legs and salivated at her throat, glancing now and then at Wayne, baiting him good.

"Okay, you creep," Wayne said.

He stood up and started through the haze. The psycho leaped and a table crashed. Wayne's .38 dropped from its spring-clip holster and the blast filled the room. The psycho screamed and stumbled toward the door holding something in. The mouse darted by, eluded Wayne's grasp and was out the door.

Wayne went out after her in a laughing frenzy of release. He felt the cold strange breath of moist air on his sweating skin as he sprinted down the alley into a wind full of blowing wet.

He ran laughing under the crazy starlight and glimpsed her now and then, fading in and out of shadows, jumping, crawling, running with the life-or-death animation of a wild deer.

Up and down alleys, a rat's maze. A rabbit run. Across vacant lots. Through shattered tenement ruins. Over a fence. There she was, falling, sliding down a brick shute.

He gained. He moved up. His labored breath pumped more fire. And her scream was a rejuvenation hypo in his blood.

CHAPTER FIVE

She quivered above him on the stoop, panting, her eyes afire with terror.

"You, baby," Wayne gasped. "I gotcha."

She backed into darkness, up there against the sagging tenement wall, her arms out and poised like crippled wings. Wayne crept up. She gave a squeaking sob, turned, ran. Wayne leaped into gloom. Wood cracked. He clambered over rotten lumber. The doorway sagged and he hesitated in the musty dark. A few feet away was the sound of loose trickling plaster, a whimpering whine.

"No use running," Wayne said. "Go loose. Give, baby. Give now."

She scurried up sagging stairs. Wayne laughed and dug up after her, feeling his way through debris. Dim moonlight filtered through a sagging stairway from a shattered skylight three floors up. The mouse's shadow floated ahead.

He started up. The entire stair structure canted sickeningly. A railing ripped and he nearly went with it back down to the first floor. He heard a scream as rotten boards crumbled and dust exploded from cracks. A rat ran past Wayne and fell into space. He burst into the third-floor hallway and saw her half-falling through a door under the jagged skylight.

Wayne took his time. He knew how she felt waiting in there, listening to his creeping, implacable footfalls.

Then he yelled and slammed open the door.

Dust and stench, filth so awful it made nothing of the dust. In the corner he saw something hardly to be called a bed. More like a nest. A dirty, lumpy pile of torn mattress, felt, excelsior, shredded newspapers and rags. It seemed to crawl a little under the moon-streaming skylight.

She crouched in the corner panting. He took his time moving in. He snickered as he flashed the switchblade and circled it like a serpent's tongue. He watched what was left of her nerves go to pieces like rotten cloth.

"Do it quick, hunter," she whispered. "Please do it quick."

"What's that, baby?"

"I'm tired running. Kill me first. Beat me after. They won't know the difference."

"I'm gonna bruise and beat you," he said.

"Kill me first," she begged. "I don't want—" She began to cry. She cried right up in his face, her wide eyes unblinking, and her mouth open.

"You got bad blood, baby," he snarled. He laughed but it didn't sound like him and something was wrong with his belly. It was knotting up.

"Bad, I know! So get it over with, please. Hurry, hurry."

She was small and white and quivering. She moaned but kept staring up at him.

He ripped off his rivet-studded belt and swung once, then groaned and shuffled away from her.

He kept backing toward the door. She crawled after him, begging and clutching with both arms as she wriggled forward on her knees.

"Don't run. Please. Kill me! It'll be someone else if you don't. Oh, God, I'm so tired waiting and running!"

"I can't," he said, and sickness soured in his throat.

"Please."

"I can't, I can't!"

He turned and ran blindly, half-fell down the cracking stairs.

CHAPTER SIX

Doctor Burns, head of the readjustment staff at the Youth Center, studied Wayne with abstract interest.

"You enjoyed the hunt, Seton? You got your kicks?"

"Yes, sir."

"But you couldn't execute them?"

"No, sir."

"They're undesirables. Incurables. You know that, Seton?"

"Yes, sir."

"The psycho you only wounded. He's a five-times murderer. And that girl killed her father when she was twelve. You realize there's nothing can be done for them? That they have to be executed?"

"I know."

"Too bad," the doctor said. "We all have aggressive impulses, primitive needs that must be expressed early, purged. There's murder in all of us, Seton. The impulse shouldn't be denied or suppressed, but *educated*. The state used to kill them. Isn't it better all around,

Seton, for us to do it, as part of growing up? What was the matter, Seton?"

"I—felt sorry for her."

"Is that all you can say about it?"

"Yes, sir."

The doctor pressed a buzzer. Two men in white coats entered.

"You should have got it out of your system, Seton, but now it's still in there. I can't turn you out and have it erupt later—and maybe shed clean innocent blood, can I?"

"No, sir," Wayne mumbled. He didn't look up. "I'm sorry I punked out."

"Give him the treatment," the doctor said wearily. "And send him back to his mother."

Wayne nodded and they led him away. His mind screamed still to split open some prison of bone and lay bare and breathing wide. But there was no way out for the trapped. Now he knew about the old man and his poker-playing pals.

They had all punked out.

Like him.

THE VICTOR

The Victor by Bryce Walton

First published in 1953

This Edition Copyright @2020 by Eli Jayne

All rights reserved.

Cover art by Eli Jayne

Under the new system of the Managerials, the fight was not for life but for death! And great was the ingenuity of—The Victor.

CHAPTER ONE

Charles Marquis had a fraction of a minute in which to die. He dropped through the tubular beams of alloydem steel and hung there, five thousand feet above the tiers and walkways below. At either end of the walkway crossing between the two power-hung buildings, he saw the plainclothes security officers running in toward him.

He grinned and started to release his grip. He would think about them on the way down. His fingers wouldn't work. He kicked and strained and tore at himself with his own weight, but his hands weren't his own any more. He might have anticipated that. Some paralysis beam freezing his hands into the metal.

He sagged to limpness. His chin dropped. For an instant, then, the fire in his heart almost went out, but not quite. It survived that one terrible moment of defeat, then burned higher. And perhaps something in that desperate resistance was the factor that kept it burning where it was thought no flame could burn. He felt the rigidity of paralysis leaving his arms as he was lifted, helped along the walkway to a security car.

The car looked like any other car. The officers appeared like all the other people in the clockwork culture of the mechanized New System.

Marquis sought the protection of personal darkness behind closed eyelids as the monorail car moved faster and faster through the high clean air. Well—he'd worked with the Underground against the System for a long time. He had known that eventually he would be caught. There were rumors of what happened to men then, and even the vaguest, unsubstantiated rumors were enough to indicate that death was preferable. That was the Underground's philosophy—better to die standing up as a man with some degree of personal integrity and freedom than to go on living as a conditioned slave of the state.

He'd missed—but he wasn't through yet though. In a hollow tooth was a capsule containing a very high-potency poison. A little of that would do the trick too. But he would have to wait for the right time....

CHAPTER TWO

The Manager was thin, his face angular, and he matched up with the harsh steel angles of the desk and the big room somewhere in the Security Building. His face had a kind of emotion—cold, detached, cynically superior.

"We don't get many of your kind," he said. "Political prisoners are becoming more scarce all the time. As your number indicates. From now on, you'll be No. 5274."

He looked at some papers, then up at Marquis. "You evidently found out a great deal. However, none of it will do you or what remains of your Underground fools any good." The Manager studied Marquis with detached curiosity. "You learned things concerning the Managerials that have so far remained secret."

It was partly a question. Marquis' lean and darkly inscrutable face smiled slightly. "You're good at understatement. Yes—I found out what we've suspected for some time. That the Managerial class has found some way to stay young. Either a remarkable longevity, or immortality. Of all the social evils that's the worst of all. To deny the people knowledge of such a secret."

The Manager nodded. "Then you did find that out? The Underground knows? Well, it will do no good."

"It will, eventually. They'll go on and someday they'll learn the secret." Marquis thought of Marden. Marden was as old as the New System of statism and inhumanity that had started off disguised as social-democracy. Three-hundred and three years old to be exact.

The Manager said, "No. 5274—you will be sent to the work colony on the Moon. You won't be back. We've tried re-conditioning rebels, but it doesn't work. A rebel has certain basic deviant characteristics and we can't overcome them sufficiently to make happy, well-adjusted workers out of you. However on the Moon—you will conform. It's a kind of social experiment there in associative reflex culture, you might say. You'll conform all right."

He was taken to a small, naked, gray-steel room. He thought about taking the capsule from his tooth now, but decided he might be observed. They would rush in an antidote and make him live. And he might not get a chance to take his life in any other way. He would try of course, but his knowledge of his future situation was vague—except that in it he would conform. There would be extreme conditioned-reflex therapeutic techniques. And it would be pretty horrible. That was all he knew.

He didn't see the pellet fall. He heard the slight sound it made and then saw the almost colorless gas hissing softly, clouding the room. He tasted nothing, smelled or felt nothing.

He passed out quickly and painlessly.

CHAPTER THREE

He was marched into another office, and he knew he was on the Moon. The far wall was spherical and was made up of the outer shell of the pressure dome which kept out the frigid cold nights and furnace-hot days. It was opaque and Marquis could see the harsh black and white shadows out there—the metallic edges of the far crater wall.

This Manager was somewhat fat, with a round pink face and cold blue eyes. He sat behind a chrome shelf of odd shape suspended from the ceiling with silver wires.

The Manager said, "No. 5274, here there is only work. At first, of course, you will rebel. Later you will work, and finally there will be nothing else. Things here are rigidly scheduled, and you will learn the routines as the conditioning bells acquaint you with them. We are completely self-sufficient here. We are developing the perfect scientifically-controlled society. It is a kind of experiment. A closed system to test to what extremes we can carry our mastery of associative reflex to bring man security and happiness and freedom from responsibility."

Marquis didn't say anything. There was nothing to say. He knew he couldn't get away with trying to kill this particular Managerial specimen. But one man, alone, a rebel, with something left in him that still burned, could beat the system. *He had to!*

"Our work here is specialized. During the indoctrination period you will do a very simple routine job in coordination with the cybernetics machines. There, the machines and the nervous system of the workers become slowly cooperative. Machine and man learn to work very intimately together. Later, after the indoctrination—because of your specialized knowledge of food-concentrate preparation—we will transfer you to the food-mart. The period of indoctrination varies in length with the individuals. You will be screened now and taken to the indoctrination ward. We probably won't be seeing one another again. The bells take care of everything here. The bells and the machines. There is never an error—never any mistakes. Machines do not make mistakes."

He was marched out of there and through a series of rooms. He was taken in by generators, huge oscilloscopes. Spun like a living tube through curtains of vacuum tube voltmeters, electronic power panels. Twisted and squeezed through rolls of skeins of hook-up wire. Bent through shieldings of every color, size and shape. Rolled over panel plates, huge racks of glowing tubes, elaborate transceivers. Tumbled down long surfaces of gleaming bakelite. Plunged through color-indexed files of resistors and capacitances....

... here machine and man learn to work very intimately together.

As he drifted through the machine tooled nightmare, Marquis knew *what* he had been fighting all his life, what he would continue to fight with every grain of ingenuity. Mechanization—the horror of losing one's identity and becoming part of an assembly line.

He could hear a clicking sound as tubes sharpened and faded in intensity. The clicking—rhythm, a hypnotic rhythm like the beating of his own heart—the throbbing and thrumming, the contracting and expanding, the pulsing and pounding....

... the machines and the nervous system of the workers become slowly cooperative.

CHAPTER FOUR

Beds were spaced ten feet apart down both sides of a long gray metal hall. There were no cells, no privacy, nothing but beds and the gray metalene suits with numbers printed across the chest.

His bed, with his number printed above it, was indicated to him, and the guard disappeared. He was alone. It was absolutely silent. On his right a woman lay on a bed. No. 329. She had been here a long time. She appeared dead. Her breasts rose and fell with a peculiarly steady rhythm, and seemed to be coordinated with the silent, invisible throbbing of the metal walls. She might have been attractive once. Here it didn't make any difference. Her face was gray, like metal. Her hair was cropped short. Her uniform was the same as the man's on Marquis' left.

The man was No. 4901. He hadn't been here so long. His face was thin and gray. His hair was dark, and he was about the same size and build as Marquis. His mouth hung slightly open and his eyes were closed and there was a slight quivering at the ends of the fingers which were laced across his stomach.

When the bells rang they would arise....

"Hello," Marquis said. The man shivered, then opened dull eyes and looked up at Marquis. "I just got in. Name's Charles Marquis."

The man blinked. "I'm—I'm—No. 4901." He looked down at his chest, repeated the number. His fingers shook a little as he touched his lips.

Marquis said. "What's this indoctrination?"

"You—learn. The bells ring—you forget—and learn—"

"There's absolutely no chance of escaping?" Marquis whispered, more to himself than to 4901.

"Only by dying," 4901 shivered. His eyes rolled crazily, then he turned over and buried his face in his arms.

The situation had twisted all the old accepted values squarely around. Preferring death over life. But not because of any anti-life attitude, or pessimism, or defeatism. None of those negative attitudes that would have made the will-to-die abnormal under conditions in which there would have been hope and some faint chance of a bearable future. Here to keep on living was a final form of de-humanized indignity, of humiliation, of ignominy, of the worst thing of all—loss of one's-self—of one's individuality. To die as a human being was much more preferable over continuing to live as something else—something neither human or machine, but something of both, with none of the dignity of either.

CHAPTER FIVE

The screening process hadn't detected the capsule of poison in Marquis' tooth. The capsule contained ten grains of poison, only one of which was enough to bring a painless death within sixteen hours or so. That was his ace in the hole, and he waited only for the best time to use it.

Bells rang. The prisoners jumped from their beds and went through a few minutes of calisthenics. Other bells rang and a tray of small tins of food-concentrates appeared out of a slit in the wall by each bed. More bells rang, different kinds of bells, some deep and brazen, others high and shrill. And the prisoners marched off to specialized jobs co-operating with various machines.

You slept eight hours. Calisthenics five minutes. Eating ten minutes. Relaxation to the tune of musical bells, ten minutes. Work period eight hours. Repeat. That was all of life, and after a while Marquis knew, a man would not be aware of time, nor of his name, nor that he had once been human.

Marquis felt deep lancing pain as he tried to resist the bells. Each time the bells rang and a prisoner didn't respond properly, invisible rays of needle pain punched and kept punching until he reacted properly.

And finally he did as the bells told him to do. Finally he forgot that things had ever been any other way.

Marquis sat on his bed, eating, while the bells of eating rang across the bowed heads in the gray uniforms. He stared at the girl, then at the man, 4901. There were many opportunities to take one's own life here. That had perplexed him from the start—*why hasn't the girl, and this man, succeeded in dying?*

And all the others? They were comparatively new here, all these in this indoctrination ward. Why weren't they trying to leave in the only dignified way of escape left?

No. 4901 tried to talk, he tried hard to remember things. Sometimes memory would break through and bring him pictures of other times, of happenings on Earth, of a girl he had known, of times when he was a child. But only the mildest and softest kind of recollections....

Marquis said, "I don't think there's a prisoner here who doesn't want to escape, and death is the only way out for us. We know that."

For an instant, No. 4901 stopped eating. A spoonful of food concentrate hung suspended between his mouth and the shelf. Then the food moved again to the urging of the bells. Invisible pain needles gouged Marquis' neck, and he ate again too, automatically, talking between tasteless bites. "A man's life at least is his own," Marquis said. "They can take everything else. But a man certainly has a right and a duty to take that life if by so doing he can retain his integrity as a human being. Suicide—"

No. 4901 bent forward. He groaned, mumbled "Don't—don't—" several times, then curled forward and lay on the floor knotted up into a twitching ball.

The eating period was over. The lights went off. Bells sounded for relaxation. Then the sleep bells began ringing, filling up the absolute darkness.

Marquis lay there in the dark and he was afraid. He had the poison. He had the will. But he couldn't be unique in that respect. What was the matter with the others? All right, the devil with them. Maybe they'd been broken too soon to act. He could act. Tomorrow, during the work period, he would take a grain of the poison. Put the capsule back in the tooth. The poison would work slowly, painlessly, paralyzing the nervous system, finally the heart. Sometime during the beginning of the next sleep period he would be dead. That would leave six or seven hours of darkness and isolation for him to remain dead, so they couldn't get to him in time to bring him back.

He mentioned suicide to the girl during the next work period. She moaned a little and curled up like a fetus on the floor. After an hour, she got up and began inserting punch cards into the big machine again. She avoided Marquis.

Marquis looked around, went into a corner with his back to the room, slipped the capsule out and let one of the tiny, almost invisible grains, melt on his tongue. He replaced the capsule and returned to the machine. A quiet but exciting triumph made the remainder of the work period more bearable.

Back on his bed, he drifted into sleep, into what he knew was the final sleep. He was more fortunate than the others. Within an hour he would be dead.

CHAPTER SIX

Somewhere, someone was screaming.

The sounds rose higher and higher. A human body, somewhere ... pain unimaginable twisting up through clouds of belching steam ... muscles quivering, nerves twitching ... and somewhere a body floating and bobbing and crying ... sheets of agony sweeping and returning in waves and the horror of unescapable pain expanding like a volcano of madness....

Somewhere was someone alive who should be dead.

And then in the dark, in absolute silence, Marquis moved a little. He realized, vaguely, that the screaming voice was his own.

He stared into the steamy darkness and slowly, carefully, wet his lips. He moved. He felt his lips moving and the whisper sounding loud in the dark.

I'm alive!

He managed to struggle up out of the bed. He could scarcely remain erect. Every muscle in his body seemed to quiver. He longed to slip down into the darkness and escape into endless sleep. But he'd tried that. And he was still alive. He didn't know how much time had passed. He was sure of the poison's effects, but he wasn't dead. They had gotten to him in time.

Sweat exploded from his body. He tried to remember more. Pain. He lay down again. He writhed and perspired on the bed as his tortured mind built grotesque fantasies out of fragments of broken memory.

The routine of the unceasing bells went on. Bells, leap up. Bells, calisthenics. Bells, eat. Bells, march. Bells, work. He tried to shut out the bells. He tried to talk to 4901. 4901 covered up his ears and wouldn't listen. The girl wouldn't listen to him.

There were other ways. And he kept the poison hidden in the capsule in his hollow tooth. He had been counting the steps covering the length of the hall, then the twenty steps to the left, then to the right to where the narrow corridor led again to the left where he had seen the air-lock.

After the bells stopped ringing and the darkness was all around him, he got up. He counted off the steps. No guards, no alarms, nothing to stop him. They depended on the conditioners to take care of everything. This time he would do it. This time they wouldn't bring him back.

No one else could even talk with him about it, even though he knew they all wanted to escape. Some part of them still wanted to, but they couldn't. So it was up to him. He stopped against the smooth, opaque, up-curving glasite dome. It had a brittle bright shine that reflected from the Moon's surface. It was night out there, with an odd metallic reflection of Earthlight against the naked crags.

He hesitated. He could feel the intense and terrible cold, the airlessness out there fingering hungrily, reaching and whispering and waiting.

He turned the wheel. The door opened. He entered the air-lock and shut the first door when the air-pressure was right. He turned the other wheel and the outer lock door swung outward. The out-rushing air spun him outward like a balloon into the awful airless cold and naked silence.

His body sank down into the thick pumice dust that drifted up around him in a fine powdery blanket of concealment. He felt no pain. The cold airlessness dissolved around him in deepening darkening pleasantness. This time he was dead, thoroughly and finally and gloriously dead, even buried, and they couldn't find him. And even if they did finally find him, what good would it do them?

Some transcendental part of him seemed to remain to observe and triumph over his victory. This time he was dead to stay.

CHAPTER SEVEN

This time he knew at once that the twisting body in the steaming pain, the distorted face, the screams rising and rising were all Charles Marquis.

Maybe a dream though, he thought. So much pain, so much screaming pain, is not real. In some fraction of a fraction of that interim between life and death, one could dream of so much because dreams are timeless.

Yet he found himself anticipating, even through the shredded, dissociated, nameless kind of pain, a repetition of that other time.

The awful bitterness of defeat.

He opened his eyes slowly. It was dark, the same darkness. He was on the same bed. And the old familiar dark around and the familiar soundlessness that was now heavier than the most thunderous sound.

Everything around him then seemed to whirl up and go down in a crash. He rolled over to the floor and lay there, his hot face cooled by the cold metal.

As before, some undeterminable interim of time had passed. And he knew he was alive. His body was stiff. He ached. There was a drumming in his head, and then a ringing in his ears as he tried to get up, managed to drag himself to an unsteady stance against the wall. He felt now an icy surety of horror that carried him out to a pin-point in space.

A terrible fatigue hit him. He fell back onto the bed. He lay there trying to figure out how he could be alive.

He finally slept pushed into it by sheer and utter exhaustion. The bells called him awake. The bells started him off again. He tried to talk again to 4901. They avoided him, all of them. But they weren't really alive any more. How long could he maintain some part of himself that he knew definitely was Charles Marquis?

He began a ritual, a routine divorced from that to which all those being indoctrinated were subjected. It was a little private routine of his own. Dying, and then finding that he was not dead.

He tried it many ways. He took more grains of the poison. But he was always alive again.

"You—4901! Damn you—talk to me! You know what's been happening to me?"

The man nodded quickly over his little canisters of food-concentrate.

"This indoctrination—you, the girl—you went crazy when I talked about dying—what—?"

The man yelled hoarsely. "Don't ... don't say it! All this—what you've been going through, can't you understand? All that is part of indoctrination. You're no different than the rest of us! We've all had it! All of us. All of us! Some more maybe than others. It had to end. You'll have to give in. Oh God, I wish you didn't. I wish you could win. But you're no smarter than the rest of us. *You'll have to give in!*"

It was 4901's longest and most coherent speech. Maybe I can get somewhere with him, Marquis thought. I can find out something.

But 4901 wouldn't say any more. Marquis kept on trying. No one, he knew, would ever realize what that meant—to keep on trying to die when no one would let you, when you kept dying, and then kept waking up again, and you weren't dead. No one could ever understand the pain that went between the dying and the living. And even Marquis couldn't remember it afterward. He only knew how painful it had been. And knowing that made each attempt a little harder for Marquis.

He tried the poison again. There was the big stamping machine that had crushed him beyond any semblance of a human being, but he had awakened, alive again, whole again. There was the time he grabbed the power cable and felt himself, in one blinding flash, conquer life in a burst of flame. He slashed his wrists at the beginning of a number of sleep periods.

When he awakened, he was whole again. There wasn't even a scar.

He suffered the pain of resisting the eating bells until he was so weak he couldn't respond, and he knew that he died that time too—from pure starvation.

But I can't stay dead!

"... *You'll have to give in!*"

CHAPTER EIGHT

He didn't know when it was. He had no idea now how long he had been here. But a guard appeared, a cold-faced man who guided Marquis back to the office where the fat, pink-faced little Manager waited for him behind the shelf suspended by silver wires from the ceiling.

The Manager said. "You are the most remarkable prisoner we've ever had here. There probably will not be another like you here again."

Marquis' features hung slack, his mouth slightly open, his lower lip drooping. He knew how he looked. He knew how near he was to cracking completely, becoming a senseless puppet of the bells. "Why is that?" he whispered.

"You've tried repeatedly to—you know what I mean of course. You have kept on attempting this impossible thing, attempted it more times than anyone else here ever has! Frankly, we didn't think any human psyche had the stuff to try it that many times—to resist that long."

The Manager made a curious lengthened survey of Marquis' face. "Soon you'll be thoroughly indoctrinated. You are, for all practical purposes, now. You'll work automatically then, to the bells, and think very little about it at all, except in a few stereotyped ways to keep your brain and nervous system active enough to carry out simple specialized work duties. Or while the New System lasts. And I imagine that will be forever."

"Forever...."

"Yes, yes. You're immortal now," the Manager smiled. "Surely, after all this harrowing indoctrination experience, you realize *that*!"

Immortal. I might have guessed. I might laugh now, but I can't. We who pretend to live in a hell that is worse than death, and you, the Managerials who live in paradise. We two are immortal.

"That is, you're immortal as long as we desire you to be. You'll never grow any older than we want you to, never so senile as to threaten efficiency. That was what you were so interested in finding out on Earth, wasn't it? The mystery behind the Managerials? Why they never seemed to grow old. Why we have all the advantage, no senility, no weakening, the advantage of accumulative experience without the necessity of re-learning?"

"Yes," Marquis whispered.

The Manager leaned back. He lit a paraette and let the soothing nerve-tonic seep into his lungs. He explained.

"Every one of you political prisoners we bring here want, above everything else, to die. It was a challenge to our experimental social order here. We have no objection to your killing yourself. We have learned that even the will to die can be conditioned out of the most determined rebel. As it has been conditioned out of you. You try to die enough times, and you do die, but the pain of resurrection is so great that finally it is impossible not only to kill yourself, but even to think of attempting it."

Marquis couldn't say anything. The memory called up by the mention of self-destruction rasped along his spine like chalk on a blackboard. He could feel the total-recall of sensation, the threatening bursts of pain. "No...." he whispered over and over. "No—please—no—"

The Manager said. "We won't mention it anymore. You'll never be able to try any overt act of self-destruction again."

The bright light from the ceiling lanced like splinters into the tender flesh of Marquis' eyeballs, danced about the base of his brain in reddened choleric circles. His face had drawn back so that his cheekbones stood out and his nose was beak-like. His irises became a bright painful blue in the reddened ovals of his eyes.

The Manager yawned as he finished explaining. "Each prisoner entering here has an identification punch-plate made of his unique electro-magnetic vibratory field. That's the secret of our immortality and yours. Like all matter, human difference is in the electro-magnetic, vibratory rates. We have these punch-plates on file for every prisoner. We have one of you. Any dead human body we merely put in a tank which dissolves it into separate cells, a mass of stasis with potentiality to be reformed into any type of human being of which we have an identification punch-plate, you see? This tank of dissociated cells is surrounded by an electro-magnetic field induced from a machine by one of the identification punch-plates. That particular human being lives again, the body, its mind, its life pattern identical to that from which the original punch-plate was made. Each time you have died, we reduced your body, regardless of its condition, to dissociated cells in the tank. The identification punch-plate was put in the machine. Your unique electro-magnetic field reformed the cells into you. It could only be you, as you are now. From those cells we can resurrect any one of whom we have an identification plate.

"That is all, No. 5274. Now that you're indoctrinated, you will work from now on in the food-mart, because of your experience."

CHAPTER NINE

For an undeterminable length of time, he followed the routines of the bells. In the big food-mart, among the hydroponic beds, and the canning machines; among the food-grinders and little belts that dropped cans of food-concentrate into racks and sent them off into the walls.

He managed to talk more and more coherently with No. 4901. He stopped referring to suicide, but if anyone had the idea that Marquis had given up the idea of dying, they were wrong. Marquis was stubborn. Somewhere in him the flame still burned. He wouldn't let it go out. The bells couldn't put it out. The throbbing machines couldn't put it out. And now he had at last figured out a way to beat the game.

During an eating period, Marquis said to 4901. "You want to die. Wait a minute—I'm talking about something we can both talk and think about. A murder agreement. You understand? We haven't been conditioned against killing each other. It's only an overt act of selfdes —all right, we don't think about that. But we can plan a way to kill each other."

4901 looked up. He stopped eating momentarily. He was interested.

"What's the use though?" Pain shadowed his face. "We only go through it—come back again—"

"I have a plan. The way I have it worked out, they'll never bring either one of us back."

That wasn't exactly true. *One* of them would have to come back. Marquis hoped that 4901 wouldn't catch on to the fact that he would have to be resurrected, but that Marquis never would. He hoped that 4901's mind was too foggy and dull to see through the complex plan. And that was the way it worked.

Marquis explained. 4901 listened and smiled. It was the first time Marquis had ever seen a prisoner smile.

He left what remained of the capsule of poison where 4901 could get it. During one of the next four eating periods, 4901 was to slip the poison into Marquis' food can. Marquis wouldn't know what meal, or what can. He had to eat. The bells had conditioned him that much. And not to eat would be an overt act of self-destruction.

He wasn't conditioned not to accept death administered by another.

And then, after an eating period, 4901 whispered to him. "You're poisoned. It was in one of the cans you just ate."

"Great!" almost shouted Marquis. "All right. Now I'll die by the end of the next work period. That gives us this sleep period and all the next work period. During that time I'll dispose of you as I've said."

4901 went to his bed and the bells rang and the dark came and both of them slept.

CHAPTER TEN

Number 4901 resisted the conditioners enough to follow Marquis past his regular work room into the food-mart. As planned, 4901 marched on and stood in the steaming shadows behind the hydroponic beds.

Marquis worked for a while at the canning machines, at the big grinding vats. Then he went over to 4901 and said. "Turn around now."

4901 smiled. He turned around. "Good luck," he said. "Good luck—to you!"

Marquis hit 4901 across the back of the neck with an alloy bar and killed him instantly. He changed clothes with the dead man. He put his own clothes in a refuse incinerator. Quickly, he dragged the body over and tossed it into one of the food-grinding vats. His head bobbed up above the gray swirling liquid once, then the body disappeared entirely, was ground finely and mixed with the other foodstuff.

Within eight hours the cells of 4901 would be distributed minutely throughout the contents of thousands of cans of food-concentrate. Within that time much of it would have been consumed by the inmates and Managers.

At the end of that work period, Marquis returned to his cell. He went past his own bed and stopped in front of 4901's bed.

The sleep bells sounded and the dark came again. This would be the final dark, Marquis knew. This time he had beat the game. The delayed-action poison would kill him. He had on 4901's clothes with his identification number. He was on 4901's bed.

He would die—as 4901. The guards would finally check on the missing man in the food-mart. But they would never find him. They would find 4901 dead, a suicide. And they would put the body labeled 4901 in the tank, dissolve it into dissociated cells and they would subject those cells to the electro-magnetic field of 4901.

And they would resurrect—4901.

Not only have I managed to die, Marquis thought, but I've managed the ultimate suicide. There won't even be a body, no sign anywhere that I have ever been at all. Even my cells will have been resurrected as someone else. As a number 4901.

CHAPTER ELEVEN

"And that's the way it was," No. 4901 would tell new prisoners coming in. Sometimes they listened to him and seemed interested, but the interest always died during indoctrination. But No. 4901's interest in the story never died.

He knew that now he could never let himself die as a human being either, that he could never let himself become completely controlled by the bells. He'd been nearly dead as an individual, but No. 5274 had saved him from that dead-alive anonymity. He could keep alive, and maintain hope now by remembering what 5274 had done. He clung to that memory. As long as he retained that memory of hope—of triumph—at least some part of him would keep burning, as something had kept on burning within the heart of 5274.

So every night before the sleep bells sounded, he would go over the whole thing in minute detail, remembering 5274's every word and gesture, the details of his appearance. He told the plan over to himself every night, and told everyone about it who came in to the indoctrination ward.

Swimming up through the pain of resurrection, he had been a little mad at 5274 at first, and then he had realized that at least the plan had enabled one man to beat the game.

"He will always be alive to me. Maybe, in a way, he's part of me. Nobody knows. But his memory will live. He succeeded in a kind of ultimate dying—no trace of him anywhere. But the memory of him and what he did will be alive when the New System and the Managers are dead. That spirit will assure the Underground of victory—someday. And meanwhile, I'll keep 5274 alive.

"He even knew the psychology of these Managers and their System. That they can't afford to make an error. He knew they'd still have that identification punch-plate of him. That they would have one more plate than they had prisoners. But he anticipated what they would do there too. To admit there was one more identification plate than there were prisoners would be to admit a gross error. Of course they could dissolve one of the other prisoners and use 5274's plate and resurrect 5274. But they'd gain nothing. There would still be an extra plate. You see?

"So they destroyed the plate. He knew they would. And they also had to go back through the records, to Earth, through the security files there, through the birth records, everything. And they destroyed every trace, every shred of evidence that No. 5274 ever existed."

So he kept the memory alive and that kept 4901 alive while the other prisoners become automatons, hearing, feeling, sensing nothing except the bells. Remembering nothing, anticipating nothing.

But 4901 could remember something magnificent, and so he could anticipate, and that was hope, and faith. He found that no one really believed him but he kept on telling it anyway, the story of the Plan.

"Maybe this number didn't exist," someone would say. "If there's no record anywhere—"

4901 would smile. "In my head, there's where the record is. *I* know. *I* remember."

And so it was that 4901 was the only one who still remembered and who could still smile when sometime after that—no one in the prison colony knew how long—the Underground was victorious, and the Managerial System crumbled.

THY NAME IS WOMAN

Thy Name Is Woman by Bryce Walton

First published in 1953

This Edition Copyright @2020 by Eli Jayne

All rights reserved.

Cover art by Eli Jayne

There wasn't a woman left on earth. They had just packed their bags and left.

CHAPTER ONE

After the Doctor gave him the hypo and left the ship, Bowren lay in absolute darkness wondering when the change would start. There would be pain, the Doctor had said. "Then you won't be aware of anything—anything at all."

That was a devil of a thing, Bowren thought, not to be aware of the greatest adventure any man ever had. He, Eddie Bowren, the first to escape the Earth into space, the first man to Mars!

He was on his back in a small square steel cubicle, a secretly constructed room in the wall of the cargo bin of the big spaceship cradled at the New Chicago Port. He was not without fear. But before the ship blasted he wouldn't care—he would be changed by then. He would start turning any minute now, becoming something else; he didn't know exactly what, but that wouldn't matter. After it was over, he wouldn't remember because the higher brain centers, the cortex, the analytical mind, would be completely cut off, short-circuited, during the alteration.

The cubicle was close, hot, sound-proofed, like a tomb. "You will probably make loud unpleasant noises," the Doctor had said, "but no one will hear you. Don't worry about anything until you get to Mars."

That was right, Bowren thought. My only problem is to observe, compute, and get back into this dungeon without being observed, and back to Earth.

The idea was to keep it from the women. The women wouldn't go for this at all. They would object. The women would be able to bring into effect several laws dealing with spaceflight, among them the one against stowaways, and especially that particular one about aberrated males sneaking into space and committing suicide.

A lot of men had tried it, in the beginning. Some of them had managed it, but they had all died. For a long time, the men's egos hadn't been able to admit that the male organism was incapable of standing the rigors of acceleration. Women had had laws passed, and if the women caught him doing this, the punishment would be extreme for him, personally, and a lot more extreme for Earth civilization in general. If you could call it a civilization. You could call it anything, Bowren groaned—but it didn't make sense. A world without women. A birthrate reduced to zero.

A trickle of sweat slid past Bowren's eyes, loosening a nervous flush along his back that prickled painfully. His throat was tense and his heart pounded loud in the hot dark.

A sharp pain ran up his body and exploded in his head. He tried to swallow, but something gagged in his throat. He was afraid of retching. He lay with his mouth open, spittle dribbling over his lips. The pain returned, hammered at his entrails. He fought the pain numbly, like a man grappling in the dark.

The wave subsided and he lay there gasping, his fists clenched.

"The pain will come in increasingly powerful waves," the Doctor had said. "At a certain point, it will be so great, the analytical mind will completely short-circuit. It will stay that way enroute to Mars, and meanwhile your body will rapidly change into that of a beast. Don't worry about it. A catalytic agent will return you to normal before you reach the planet. If you live, you'll be human again."

CHAPTER TWO

A male human couldn't stand the acceleration. But a woman could. Animals could. They had experimented on human males and animals in the giant centrifuges, and learned what to do. Animals could stand 25 "G" consistently, or centrifugal forces as high as 120 revolutions a minute. About 10 "G" was the limit of female endurance. Less for men.

It had never been thoroughly determined why women had been able to stand higher acceleration. But human females had the same physical advantages over men as female rats, rabbits, and cats over males of the same species. A woman's cellular structure was different; her center of gravity was different, the brain waves given off during acceleration were different. It was suspected that the autonomic nervous system in women could function more freely to protect the body during emergency situations. The only certainty about it was that no man had ever been able to get into space and live.

But animals could so they had worked on it and finally they decided to change a man into an animal, at least temporarily. Geneticists and biochemists and other specialists had been able to do a lot with hormones and hard radiation treatment. Especially with hormones. You could shoot a man full of some fluid or another, and do almost anything to his organism. You could induce atavism, regression to some lower form of animal life—a highly speeded up regression. When you did that, naturally the analytical mind, the higher thought centers of a more recent evolutionary development, blanked out and the primal mind took over. The body changed too, considerably.

Bowren was changing. Then the pain came and he couldn't think. He felt his mind cringing—giving way before the onslaught of the pain. Dimly he could feel the agony in his limbs, the throbbing of his heart, the fading power of reason.

He retched, languished through flaccid minutes. There were recurring spasms of shivering as he rolled his thickened tongue in the arid cavity of his mouth. And then, somewhere, a spark exploded, and drowned him in a pool of streaming flame.

CHAPTER THREE

Consciousness returned slowly—much as it had gone—in waves of pain. It took a long time. Elements of reason and unreason fusing through distorted nightmares until he was lying there able to remember, able to wonder, able to think.

Inside the tiny compartment were supplies. A hypo, glucose, a durolene suit neatly folded which he put on. He gave himself a needle, swallowed the tablets, and waited until energy and a sense of well-being gave him some degree of confidence.

It was very still. The ship would be cradled on Mars now. He lay there, relaxing, preparing for the real challenge. He thought of how well the Earth Investigation Committee had planned the whole thing.

The last desperate attempt of man to get into space—to Mars—a woman's world. At least it was supposed to be. Whatever it was, it wasn't a man's world.

The women didn't want Earth anymore. They had something better. But what? There were other questions, and Bowren's job was to find the answers, remain unobserved and get back aboard this ship. He would then hypo himself again, and when the ship blasted off to Earth, he would go through the same transition all over again.

He put on the soft-soled shoes as well as the durolene suit and crawled through the small panel into the big cargo bin. It was empty. Only a dim yellow light shone on the big cargo vices along the curved walls.

He climbed the ladders slowly, cautiously, through a gnawing silence of suspense, over the mesh grid flooring along the tubular corridors. He wondered what he would find.

Could the women have been influenced by some alien life form on Mars?

That could explain the fact that women had divorced themselves completely from all men, from the Earth. Something had to explain it.

There was one other possibility. That the women had found human life on Mars. That was a very remote possibility based on the idea that perhaps the Solar system had been settled by human beings from outer space, and had landed on two worlds at least.

Bowren remembered how his wife, Lora, had told him he was an idiot and a bore, and had walked out on him five years before; taken her three months course in astrogation, and left Earth. He hadn't heard of her or from her since. It was the same with every other man, married or not. The male ego had taken a beating for so long that the results had been psychologically devastating.

The ship seemed to be empty of any human being but Bowren. He reached the outer lock door. It was ajar. Thin cold air came through and sent a chill down his arms, tingling in his fingers. He looked out. It was night on Mars, a strange red-tinted night, the double moons throwing streaming color over the land.

Across the field, he saw the glowing Luciferin-like light of a small city. Soaring spherical lines. Nothing masculine about its architecture. Bowren shivered.

He climbed down the ladder, the air biting into his lungs. The silence down there on the ground under the ship was intense.

He stood there a minute. The first man on Mars. Man's oldest dream realized.

But the great thrill he had anticipated was dulled somewhat by fear. A fear of what the women had become, and of what might have influenced their becoming.

He took out a small neurogun and walked. He reached what seemed to be a huge park that seemed to surround the city. It grew warmer and a soft wind whispered through the strange wide-spreading trees and bushes and exotic blossoms. The scent of blossoms drifted on the wind and the sound of running water, of murmuring voices.

The park thickened as Bowren edged into its dark, languid depth. It seemed as though the city radiated heat. He dodged suddenly behind a tree, knelt down. For an instant he was embarrassed seeing the two shadowy figures in each others arms on a bench in the moonlight. This emotion gave way to shock, anger, fear.

One of them was a—man!

Bowren felt the perspiration start from his face. An intense jealousy surrendered to a start of fearful curiosity. Where had the man come from?

Bowren's long frustration, the memory of his wife, the humiliation, the rejection, the abandonment, the impotent rage of loneliness—it all came back to him.

He controlled his emotion somehow. At least he didn't manifest it physically. He crept closer, listened.

"This was such a sweet idea," the woman was whispering. "Bringing me here to the park tonight. That's why I love you so, Marvin. You're always so romantic."

"How else could I think of you, darling," the man said. His voice was cultured, precise, soft, thick with emotion.

"You're so sweet, Marvin."

"You're so beautiful, darling. I think of you every minute that you're away on one of those space flights. You women are so wonderful to have conquered space, but sometimes I hate the ships that take you away from me."

The woman sighed. "But it's so nice to come back to you. So exciting, so comfortable."

The kiss was long and deep. Bowren backed away, almost smashing into the tree. He touched his forehead. He was sweating heavily. His beard dripped moisture. There was a hollow panicky feeling in his stomach. Now he was confused as well as afraid.

Another couple was sitting next to a fountain, and a bubbling brook ran past them, singing into the darkness. Bowren crouched behind a bush and listened. It might have been the man he had just left, still talking. The voice was slightly different, but the dialogue sounded very much the same.

"It must be wonderful to be a woman, dear, and voyage between the stars. But as I say, I'm glad to stay here and tend the home and mind the children, glad to be here, my arms open to you when you come back."

"It's so wonderful to know that you care so much. I'm so glad you never let me forget that you love me."

"I love you, every minute of every day. Just think—two more months and one week and we will have been married ten years."

"It's so lovely," she said. "It seems like ten days. Like those first thrilling ten days, darling, going over and over again."

"I'll always love you, darling."

"Always?"

"Always."

The man got up, lifted the woman in his arms, held her high. "Darling, let's go for a night ride across the desert."

"Oh, you darling. You always think of these little adventures."

"All life with you is an adventure."

"But what about little Jimmie and Janice?"

"I've arranged a sitter for them."

"But darling—you mean you—Oh, you're so wonderful. You think of everything. So practical, yet so romantic ... so—"

He kissed her and ran away, holding her high in the air, and her laughter bubbled back to where Bowren crouched behind the bush. He kept on crouching there, staring numbly at the vacancy the fleeing couple had left in the shadows. "Good God," he whispered. "After ten years—"

He shook his head and slowly licked his lips. He'd been married five years.

It hadn't been like this. He'd never heard of any marriage maintaining such a crazy high romantic level of manic neuroticism as this for very long. Of course the women had always expected it to. But the men—

And anyway—*where did the men come from?*

CHAPTER FOUR

Bowren moved down a winding lane between exotic blossoms, through air saturated with the damp scent of night-blooming flowers. He walked cautiously enough, but in a kind of daze, his mind spinning. The appearance of those men remained in his mind. When he closed his eyes for a moment, he could see them.

Perfectly groomed, impeccably dressed, smiling, vital, bronze-skinned, delicate, yet strong features; the kind of male who might be considered, Bowren thought, to be able to assert just the right degree of aggressiveness without being indelicate.

Why, he thought, they've found perfect men, their type of men.

He dodged behind a tree. Here it was again. Same play, same scene practically, only the players were two other people. A couple standing arm in arm beside a big pool full of weird darting fish and throwing upward a subdued bluish light. Music drifted along the warm currents of air. The couple were silhouetted by the indirect light. The pose is perfect, he thought. The setting is perfect.

"You're so wonderful, darling," the man was saying, "and I get so lonely without you. I always see your face, hear your voice, no matter how long you're away."

"Do you? Do you?"

"Always. Your hair so red, so dark it seems black in certain lights. Your eyes so slanted, so dark a green they seem black usually too. Your nose so straight, the nostrils flaring slightly, the least bit too much sometimes. Your mouth so red and full. Your skin so smooth and dark. And you're ageless, darling. Being married to you five years, it's one exciting adventure."

"I love you so," she said. "You're everything any woman could want in a husband. Simply everything, yet you're so modest with it all. I still remember how it used to be. Back there ... with the other men I mean?"

"You should forget about *them*, my dear."

"I'm forgetting, slowly though. It may take a long time to forget completely. Oh, he was such an unpleasant person, so uninteresting after a while. So inconsiderate, so self-centered. He wasn't romantic at all. He never said he loved me, and when he kissed me it was mere routine. He never thought about anything but his work, and when he did come home at night, he would yell at me about not having ordered the right dinner from the cafelator. He didn't care whether he used hair remover on his face in the mornings or not. He was surly and sullen and selfish. But I could have forgiven everything else if he had only told me every day that he loved me, that he could never love anyone else. The things that you do and say, darling."

"I love you," he said. "I love you, I love you. But please, let's not talk about *him* anymore. It simply horrifies me!"

Bowren felt the sudden sickening throbbing of his stomach. The description. Now the slight familiarity of voice. And then he heard the man say, murmuring, "Lois ... darling Lois...."

Lois! LOIS!

Bowren shivered. His jowls darkened, his mouth pressed thin by the powerful clamp of his jaws. His body seemed to loosen all over and he fell into a crouch. Tiredness and torn nerves and long-suppressed emotion throbbed in him, and all the rage and suppression and frustration came back in a wave. He yelled. It was more of a sound, a harsh prolonged animal roar of pain and rage and humiliation.

"Lois ..." He ran forward.

She gasped, sank away as Bowren hit the man, hard. The man sighed and gyrated swinging his arms, teetering and flipped backward into the pool among the lights and the weird fish. A spray of cold water struck Bowren, sobering him a little, sobered his burst of mindless passion enough that he could hear the shouts of alarm ringing through the trees. He turned desperately.

Lois cringed. He scarcely remembered her now, he realized. She was different. He had forgotten everything except an image that had changed with longing. She hadn't been too impressive anyway, maybe, or maybe she had. It didn't matter now.

He tried to run, tried to get away. He heard Lois' voice, high and shrill. Figures closed in around him. He fought, desperately. He put a few temporarily out of the way with the neurogun, but there were always more. Men, men everywhere. Hundreds of men where there should be no men at all. Well-groomed, strong, bronzed, ever-smiling men. It gave him intense pleasure to crack off a few of the smiles. To hurl the gun, smash with his fists.

Then the men were swarming all over him, the clean faces, the smiling fragrant men, and he went down under the weight of men.

He tried to move. A blow fell hard and his head smashed against the rocks. He tried to rise up, and other blows beat him down and he was glad about the darkness, not because it relieved the pain, but because it curtained off the faces of men.

CHAPTER FIVE

After a time it was as though he was being carried through a dim half-consciousness, able to think, too tired to move or open his eyes. He remembered how the men of Earth had rationalized a long time, making a joke out of it. Laughing when they hadn't wanted to laugh, but to hate. It had never been humorous. It had been a war between the sexes, and the women had finally won, destroying the men psychologically, the race physically. Somehow they had managed to go on with a culture of their own.

The war between the sexes had never really been a joke. It had been deadly serious, right from the beginning of the militant feminist movements, long before the last big war. There had always been basic psychological and physiological differences. But woman had refused to admit this, and had tried to be the "equal" if not the better of men. For so long woman had made it strictly competitive, and in her subconscious mind she had regarded men as wonderful creatures, capable of practically anything, and that woman could do nothing better than to emulate them in every possible way. There was no such thing as a woman's role unless it had been the same as a man's. That had gone on a long time. And it hadn't been a joke at all.

How ironic it was, there at the last! All of man's work through the ages had been aimed at the stars. And the women had assumed the final phase of conquest!

For a long time women had been revolting against the masculine symbols, the levers, pistons, bombs, torpedoes and hammers, all manifestations of man's whole activity of overt, aggressive power.

The big H-bombs of the last great war had seemed to be man's final symbol, destructive. And after that, the spaceships, puncturing space, roaring outward, the ultimate masculine symbol of which men had dreamed for so long, and which women had envied.

And then only the women could stand the acceleration. It was a physiological fact. Nothing could change it. Nothing but what they had done to Bowren.

All of man's evolutionary struggle, and the women had assumed the climax, assumed all the past wrapped up in the end, usurped the effect, and thereby psychologically assuming also all the thousands of years of causation.

For being held down, being made neurotic by frustration and the impossibility of being the "equal" of men, because they were fundamentally psychologically and physiologically different, women had taken to space with an age-old vengeance. Personal ego salvation.

But they hadn't stopped there. What had they done? What about the men? A man for every woman, yet no men from Earth. That much Bowren knew. Native Martians? What?

He had been transported somewhere in a car of some kind. He didn't bother to be interested. He couldn't get away. He was held fast. He refused to open his eyes because he didn't want to see the men who held him, the men who had replaced him and every other man on Earth. The men who were destroying the civilization of Earth.

The gimmicks whereby the women had rejected Earth and left it to wither and die in neglect and bitter, bitter wonderment.

He was tired, very tired. The movement of the car lulled him, and he drifted into sleep.

He opened his eyes and slowly looked around. Pretty pastel ceiling. A big room, beautiful and softly furnished, with a marked absence of metal, of shiny chrome, of harshness or brittle angles. It was something of an office, too, with a desk that was not at all business-like, but still a desk. A warm glow suffused the room, and the air was pleasantly scented with natural smelling perfumes.

A woman stood in the middle of the room studying him with detached interest. She was beautiful, but in a hard, mature, withdrawn way. She was dark, her eyes large, liquid black and dominating her rather small sharply-sculptured face. Her mouth was large, deeply red. She had a strong mouth.

He looked at her a while. He felt only a deep, bitter resentment. He felt good though, physically. He had probably been given something, an injection. He sat up. Then he got to his feet.

She kept on studying him. "A change of clothes, dry detergent, and hair remover for your face are in there, through that door," she said.

He said: "Right now I'd rather talk."

"But don't you want to take off that awful—beard?"

"The devil with it! Is that so important? It's natural isn't it for a man to have hair on his face? I like hair on my face."

She opened her mouth a little and stepped back a few steps.

"And anyway, what could be less important right now than the way I look?"

"I'm—I'm Gloria Munsel," she said hesitantly. "I'm President of the City here. And what is your name, please?"

"Eddie Bowren. What are you going to do with me?"

She shrugged. "You act like a mad man. I'd almost forgotten what you men of Earth were like. I was pretty young then. Well, frankly, I don't know what we're going to do with you. No precedent for the situation. No laws concerning it. It'll be up to the Council."

"It won't be pleasant for me," he said, "I can be safe in assuming that."

She shrugged again and crossed her arms. He managed to control his emotions somehow as he looked at the smooth lines of her body under the long clinging gown. She was so damn beautiful! A high proud body in a smooth pink gown, dark hair streaming back and shiny and soft.

CHAPTER SIX

It was torture. It had been for a long time, for him, for all the others. "Let me out of here!" he yelled harshly. "Put me in a room by myself!"

She moved closer to him and looked into his face. The fragrance of her hair, the warmth of her reached out to him. Somehow, he never knew how, he managed to grin. He felt the sweat running down his dirty, bearded, battered face. His suit was torn and dirty. He could smell himself, the stale sweat, the filth. He could feel his hair, shaggy and long, down his neck, over his ears.

Her lips were slightly parted, and wet, and she had a funny dark look in her eyes, he thought. She turned quickly as the door opened, and a man came in. He was only slightly taller than Gloria and he nodded, smiled brightly, bowed a little, moved forward. He carried a big bouquet of flowers and presented them to her.

She took the flowers, smiled, thanked him, and put them on the table. The man said. "So sorry, darling, to intrude. But I felt I had to see you for a few minutes. I left the children with John, and dashed right up here. I thought we might have lunch together."

"You're so thoughtful, dear," she said.

The man turned a distasteful look upon Bowren. He said. "My dear, what is *this*?"

"A man," she said, and then added. "From Earth."

"What? Good grief, you mean they've found a way—?"

"I don't know. You'd better go back home and tend the yard today, Dale. I'll tell you all about it when I come home this evening. All right?"

"Well I—oh, oh yes, of course, if you say so, darling."

"Thank you, dear." She kissed him and he bowed out.

She turned and walked back toward Bowren. "Tell me," she said. "How did you get here alive?"

Why not tell her? He was helpless here. They'd find out anyway, as soon as they got back to Earth on the cargo run. And even if they didn't find out, that wouldn't matter either. They would be on guard from now on. No man would do again what Bowren had done. The only chance would be to build secret spaceships of their own and every time one blasted, have every member of the crew go through what Bowren had. It couldn't last. Too much injury and shock.

As he talked he studied the office, and he thought of other things. An office that was like a big beautiful living room. A thoroughly feminine office. Nor was it the type of office a woman would fix for a man. It was a woman's office. Everything, the whole culture here, was feminine. When he had finished she said, "Interesting. It must have been a very unpleasant experience for you."

He grinned. "I suffered. But even though I've failed, it's worth all the suffering, if you'll tell me—where did all the ah—men come from?"

She told him. It was, to say the least, startling, and then upon reflection, he realized how simple it all was. No aliens. No native Martians. A very simple and thoroughly logical solution, and in a way, typically feminine.

Hormone treatment and genetic manipulation, plus a thorough reconditioning while the treatment was taking place.

And the women had simply turned approximately half of their number into men!

She paused, then went on. "It was the only way we could see it, Mr. Bowren. Earth was a man's world, and we could never have belonged in it, not the way we wanted to. Men wouldn't stand it anyway, down there, having us going into space, usurping their masculine role. And anyway—you men of Earth had become so utterly unsatisfactory as companions, lovers, and husbands, that it was obvious nothing could ever be done about it. Not unless we set up our own culture, our own civilization, our way."

"But meanwhile we die down there," Bowren said. "Logic is nice. But mass murder, and the death of a whole world civilization seems pretty cold from where I'm standing. It's pathological, but it's too late to think about that. It's done now."

"But we're happy here," she said. "For the first time in a long, long time, we women feel like ourselves. We feel truly independent. The men around us are the kind of men we want, instead of us being what they want us to be, or even worse, the men being what we want them to be but resenting it and making life unbearable for both. All through the process of being changed into men, our women undergo such a thorough conditioning that they can never be anything else but model men in every sense. Their attitude as women with which they started treatment helped. They knew what they wanted in men, and they became what we wanted them to be, as men."

"Very logical," Bowren said. "It smells to heaven it's so logical." It was purely impulse, what he did then. He couldn't help it. It wasn't logical either. It was emotional and he did it because he had to do it and because he didn't see any reason why he shouldn't.

He put his arm out suddenly, hooked her slim waist, and pulled her to him. Her face flushed and his eyes were very wide and dark as she looked up at him.

"Listen," he said. "The whole thing's insane. The lot of you are mad, and though I can't help it, I hate to see it happen this way. What kind of men are these? These smiling robots, these goons who are nothing else but reflections in a woman's mirror? Who'd want to be a man like that. Who would really want a man like that? And who would want a woman who was just what a man wanted her to be? Where's the fire? Where's the individuality? Where's the conflict, the fighting and snarling and raging that makes living. All this is apathy, this is death! You don't grow by being agreeable, but by conflict."

"What are you trying to sell now?" she whispered.

He laughed. It was wild sounding to him, not very humorous really, but still it was laughter. "Selling nothing, buying nothing." He pulled her closer and kissed her. Her lips parted slightly and he could feel the warmth of her and the quick drawing of breath. Then she pushed him away. She raised her hand and brushed it over his face.

She shook her head slowly. "It feels rather interesting," she said, "your face. I've never felt a man's face before, that wasn't smooth, the way it should be."

He laughed again, more softly this time. "Why reform your men? You women always wanted to do that."

"We don't reform men here," she said. "We start them out right—from the beginning."

She backed away from him. She raised her hand to her face and her fingers touched her lips. Wrinkles appeared between her eyes and she shook her head again. Not at him, but at something, a thought perhaps, he couldn't tell.

Finally she said. "That was an inexcusable, boorish thing to do. A typical thoughtless egomanical Earth-male action if there ever was one. Our men are all perfect here, and in comparison to them, you're a pretty miserable specimen. I'm glad you showed up here. It's given me, and other women, a good chance for comparison. It makes our men seem so much better even than they were to us before."

He didn't say anything.

"Our men are perfect! Perfect you understand? What are you smiling about? Their character is good. They're excellent conversationalists, well informed, always attentive, moderate, sympathetic, interested in life, and always interested in *us*."

"And I suppose they are also—human?"

"This is nonsense," she said, her voice rising slightly. "You will take that door out please. The Council will decide what's to be done with you."

He nodded, turned, and went through the door. There were two men there waiting for him. They were both blond, with light blue eyes, just medium height, perfectly constructed physically, perfectly groomed, impeccably dressed. They smiled at him. Their teeth had been brushed every morning. One of them wrinkled his nose, obviously as a reaction to Bowren. The other started to reach, seemed reluctant to touch him.

"Then don't touch me, brother," Bowren said. "Put a hand on me, and I'll slug you." The man reached away, and it gave Bowren an ecstatic sensation to send his fist against the man's jaw. It made a cracking sound and the man's head flopped back as his knees crumbled and he swung around and stretched out flat on his face on the long tubular corridor.

"Always remember your etiquette," Bowren said. "Keep your hands off people. It isn't polite."

The other man grunted something, still managing to smile, as he rushed at Bowren. Bowren side-stepped, hooked the man's neck in his arm and ran him across the hall and smashed his head into the wall.

He turned, opened the door into Munsel's office, dragged both of them in and shut the door again. He walked down the corridor several hundred feet before a woman appeared, in some kind of uniform, and said. "Will you come this way please?"

He said he would.

CHAPTER SEVEN

It was a small room, comfortably furnished. Food came through a panel in the wall whenever he pressed the right button. A telescreen furnished entertainment when he pushed another button. Tasty mixed drinks responded to other buttons.

He never bothered to take advantage of the facilities offered for removing his beard, bathing, or changing clothes. Whatever fate was going to befall him, he would just as soon meet it as the only man on Mars who looked the part—according to Bowren's standards, at least—at least by comparison.

He thought of trying to escape. If he could get away from the city and into the Martian hills, he could die out there with some dignity. It was a good idea, but he knew it was impossible. At least so far, it was impossible. Maybe something would come up. An opportunity and he would take it. That was the only thing left for him.

He was in there for what seemed a long time. It was still, the light remaining always the same. He slept a number of times and ate several times. He did a lot of thinking too. He thought about the men on Earth and finally he decided it didn't matter much. They had brought it on themselves in a way, and if there was anything like cause and effect operating on such a scale, they deserved no sympathy. Man had expressed his aggressive male ego until he evolved the H-bombs and worse, and by then the whole world was neurotic with fear, including the women. Women had always looked into the mirror of the future (or lack of it), of the race, and the more she had looked, the more the insecurity. The atomic wars had created a kind of final feeling of insecurity as far as men were concerned, forced them to become completely psychologically and physiologically self-sufficient. They had converted part of their own kind into men, their own kind of men, and theoretically there wouldn't be any more insecurity brought on by the kind of male psychology that had turned the Earth around for so long.

All right, drop it right there then, he thought. It's about all over. It's all over but the requiem. Sometime later he was in a mood where he didn't mind it when an impersonal face appeared on the screen and looked right at him and told him the Council's verdict. It was a woman, and her voice was cold, very cold.

"Mr. Eddie Bowren. The Council has reached a verdict regarding what is to be done with you. You are to be exterminated. It is painless and we will make it as pleasant as possible."

"Thanks," Bowren said. A woman's world was so polite, so mannerly, so remembering of all the social amenities. It would be so difficult after a while to know when anyone was speaking, or doing anything real. "Thanks," he said again. "I will do all in my power to make my extermination a matter of mutual pleasure." By now he was pretty drunk, had been drunk for some time. He raised his glass. "Here's to a real happy time of it, baby."

The screen faded. He sat there brooding, and he was still brooding when the door unlocked and opened softly. He sat there and looked at Gloria Munsel for a while, wondering why she was here. Why she would look so provocative, so enchanting, so devastating, whatever other words you cared to dream up.

She moved toward him with a slight swaying motion that further disturbed him. He felt her long white fingers rubbing over the stiff wiry beard of his face. "I dreamed about the way that beard felt last night," she said. "Silly of me wasn't it? I heard of the way you smell, of the way you yelled at me, so impolitely. Why did I dream of it, I said this morning, so now I'm here to find out why."

"Get out and let me alone," Bowren yelled. "I'm going to be exterminated. So let me alone to my own company."

"Yes, I heard about that verdict," she said. She looked away from him. "I don't know why they made that choice. Well, I do in a way, they're afraid of you, your influence. It would be very disruptive socially. Several of our men—"

"It doesn't matter why," Bowren said. "What matters is that it will be as pleasant as possible. If you're going to kill a man, be nice about it."

She stared down at him. Chills rippled down his back as her warm soft fingers continued to stroke his bearded chin and throat. He got up. It was too uncomfortable and it was torture. He said, "Get out of here. Maybe I'm not a conformist, but I'm damn human!"

She backed away. "But—but what do you mean?"

He got up and put the flat of his hands cupping her shoulder blades. Her eyes stared wildly, and her lips were wet and she was breathing heavily. He could see the vein pulsing faster in her slim throat. She had an exciting body.

He saw it then, the new slow smile that crept across her face. His left hand squirmed at the thick piled hair on her shoulders and he tugged and her face tilted further and he looked at the parted pouting lips. The palm of his right hand brushed her jaw and his fingers took her cheeks and brought her face over and he spread his mouth hard over her mouth. Her lips begged. Hammers started banging away in his stomach.

Music from the screen was playing a crescendo into his pulse. They swayed together to the music, her head thrown back, her eyes closed. She stepped back, dropped her arms limply at her sides. There was the clean sweet odor of her hair.

"I'd better go now," she whispered. "Before I do something that would result in my not being President anymore."

CHAPTER EIGHT

He wiped his face. Don't beg, he thought. The devil with her and the rest. A man could lose everything, all the women, not one, but all of them. He could live alone, a thousand miles from nowhere, at the North Pole like Amundsen, and it didn't matter. He could be killed pleasantly or unpleasantly, that didn't matter either. All that mattered was that he maintain some dignity, as a man.

He stood there, not saying anything. He managed to grin. Finally he said, "Goodbye, and may your husband never say a harsh word to you or do anything objectionable as long as you both shall live, and may he love you every hour of every day, and may he drop dead."

She moved in again, put her arms around him. There were tears in her eyes. She placed her cheek on his shoulder. "I love you," she whispered. "I know that now."

He felt a little helpless. Tears, what could you do with a woman's tears?

She sobbed softly, talking brokenly. Maybe not to him, but to someone, somewhere. A memory, a shadow out of a long time back....

"Maybe it's ... it's all a mistake after all ... maybe it is. I've never been too sure, not for a while now. And then you—the way you talked and looked—the excitement. I don't know why. But the touch of your beard—your voice. I don't know what happened. We've carried it to extremes, extremes, Eddie. It was always this way with us—once we were sure of our man, and even before, when he was blinded by new love, we tried to make him over, closer to *our* idea of what was right. But now I know something ... those faults and imperfections, most of them were men's, the real men's chief attractions. Individuality, that's the thing, Eddie, that's it after all. And it's imperfections too, maybe more than anything else. Imperfections.... Oh, Eddie, you're close, much closer to human nature, to real vitality, through *your* imperfections. Not imperfections. Eddie—your beard is beautiful, your dirt is lovely, your yelling insults are wonderful —and...."

She stopped a minute. Her hands ran through his hair. "When you get a man made over, he's never very nice after that, Eddie. Never—"

She sobbed, pulled his lips down. "Eddie—I can't let them kill you."

"Forget it," he said. "No one can do anything. Don't get yourself in a jam. You'll forget this in a little while. There's nothing here for a guy like me, and I'm not for you."

She stepped way, her hands still on his shoulders. "No—I didn't mean that. I've got to go on living in the world I helped make, among the men we all decided we would always want. I've got to do that. Listen, Eddie, how did you intend to get back to Earth?"

He told her.

"Then it's just a matter of getting back aboard that same ship, and into this secret room unobserved?"

"That's all, Gloria. That and keep from being exterminated first."

"I can get you out of here. We'll have to do it right now. Take that beard off, and get that hair smoothed down somehow. I hate to see it happen, but I've got to get you out of here, and the only way to do it is for you to be like one of the men here."

He went to work on his face and hair. She went out and returned with a suit like the other men wore. He got into it. She smiled at him, a hesitant and very soft smile, and she kissed him before they left the room and cautiously went out of the City.

CHAPTER NINE

The way was clear across the moonlit field and under the deep dark shadow of the ship. He kissed her and then took hold of the ladder. She slipped a notebook of velonex, full of micro-film, into his hands. "Goodbye, Eddie," she said. "Take this with you. It may give you men down there a way out. I never thought much before of how mad it must be for you."

He took the folder. He looked up at the double moons painting the night a fantastic shifting wave of changing light. And then he looked down at Gloria Munsel again, at the glinting shine of her hair.

"Goodbye," he said. "I might stay after all—except that a lot of men on Earth are waiting for me to tell them something. They'll be surprised. I —" He hesitated. Her eyes widened. Warmth of emotion moved him and he said, or started to say, "I love you," and many other things, but she interrupted him.

"Don't please, Eddie. Anything you said now would sound just like what my devoted husband says, every day. I'd rather you wouldn't say anything at all now, Eddie, just goodbye."

"Goodbye then," he said again.

He looked back from the opened door in the ship's cargo bin. Her face was shining up at him, her lips slightly parted, her cheeks wet. It was a picture he would never be able to forget, even if he wanted to.

"When you forget to shave in the mornings, Eddie, think of me."

CHAPTER TEN

Bowren stood up and addressed the investigation committee which had sent him to Mars. He hadn't made any statements at all up to this moment. The ten members of the Committee sat there behind the half-moon table. None of them moved. Their faces were anxious. Some of them were perspiring.

Eddie told them what he had seen, what he had heard, his own impressions about the whole thing, about his escape. He left out certain personal details that were, to him, unnecessary to this particular report.

The Committee sat there a while, then started to talk. They talked at once for a while, then the Chairman rapped for order and stood up. His face had an odd twist to it, and his bald head was pocked with perspiration.

Eddie Bowren took the book of micro-film from under his arm, the one Gloria Munsel had given him. He put it on the table. "That has been thoroughly checked by scientists, and their report is included. I thought it surely was a false report, until they checked it. The first page there gives a brief outline of what the micro-film contains."

The Chairman read, then looked up. He coughed. He mopped at his head.

Eddie said. "As I saw it up there, this is the way it's going to stay. We'll never get into space, not without using the methods that were used with me. And they're too destructive. I've been examined. I could never go through it again and live. And that's the only way Earth men can ever get into space. The women aren't coming back to us. They have husbands of their own now. Believe me, those women aren't going to leave their perfect husbands. They've set up a completely feminine culture. It's theirs, all theirs. They'll never give it up to return to a masculine world, and that's what Earth will always be to them. There are only a few women left on Earth, and they're of such subnormal intelligence as to be only a menace to any possible future progeny. Our birthrate has stopped. We are living under extremely abnormal circumstances without women. I have, as I said before, but one recommendation to this Committee, and you take it for what it's worth. I personally don't care—much—and that isn't important either."

"What is your recommendation, Bowren?"

"I assure you that the formulas in that book will work for us, Mr. Chairman. Will you accept the reports of the scientists who investigated those formulas?"

"I will," the Chairman said hoarsely. "I'll accept it. Why not—?"

Bowren grinned thinly at the ten men. "There's the secret of doing what the women have done. It'll work for us too. Our only chance for survival is to follow their procedure. We've got to start turning at least a percentage of ourselves into women."

One man leaned forward and put his head on his arms. The others sat there, in a kind of stunned numb attitude, their eyes drifting vaguely.

The Chairman coughed and looked around the silent hall, and at the other ten men in it.

"Any volunteers?" he whispered.

TO EACH HIS STAR

To Each His Star by Bryce Walton

First published in 1952

This Edition Copyright @2020 by Eli Jayne

All rights reserved.

Cover art by Eli Jayne

"Nothing around those other suns but ashes and dried blood," old Dunbar told the space-wrecked, desperate men. *"Only one way to go, where we can float down through the clouds to Paradise. That's straight ahead to the sun with the red rim around it."*

But Dunbar's eyes were old and uncertain. How could they believe in his choice when every star in this forsaken section of space was surrounded by a beckoning red rim?

CHAPTER ONE

There was just blackness, frosty glimmering terrible blackness, going out and out forever in all directions. Russell didn't think they could remain sane in all this blackness much longer. Bitterly he thought of how they would die—not knowing within maybe thousands of light years where they were, or where they were going.

After the wreck, the four of them had floated a while, floated and drifted together, four men in bulbous pressure suits like small individual rockets, held together by an awful pressing need for each other and by the "gravity-rope" beam.

Dunbar, the oldest of the four, an old space-buster with a face wrinkled like a dried prune, burned by cosmic rays and the suns of worlds so far away they were scarcely credible, had taken command. Suddenly, Old Dunbar had known where they were. Suddenly, Dunbar knew where they were going.

They could talk to one another through the etheric transmitters inside their helmets. They could live ... if this was living ... a long time, if only a man's brain would hold up, Russell thought. The suits were complete units. 700 pounds each, all enclosing shelters, with atmosphere pressure, temperature control, mobility in space, and electric power. Each suit had its own power-plant, reprocessing continuously the precious air breathed by the occupants, putting it back into circulation again after enriching it. Packed with food concentrates. Each suit a rocket, each human being part of a rocket, and the special "life-gun" that went with each suit each blast of which sent a man a few hundred thousand miles further on toward wherever he was going.

Four men, thought Russell, held together by an invisible string of gravity, plunging through a lost pocket of hell's dark where there had never been any sound or life, with old Dunbar the first in line, taking the lead because he was older and knew where he was and where he was going. Maybe Johnson, second in line, and Alvar who was third, knew too, but were afraid to admit it.

But Russell knew it and he'd admitted it from the first—that old Dunbar was as crazy as a Jovian juke-bird.

A lot of time had rushed past into darkness. Russell had no idea now how long the four of them had been plunging toward the red-rimmed sun that never seemed to get any nearer. When the ultra-drive had gone crazy the four of them had blanked out and nobody could say now how long an interim that had been. Nobody knew what happened to a man who suffered a space-time warping like that. When they had regained consciousness, the ship was pretty banged up, and the meteor-repeller shields cracked. A meteor ripped the ship down the center like an old breakfast cannister.

How long ago that had been, Russell didn't know. All Russell knew was that they were millions of light years from any place he had ever heard about, where the galactic space lanterns had absolutely no recognizable pattern. But Dunbar knew. And Russell was looking at Dunbar's suit up ahead, watching it more and more intently, thinking about how Dunbar looked inside that suit—and hating Dunbar more and more for claiming he knew when he didn't, for his drooling optimism—because he was taking them on into deeper darkness and calling their destination Paradise.

Russell wanted to laugh, but the last time he'd given way to this impulse, the results inside his helmet had been too unpleasant to repeat.

Sometimes Russell thought of other things besides his growing hatred of the old man. Sometimes he thought about the ship, lost back there in the void, and he wondered if wrecked space ships were ever found. Compared with the universe in which one of them drifted, a wrecked ship was a lot smaller than a grain of sand on a nice warm beach back on Earth, or one of those specks of silver dust that floated like strange seeds down the night winds of Venus.

And a human was smaller still, thought Russell when he was not hating Dunbar. Out here, a human being is the smallest thing of all. He thought then of what Dunbar would say to such a thought, how Dunbar would laugh that high piping squawking laugh of his and say that the human being was bigger than the Universe itself.

Dunbar had a big answer for every little thing.

When the four of them had escaped from that prison colony on a sizzling hot asteroid rock in the Ronlwhyn system, that wasn't enough for Dunbar. Hell no—Dunbar had to start talking about a place they could go where they'd never be apprehended, in a system no one else had ever heard of, where they could live like gods on a green soft world like the Earth had been a long time back.

And Dunbar had spouted endlessly about a world of treasure they would find, if they would just follow old Dunbar. That's what all four of them had been trying to find all their lives in the big cold grabbag of eternity—a rich star, a rich far fertile star where no one else had ever been, loaded with treasure that had no name, that no one had ever heard of before. And was, because of that, the richest treasure of all.

We all look alike out here in these big rocket pressure suits, Russell thought. No one for God only knew how many of millions of light years away could see or care. Still—we might have a chance to live, even now, Russell thought—if it weren't for old crazy Dunbar.

They might have a chance if Alvar and Johnson weren't so damn lacking in self-confidence as to put all their trust in that crazed old rum-dum. Russell had known now for some time that they were going in the wrong direction. No reason for knowing. Just a hunch. And Russell was sure his hunch was right.

Russell said. "Look—look to your left and to your right and behind us. Four suns. You guys see those other three suns all around you, don't you?"

"Sure," someone said.

"Well, if you'll notice," Russell said, "the one on the left also now has a red rim around it. Can't you guys see that?"

"Yeah, I see it," Alvar said.

"So now," Johnson said, "there's two suns with red rims around them."

"We're about in the middle of those four suns aren't we, Dunbar?" Russell said.

"That's right, boys!" yelled old Dunbar in that sickeningly optimistic voice. Like a hysterical old woman's. "Just about in the sweet dark old middle."

"You're still sure it's the sun up ahead ... that's the only one with life on it, Dunbar ... the only one we can live on?" Russell asked.

"That's right! That's right," Dunbar yelled. "That's the only one—and it's a paradise. Not just a place to live, boys—but a place you'll have trouble believing in because it's like a dream!"

"And none of these other three suns have worlds we could live on, Dunbar?" Russell asked. Keep the old duck talking like this and maybe Alvar and Johnson would see that he was cracked.

"Yeah," said Alvar. "You still say that, Dunbar?"

"No life, boys, nothing," Dunbar laughed. "Nothing on these other worlds but ashes ... just ashes and iron and dried blood, dried a million years or more."

"When in hell were you ever here?" Johnson said. "You say you were here before. You never said when, or why or anything!"

"It was a long time back boys. Don't remember too well, but it was when we had an old ship called the DOG STAR that I was here. A pirate ship and I was second in command, and we came through this sector. That was—hell, it musta' been fifty years ago. I been too many places nobody's ever bothered to name or chart, to remember where it is, but I been here. I remember those four suns all spotted to form a perfect circle from this point, with us squarely in the middle. We explored all these suns and the worlds that go round 'em. Trust me, boys, and we'll reach the right one. And that one's just like Paradise."

"Paradise is it," Russell whispered hoarsely.

"Paradise and there we'll be like gods, like Mercuries with wings flying on nights of sweet song. These other suns, don't let them bother you. They're Jezebels of stars. All painted up in the darkness and pretty and waiting and calling and lying! They make you think of nice green worlds all running waters and dews and forests thick as fleas on a wet dog. But it ain't there, boys. I know this place. I been here, long time back."

Russell said tightly. "It'll take us a long time won't it? If it's got air we can breath, and water we can drink and shade we can rest in—that'll be paradise enough for us. But it'll take a long time won't it? And what if it isn't there—what if after all the time we spend hoping and getting there—there won't be nothing but ashes and cracked clay?"

"I know we're going right," Dunbar said cheerfully. "I can tell. Like I said—you can tell it because of the red rim around it."

"But the sun on our left, you can see—it's got a red rim too now," Russell said.

"Yeah, that's right," said Alvar. "Sometimes I see a red rim around the one we're going for, sometimes a red rim around that one on the left. Now, sometimes I'm not sure either of them's got a red rim. You said that one had a red rim, Dunbar, and I wanted to believe it. So now maybe we're all seeing a red rim that was never there."

Old Dunbar laughed. The sound brought blood hotly to Russell's face. "We're heading to the right one, boys. Don't doubt me ... I been here. We explored all these sun systems. And I remember it all. The second planet from that red-rimmed sun. You come down through a soft atmosphere, floating like in a dream. You see the green lakes coming up through the clouds and the women dancing and the music playing. I remember seeing a ship there that brought those women there, a long long time before ever I got there. A land like heaven and women like angels singing and dancing and laughing with red lips and arms white as milk, and soft silky hair floating in the winds."

Russell was very sick of the old man's voice. He was at least glad he didn't have to look at the old man now. His bald head, his skinny bobbing neck, his simpering watery blue eyes. But he still had to suffer that immutable babbling, that idiotic cheerfulness ... and knowing all the time the old man was crazy, that he was leading them wrong.

I'd break away, go it alone to the right sun, Russell thought—but I'd never make it alone. A little while out here alone and I'd be nuttier than old Dunbar will ever be, even if he keeps on getting nuttier all the time.

Somewhere, sometime then ... Russell got the idea that the only way was to get rid of Dunbar.

CHAPTER TWO

"You mean to tell us there are people living by that red-rimmed sun," Russell said.

"Lost people ... lost ... who knows how long," Dunbar said, as the four of them hurtled along. "You never know where you'll find people on a world somewhere nobody's ever named or knows about. Places where a lost ship's landed and never got up again, or wrecked itself so far off the lanes they'll never be found except by accident for millions of years. That's what this world is, boys. Must have been a ship load of beautiful people, maybe actresses and people like that being hauled to some outpost to entertain. They're like angels now, living in a land all free from care. Every place you see green forests and fields and blue lakes, and at nights there's three moons that come around the sky in a thousand different colors. And it never gets cold ... it's always spring, always spring, boys, and the music plays all night, every night of a long long year...."

Russell suddenly shouted. "Keep quiet, Dunbar. Shut up will you?"

Johnson said. "Dunbar—how long'll it take us?"

"Six months to a year, I'd say," Dunbar yelled happily. "That is—of our hereditary time."

"What?" croaked Alvar.

Johnson didn't say anything at all.

Russell screamed at Dunbar, then quieted down. He whispered. "Six months to a year—out here—cooped up in these damn suits. You're crazy as hell, Dunbar. Crazy ... crazy! Nobody could stand it. We'll all be crazier than you are—"

"We'll make it, boys. Trust ole' Dunbar. What's a year when we know we're getting to Paradise at the end of it? What's a year out here ... it's paradise ain't it, compared with that prison hole we were rotting in? We can make it. We have the food concentrates, and all the rest. All we need's the will, boys, and we got that. The whole damn Universe isn't big enough to kill the will of a human being, boys. I been over a whole lot of it, and I know. In the old days—"

"The hell with the old days," screamed Russell.

"Now quiet down, Russ," Dunbar said in a kind of dreadful crooning whisper. "You calm down now. You younger fellows—you don't look at things the way we used to. Thing is, we got to go straight. People trapped like this liable to start meandering. Liable to start losing the old will-power."

He chuckled.

"Yeah," said Alvar. "Someone says maybe we ought to go left, and someone says to go right, and someone else says to go in another direction. And then someone says maybe they'd better go back the old way. An' pretty soon something breaks, or the food runs out, and you're a million million miles from someplace you don't care about any more because you're dead. All frozen up in space ... preserved like a piece of meat in a cold storage locker. And then maybe in a million years or so some lousy insect man from Jupiter comes along and finds you and takes you away to a museum...."

"Shut up!" Johnson yelled.

Dunbar laughed. "Boys, boys, don't get panicky. Keep your heads. Just stick to old Dunbar and he'll see you through. I'm always lucky. Only one way to go ... an' that's straight ahead to the sun with the red-rim around it ... and then we tune in the gravity repellers, and coast down, floating and singing down through the clouds to paradise."

After that they traveled on for what seemed months to Russell, but it couldn't have been over a day or two of the kind of time-sense he had inherited from Earth.

Then he saw how the other two stars also were beginning to develop red rims. He yelled this fact out to the others. And Alvar said. "Russ's right. That sun to the right, and the one behind us ... now they ALL have red rims around them. Dunbar—" A pause and no awareness of motion.

Dunbar laughed. "Sure, they all maybe have a touch of red, but it isn't the same, boys. I can tell the difference. Trust me—"

Russell half choked on his words. "You old goat! With those old eyes of yours, you couldn't see your way into a fire!"

"Don't get panicky now. Keep your heads. In another year, we'll be there—"

"God, you gotta' be sure," Alvar said. "I don't mind dyin' out here. But after a year of this, and then to get to a world that was only ashes, and not able to go any further—"

"I always come through, boys. I'm lucky. Angel women will take us to their houses on the edges of cool lakes, little houses that sit there in the sun like fancy jewels. And we'll walk under colored fountains, pretty colored fountains just splashing and splashing like pretty rain on our hungry hides. That's worth waiting for."

Russell did it before he hardly realized he was killing the old man. It was something he had had to do for a long time and that made it easy. There was a flash of burning oxygen from inside the suit of Dunbar. If he'd aimed right, Russell knew the fire-bullet should have pierced

Dunbar's back. Now the fire was gone, extinguished automatically by units inside the suit. The suit was still inflated, self-sealing. Nothing appeared to have changed. The four of them hurtling on together, but inside that first suit up there on the front of the gravity rope, Dunbar was dead.

He was dead and his mouth was shut for good.

Dunbar's last faint cry from inside his suit still rang in Russell's ears, and he knew Alvar and Johnson had heard it too. Alvar and Johnson both called Dunbar's name a few times. There was no answer.

"Russ—you shouldn't have done that," Johnson whispered. "You shouldn't have done that to the old man!"

"No," Alvar said, so low he could barely be heard. "You shouldn't have done it."

"I did it for the three of us," Russell said. "It was either him or us. Lies ... lies that was all he had left in his crazy head. Paradise ... don't tell me you guys don't see the red rims around all four suns, all four suns all around us. Don't tell me you guys didn't know he was batty, that you really believed all that stuff he was spouting all the time!"

"Maybe he was lying, maybe not," Johnson said. "Now he's dead anyway."

"Maybe he was wrong, crazy, full of lies," Alvar said. "But now he's dead."

"How could he see any difference in those four stars?" Russell said, louder.

"He thought he was right," Alvar said. "He wanted to take us to paradise. He was happy, nothing could stop the old man—but he's dead now."

He sighed.

"He was taking us wrong ... wrong!" Russell screamed. "Angels—music all night—houses like jewels—and women like angels—"

"*Shhhh*," said Alvar. It was quiet. How could it be so quiet, Russell thought? And up ahead the old man's pressure suit with a corpse inside went on ahead, leading the other three at the front of the gravity-rope.

"Maybe he was wrong," Alvar said. "But now do we know which way is right?"

CHAPTER THREE

Sometime later, Johnson said, "We got to decide now. Let's forget the old man. Let's forget him and all that's gone and let's start now and decide what to do."

And Alvar said, "Guess he was crazy all right, and I guess we trusted him because we didn't have the strength to make up our own minds. Why does a crazy man's laugh sound so good when you're desperate and don't know what to do?"

"I always had a feeling we were going wrong," Johnson said. "Anyway, it's forgotten, Russ. It's swallowed up in the darkness all around. It's never been."

Russell said, "I've had a hunch all along that maybe the old man was here before, and that he was right about there being a star here with a world we can live on. But I've known we was heading wrong. I've had a hunch all along that the right star was the one to the left."

"I don't know," Johnson sighed. "I been feeling partial toward that one on the right. What about you, Alvar?"

"I always thought we were going straight in the opposite direction from what we should, I guess. I always wanted to turn around and go back. It won't make over maybe a month's difference. And what does a month matter anyway out here—hell there never was any time out here until we came along. We make our own time here, and a month don't matter to me."

Sweat ran down Russell's face. His voice trembled. "No—that's wrong. You're both wrong." He could see himself going it alone. Going crazy because he was alone. He'd have broken away, gone his own direction, long ago but for that fear.

"How can we tell which of us is right?" Alvar said. "It's like everything was changing all the time out here. Sometimes I'd swear none of those suns had red rims, and at other times—like the old man said, they're all pretty and lying and saying nothing, just changing all the time. Jezebel stars, the old man said."

"I know I'm right," Russell pleaded. "My hunches always been right. My hunch got us out of that prison didn't it? Listen—I tell you it's that star to the left—"

"The one to the right," said Johnson.

"We been going away from the right one all the time," said Alvar.

"We got to stay together," said Russell. "Nobody could spend a year out here ... alone...."

"Ah ... in another month or so we'd be lousy company anyway," Alvar said. "Maybe a guy could get to the point where he'd sleep most of the time ... just wake up enough times to give himself another boost with the old life-gun."

"We got to face it," Johnson said finally. "We three don't go on together any more."

"That's it," said Alvar. "There's three suns that look like they might be right seeing as how we all agree the old man was wrong. But we believe there is one we can live by, because we all seem to agree that the old man might have been right about that. If we stick together, the chance is three to one against us. But if each of us makes for one star, one of us has a chance to live. Maybe not in paradise like the old man said, but a place where we can live. And maybe there'll be intelligent life, maybe even a ship, and whoever gets the right star can come and help the other two...."

"No ... God no...." Russell whispered over and over. "None of us can ever make it alone...."

Alvar said, "We each take the star he likes best. I'll go back the other way. Russ, you take the left. And you, Johnson, go to the right."

Johnson started to laugh. Russell was yelling wildly at them, and above his own yelling he could hear Johnson's rising laughter. "Every guy's got a star of his own," Johnson said when he stopped laughing. "And we got ours. A nice red-rimmed sun for each of us to call his very own."

"Okay," Alvar said. "We cut off the gravity rope, and each to his own sun."

Now Russell wasn't saying anything.

"And the old man," Alvar said, "can keep right on going toward what he thought was right. And he'll keep on going. Course he won't be able to give himself another boost with the life-gun, but he'll keep going. Someday he'll get to that red-rimmed star of his. Out here in space, once you're going, you never stop ... and I guess there isn't any other body to pull him off his course. And what will time matter to old Dunbar? Even less than to us, I guess. He's dead and he won't care."

"Ready," Johnson said. "I'll cut off the gravity rope."

"I'm ready," Alvar said. "To go back toward whatever it was I started from."

"Ready, Russ?"

Russell couldn't say anything. He stared at the endless void which now he would share with no one. Not even crazy old Dunbar.

"All right," Johnson said. "Good-bye."

Russell felt the release, felt the sudden inexplicable isolation and aloneness even before Alvar and Johnson used their life-guns and shot out of sight, Johnson toward the left and Alvar back toward that other red-rimmed sun behind them.

And old Dunbar shooting right on ahead. And all three of them dwindling and dwindling and blinking out like little lights.

Fading, he could hear their voices. "Each to his own star," Johnson said. "On a bee line."

"On a bee line," Alvar said.

Russell used his own life-gun and in a little while he didn't hear Alvar or Johnson's voices, nor could he see them. They were thousands of miles away, and going further all the time.

Russell's head fell forward against the front of his helmet, and he closed his eyes. "Maybe," he thought, "I shouldn't have killed the old man. Maybe one sun's as good as another...."

Then he raised his body and looked out into the year of blackness that waited for him, stretching away to the red-rimmed sun. Even if he were right—he was sure now he'd never make it alone.

CHAPTER FOUR

The body inside the pressure suit drifted into a low-level orbit around the second planet from the sun of its choice, and drifted there a long time. A strato-cruiser detected it by chance because of the strong concentration of radio-activity that came from it.

They took the body down to one of the small, quiet towns on the edge of one of the many blue lakes where the domed houses were like bright joyful jewels. They got the leathery, well-preserved body from the pressure suit.

"An old man," one of them mused. "A very old man. From one of the lost sectors. I wonder how and why he came so very far from his home?"

"Wrecked a ship out there, probably," one of the others said. "But he managed to get this far. It looks as though a small meteor fragment pierced his body. Here. You see?"

"Yes," another of them said. "But what amazes me is that this old man picked this planet out of all the others. The only one in this entire sector that would sustain life."

"Maybe he was just a very lucky old man. Yes ... a man who attains such an age was usually lucky. Or at least that is what they say about the lost sectors."

"Maybe he knew the way here. Maybe he was here before—sometime."

The other shook his head. "I don't think so. They say some humans from that far sector did land here—but that's probably only a myth. And if they did, it was well over a thousand years ago."

Another said. "He has a fine face, this old man. A noble face. Whoever he is ... wherever he came from, he died bravely and he knew the way, though he never reached this haven of the lost alive."

"Nor is it irony that he reached here dead," said the Lake Chieftain. He had been listening and he stepped forward and raised his arm. "He was old. It is obvious that he fought bravely, that he had great courage, and that he knew the way. He will be given a burial suitable to his stature, and he will rest here among the brave.

"Let the women dance and the music play for this old man. Let the trumpets speak, and the rockets fly up. And let flowers be strewn over the path above which the women will carry him to rest."

WAR GAME

War Game by Bryce Walton

First published in 1957

This Edition Copyright @2020 by Eli Jayne

All rights reserved.

Cover art by Eli Jayne

The playing of war games should not be forbidden; but rather viewed as a natural outlet for emotional tensions.— Dr. L. M. Stoltz, Stanford University

CHAPTER ONE

The Minister of Peace asked the United States President if he had heard from the Secretary of State. "Yes," the President said. "I heard from Mr. Thompson only a few minutes ago."

"How's their final conference coming, Mr. President?"

"Inevitably. Operation Push Button within the hour."

The Minister of Peace blinked out the window at Washington, D.C. "So they're going to blow up the world?"

"Inevitably."

"Shall we watch it?" asked the Minister of Peace.

The President nodded, spoke to master control through the intercom box on his desk, and switched on the TV screen. They had a special pipe-line into the United Nations Cellar. They sat back, had martinis, and watched the interior of the Cellar come to life on the screen.

Three thousand miles from New Washington, under a natural camouflage of tundra and wintry hills, the U.N. Cellar was thought by its occupants to be thoroughly resistant to any offensive weapons. It was three miles underground, protected by lead, concrete and steel. Its location was known only to the U.N. Security Division that was supposed to be strictly neutral in international affairs, or so the Cellar occupants assumed. The engineers and workmen who had planned and constructed the Cellar were supposed to have been brain-washed and therefore had no memory of the great project. An occasional caribou drifted over the Cellar with the North Wind, and wolves that always follow the caribou.

In his suite, Chandler Thompson, Secretary of State, prepared himself for the global diplomacy game's final hand in which it is never so important what hand you play, as the way you play it. After years of negotiation, full agreement on Operation Push Button had been attained, and Thompson took some pride in having played a leading role in the ingenious idea.

Morten, his valet, finished shaving Thompson's pale face, helped him dress in striped trousers, cut-away, and white gardenia.

"Thank you, Morten," said the Secretary of State.

"You seem calm enough, sir. Frankly, I'm ill at ease."

"You may leave the Cellar if you wish," Thompson said, skimming through his notes. "You've served graciously. I appreciate it. But it is your privilege to return to your family outside now. I might remind you that your chance of survival if you remain here is practically 100 percent."

"It isn't that, sir. It just seems incredible that so many must die." He felt of his wallet, the pictures of his family in it.

"It's hardly a matter of principle," Thompson said. "Nor a question of ideology. It's simply a question of firmness and realistic practicality, and getting the job done once and for all. That has been my stand from the beginning and naturally it cannot be changed."

"But billions of people dying—"

"Death before dishonor, Morten."

"Yes, sir." Morten knew that in every suite in the Cellar every diplomat was saying practically the same thing. Thompson looked up from his neat notes. "People, Morten, have been properly prepared for violent death. Indeed there has been a feeling of security in numbers. The Ministry of Education working with the War Department has done such a splendid job. Now every child has grown up fully prepared to die in the holocaust. And every individual still a child regards violent death as casually as a game of marbles. The required attitude has been thoroughly conditioned in the populace. The idea was to make violence, savagery, and sudden death, an every day affair. And we have done it. Sad, but a necessary task."

Morten said nothing. Thompson looked at the neon map coruscating on the wall. "Our country is not unique in this, Morten. Annihilation will come as a shock only to the misinformed anywhere in the world."

Morten sat down. He remembered how his kids used to come home from school laughingly playing war games, manipulating toy atomic cannons and the like. They received additional marks in school for being good and cooperative during atomic bomb drills and preparations for thermonuclear disasters. They had been so proud of their dogtags that came with boxes of cereal. In the evenings out back they used to have bury-the-dead games.

Thompson was saying, "Remember juvenile delinquency? It was necessary. Millions had to be conditioned psychologically for Operation Killer. An insensitive, fatalistic attitude had to be engendered. For their own good."

Morten flicked a speck of lint from Thompson's stooped shoulder.

"Yes, sir," he said. "Maybe it will be humane, in the long run."

"One must face the hard, materialistic facts," Thompson said. "Oh, that reminds me." He went to his private switchboard and got a secret outside line to the Office of Civilian Defense. "Hello, Donnelson. Yes, I'm fine. I haven't talked with you for some time now, and I was wondering about that suggestion of mine. Yes, the household pets thing. That's right, particularly dogs. They're big morale factors in the lives of children and there may be some survivors. Well, then, issue another bulletin on that immediately. Things are reaching a head here in the Cellar. Yes, dogs should be lashed firmly to heavy pieces of furniture, away from windows. Put water where they can reach it. Hysteria under the bombing attacks can be avoided by giving sodium bromide tablets to the dogs. That's right. Survivors will need pets. Morale...."

After Thompson was through talking to Donnelson, Morten said. "You know, sir, the end will be a relief to some people. They've been blitzed by a non-stop barrage of fear bombs so long, I think they'll be glad to get it over with."

"Very perceptive, Morten. That has been one of Psychological Warfare's primary aims in preparation." Thompson got another outside line. Dawson, Civilian Defense. As he waited for Dawson to come in, he said to Morten, "Get the dueling pistols out of the cabinet, please." Morten nodded.

"Hello, Dawson. Fine, fine, things coming to a head here. How much distribution did you manage on the shrouds? Eighty percent? Excellent. I haven't heard from Harry on the details for quite a while. Wanted to check personally. As you say, I've never really lost my touch with the grass-roots. My feeling from the start was that millions of wooden coffins would be out of the question. The olive drab plastic sheets seemed to be the only practical recourse from the start. The psychological importance of getting bodies out of sight as rapidly as possible cannot be overemphasized. Oh, Dawson, one moment ... yes, I know about the public parks, playgrounds and vacant tracts in the suburbs. But what about New York City? The only way is to send the bodies up the Hudson River using piers as morgues. The problem of where to put so many bodies, particularly when they will all appear for disposal at the same time, is a considerable one. Allowing for three-by-six grave-sites, with three feet for aisles, the whole problem of adequate disposal acreage is primary." Thompson switched off the connection.

Thompson moved his fingers over the .38 caliber dueling pistols in the velvet-lined case. His eyes mellowed with nostalgia. "Gift from the old

Secretary of War. My boy, Don, learned to shoot with this one when he was only six years old. If he had lived to be an adult, he would have been a tough fighter. But he was killed by a rival delinquent gang when he was twelve. He only got there a little sooner. He had just finished reading Niebuhr, so he knew the tragic irony of history."

Thompson balanced one of the pistols in his hand. He looked at his watch. "It's time," he said religiously.

CHAPTER TWO

As Thompson entered the Hall of Ministers, the representatives of five balance of power nations arose at once in deference to the sixth. Morten sat unobtrusively in a far corner, holding the case of dueling pistols on his knees.

Thompson sat down. The minutes of the last conference were read by a mechanical secretary. A summation of their final agreement on Operation Push Button was briefly reviewed by the automatic translating secretary. No changes were suggested.

The surface of the huge conference table was somewhat like a gigantic topographical map of the world. It covered perhaps a thousand square feet and had been constructed by brain-washed artisans and engineers and scientists in perfect electronic detail. It was so realistic that it radiated a sort of sentience, seeming almost to breathe in astonishing precision with the respiration of important strategically located cities, ports, communication and manufacturing centers. Before each Minister was a console containing several buttons.

Each Minister arose, made a speech concerning the sovereign rights of the particular nation or bloc of nations he represented. In each case, the speeches seemed the same to Morten. He knew that if merely the name of the country or bloc in each speech was changed, the rest would be the same, and sound something like:

"Gentlemen, a free such-and-such people can no longer tolerate a militant rearming so-and-so. Every other possibility has been discussed and rejected. I must say now that at this moment a state of war must of necessity exist between such-and-such and so-and-so."

Morten had been hearing variations of it for years. He knew it all by heart. As each Minister made this implacable statement, he sat down, and without further ceremony, pushed a button or buttons on his private console. On the topographical map, as a button was pushed, some important section of the map, an area, a city, a port, some significant transportation, communication, or manufacturing industrial center, would shoot out realistic sparks, smoke, and then crumble into lifeless debris.

Morten tried to control the flinching and twitching of his muscles. An intricate network of electronic relays connected with thermonuclear bombs went out all over the world, and were hooked in to the map on the conference table. Millions of people were just blown up somewhere, Morten thought.

Another Minister finished his speech, sat down, pressed buttons. More smoke and flashes shot up. Millions of others out there somewhere have just been annihilated, Morten thought. It doesn't seem possible, he thought then. It's not possible. It's some kind of final madness. But it's happening.

It had been decided that this was the simple direct way, avoiding long, time-wasting programs of mobilization and warfare. If the conclusion was foregone, had been the question, then why not go directly to it by the shortest and most efficient route? And the answer was as inevitable as the question.

More Ministers stood up, made their final declarations, and pushed buttons. Little puffballs and clouds of smoke drifted over the conference table, obscuring distinctive facial outlines and turning the ministers into shadow shapes as Morten watched.

Only two of the Ministers had not yet pressed their buttons. Only two sectors of the world remain alive, Morten thought. He coughed as acrid smoke swirled about the room. He felt a kind of blessed numbed paralysis. He could almost feel the whole world turning into a radioactive hell all around him, mushrooms of gigantic size sprouting fast and furiously in the last big aftermath of rain. Yet he could scarcely imagine how it really was now, outside the Cellar. He thought vaguely about the dogs, wondering how many of them had avoided hysteria by having been tied to heavy pieces of furniture and given sodium bromide tablets. The kids who survived would need pets.

Morten sat there, trying to see through the thickening smoke. He tried to feel grateful for having been in the Cellar. But in a few more seconds America might also be destroyed. What then? And what if only America remained—would that be any better?

He had resisted such speculation, but how could he resist it any longer? The Ministers had their wives, families, lovers in the Cellar, and supplies enough to last indefinitely. But Morten's family was outside. In a few seconds they might be dead. After that nothing. Nothing at all.

He heard Thompson say in a calm voice. "Morten, the pistols."

He also heard the other Minister say in Russian that he wanted his pistol. Morten had to respect the secret agreement that Thompson and the Russian Minister had made yesterday. After the other Ministers pushed their buttons, Thompson and the Russian would fight a duel then the survivor of the duel would push his button.

"Someone should win," Thompson and the Russian had agreed. "This way, one will be the absolute victor."

If the other Ministers knew what this secret agreement was they either did not care, or did not care enough now. They got up from the conference table and drifted out of the big spheroid room to their families, wives—wherever they wanted to go.

Now only Thompson and the Russian remained in the room. They walked ten paces away from one another in the classic tradition of honorable dueling, turned, and fired. They fell almost at the same time. Morten rushed over to Thompson who was already dead, having died instantly with a bullet in his heart. Morten saw that the Russian had a bullet hole just above his left eye.

Thompson, foreseeing this possible situation, had gotten a promise from Morten that he would press the button that would annihilate Russia, in case Thompson was dead or incapacitated. That would leave the United States the sole victor in the last great global struggle to establish once and for all, world wide, the true faith.

Morten fought a brief struggle with his conscience, then ran out of the room, leaving the console untouched. The United States and Russia still survived. Morten's family was still safe. He ran toward the bank of elevators to get out of the Cellar. He hadn't been out of the Cellar for a long, long time.

CHAPTER THREE

The President of the United States switched off the TV, and poured another martini. "You want another?" he asked the Minister of Peace. "No, sir, Mr. President."

For a while they said nothing as they looked out the window at the peaceful sunshine, and watched birds settle in the trees.

"They ran their own course," the Minister of Peace said. "Just the same, it was an unpleasant thing to see."

"Inevitable," said the President. "There wasn't any other possible way to handle them."

Psychiatry would never have altered their rigid mold, he knew. It was a strangely funny thing, that spontaneous rebellion all over the world. The people putting a stop to the whole damn vicious historical show. But they had done it. The lie had been given to all the historical pessimists like Spencer and Toynbee and Marx and all the others who had said the same things, whether they really had admitted it or not. The people, acting out of intuitive realization that they faced annihilation, had reacted *en masse* and taken things over for themselves. Now you couldn't find even a water pistol anywhere in the world.

The U.N. Cellar had been walled off, turned into a kind of sanitarium. Its occupants had never known the truth about the outside. Thompson and that absurd Russian were dead. But what about the others in the Cellar, living there still and believing they were the only few survivors left in the world?

Poor bastards, the President thought. And then he thought of that statement by Sartre. The one about hell being a restaurant where you served yourself.

SCIENCE FICTION CLASSICS

ELI JAYNE
SCI FI CLASSICS

Eli Jayne is pleased to present reformatted science fiction classics.

elijayne.com

www.ingramcontent.com/pod-product-compliance
Ingram Content Group UK Ltd.
Pitfield, Milton Keynes, MK11 3LW, UK
UKHW022243030425
5313UKWH00013B/786